Fire in the Night

Center Point
Large Print

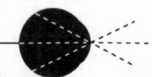

**This Large Print Book carries the
Seal of Approval of N.A.V.H.**

LANCASTER BURNING • BOOK 1

FIRE in the NIGHT

Linda Byler

CENTER POINT LARGE PRINT
THORNDIKE, MAINE

This Center Point Large Print edition is published
in the year 2015 by arrangement with
Skyhorse Publishing.

Copyright © 2013 by Good Books, Intercourse, PA 17534.

The text of this Large Print edition is unabridged.
In other aspects, this book may vary
from the original edition.
Printed in the United States of America
on permanent paper.
Set in 16-point Times New Roman type.

ISBN: 978-1-62899-625-8

Library of Congress Cataloging-in-Publication Data

Byler, Linda.
Fire in the night / Linda Byler. — Center Point Large Print edition.
  pages cm. — (Lancaster burning ; book 1)
  Summary: "Sarah Beiler's Lancaster County Amish community is
besieged by barn fires as Sarah's father, the community's minister, tries
to maintain calm"—Provided by publisher.
  ISBN 978-1-62899-625-8 (library binding : alk. paper)
  1. Amish—Fiction. 2. Arson—Fiction.
    3. Lancaster County (Pa.)—Fiction. 4. Large type books. I. Title.
PS3602.Y53F57 2015
813´.6—dc23
                                                                2015012334

Fire in the Night

Chapter 1

The flannel cloth around his neck kept bothering him that night. It smelled of the Unker's salve that was slathered all over the cloth and was supposed to soothe his sore, dry throat. He put two heavy fingers between the cloth and his neck and struggled to turn on his side before a cough tore through his sensitive throat—burning like fiery sandpaper.

Fully awake now, he turned his large, ungainly body and struggled to sit up. Lowering his legs to the side of the bed, he extended one foot, searched for his *schlippas* (slippers), and muttered to himself.

His room on the first floor used to be an enclosed porch, the place Mam and Sarah did their sewing and quilting. The spray-painted coffee cans lining the windows held blooming geraniums of various ages.

His single bed was one from the hospital with wheels on it and a crank. Whenever he was ill, they would make him comfortable by turning the handle at the foot of the bed to lower his head or to raise it when the coughing started.

A white doily with a small brown pony embroidered on it and crochet work binding the edges covered a nightstand next to the high bed.

An insulated carafe of ice water occupied a cork coaster next to a plastic tumbler with a blue bendable straw. A small battery-powered alarm clock sat invisible except for its illuminated numbers. A box of Kleenex, a bottle of Tylenol, and a tall green bottle of Swedish Bitters completed the assortment of necessities.

Levi Beiler was born with Down syndrome and gained weight easily, which was the reason he was a large man. He was the oldest of ten children, born to David and Malinda Beiler in the winter of 1977 when the snowplows opened the roads from Ronks to Gordonville in Lancaster County, Pennsylvania.

It had been a shock when their firstborn appeared different—the eyes so small and unseeing, the tongue so oversized and uncontrolled, the hands and feet square and without muscle tone.

"*Siss an mongoloid, gel?* (He's a mongoloid, right?)" she had whispered.

For some reason, it had been harder for David to accept—his firstborn son's defect a dagger to his heart. What had he done to deserve this? Was it a curse?

As was the Amish way, he examined his heart. He must have done something wrong for God to send them a "retarded" son. As always, the community rallied around them saying that God only sends special children to special couples, recognizing their outstanding abilities to care for them.

What a cute one! Grandmothers clucked and swaddled and gave advice. Grandfathers clapped David's shoulder and said He would provide strength for the coming days, and He had—far beyond anything they could imagine.

Levi was thirty-one years old now and still in reasonably good health. Except for his fiery throat.

The house was dark—no switches on the walls, no lights flicking on with the push of a finger, devoid of electricity. The small flashlight he normally kept under his bed was not in its usual place, so he turned to go to the kitchen, holding onto the doorway and then the wooden desk with his slippers sliding across the spotless linoleum.

A movement caught his eye. Something white.

Turning clumsily, he watched but could not see clearly without his glasses. Holding onto the brown recliner, he peered past the maple tree, its budding branches hanging just above his line of vision.

Well, that was a *dumba monn* (dumb man). Why would a white car drive past the house with no lights?

Moving to the window, he gripped the oak trim. Lifting the green blind slightly, he watched, his eyes narrow and brown and cunning. It was a small car, he thought. But with only a half moon

9

to provide a little light, he couldn't tell for sure.

He held his breath and waited. A cough tore through his infected throat, and he squeezed his eyes shut tightly, struggling mightily to swallow.

Should he wake Dat? Maybe they were *schtaelas* (thieves).

Ach (oh), now he needed to use the bathroom. Turning away, he shuffled carefully through the darkened house with a small yellow sliver of light from the half-opened bathroom door to guide him.

Mam kept a small kerosene lamp burning all night for Levi, and now its soft, golden glow was a sign of her love and caring. He was glad he had a good Mam.

When he was finished, he washed his hands and dried them on the brown towel that hung by the sink and decided to go back to bed.

Likely someone turning around, he thought. He put the car from his mind, replacing it with the missing flashlight.

A white form appeared at his parents' bedroom door.

"Levi, *iss sell dich*? (Is that you?)"

"*Ya.*"

"Are you alright?"

"*Nay.*"

"Do you need help?"

"No, I'm going to take Tylenol."

"Where's your flashlight?"

"Lost. *Ich bin aw base* (I am mad)."

Smiling widely in the dark living room, Mam made her way across it, touched Levi's shoulder with one hand, his forehead with the other. She clucked and then shook her head.

"You have a fever."

"I know."

Mam reached beneath Levi's pillow, retrieved the missing flashlight, and clicked it on, waiting while he poured the water and opened the pill bottle. He removed two pills and swallowed them, grimacing and moaning, watching his mother's face for any sign of sympathy, which was there, of course.

"Poor Levi. That throat of yours just acts up now and again."

"I need to eat more ice cream."

"Yes, you do."

Mam went back to bed, rolled onto her side, pulled up her knees, and fell asleep, listening to Levi settling himself in the night.

Upstairs, Sarah had left her west window open just a sliver, the crisp, spring air freshening her room with its fragrance. Her windows were covered with sheer beige panels with scarves of darker hues entwined on a heavy rod above them. So when a flickering light played across her pretty features, her wide, green eyes fluttered, squinted, and then opened completely.

At first she thought it was the swaying branches of the maple tree playing tricks with the light of

11

the half moon. But the sheer beige panels hung still. Blinking, she watched the light. Chills crept up her arms and across her shoulders. Was she being visited by some heavenly spirit? God didn't send angels now the way He had in Bible times.

The light was intensifying. In one easy movement, her tall form sat erect, her eyes wide. A crackling!

Chills ran over her entire body; her nostrils flared. When her feet hit the floor, she was already running and pushing aside the curtains. She knew before she actually saw the grim spectacle before her. Through the branches of the large tree, a hot, orange light on the barn's east side danced, the mocking tongues of flame daring her to do something about them. She could only think of demons, of hateful, vengeful destructive devils in the form of licking flames, greedy in their intent to destroy.

A scream, primal and hoarse, tore from her throat. She backed away, a hand to her mouth, as if to stop that awful sound, that implication of horror.

She was aware of the floor creaking. She wasted no time, her hands on the walls to steady herself as she descended the stairs. She called out, or thought she called, but in reality it was another hoarse scream.

"Fire! Fire!"

Her mother reached her first, a hand at the neckline of her homemade nightgown, her eyes wide with terror. By the light of the crackling flames, the kitchen had taken on an eerie, orange hue, with shadows that pulsed and danced.

Dat came to the bedroom door, his hair and beard wild in the undulating light. He yelled, then dove back to retrieve his pants, buttoning them as he reappeared.

There was a high shriek from Levi's bed. Instinctively, Sarah rushed to his bedside, telling him to stay calm. The barn was on fire, and she needed to make a phone call.

Dat was incoherent. Mam was shoving her feet into her barn shoes, crying out about dialing 911. Sarah pushed past them both, ripped open the *kesslehaus* (wash house) door, flew down the steps, and dashed across the lawn to the phone shanty beside the shed.

She tried to turn the knob three times, but it was stubborn. So she turned in the opposite direction, and the door flung inward. Turning her head, she gasped in terror as the voracious flames licked their way to the barn's rooftop.

The horses screamed. The high, intense sound scattered Sarah's senses for a second. Summoning all her strength, she focused on the telephone on the wooden shelf.

She had no flashlight. Her hands scrabbled wildly now, searching desperately for a source of light. She felt the smooth roundness of a small Bic lighter. Thank God.

Instantly, she flicked it with her thumb and held it steady. A tiny orange flame rewarded her with a small circle of light—ironically so necessary when only a few hundred feet away the same element was now destroying their livelihood.

Lifting the receiver, she jabbed hard at the 9 and then hit the 1 twice. Instantly, a dispatcher on the other end of the line spoke in clipped, precise tones. Sarah gave him articulate directions and then replaced the receiver, a terrible dread seizing her as she kicked open the door.

Acceptance would have been easier if she hadn't had to listen to the desperate cries of the horses. They thrashed and kicked, completely beside themselves with fear. Cows and heifers bawled, their raw fear transforming ordinary moos into sounds of frightful proportions. Sarah barreled straight through the stable door as flames roared overhead, the haymow fully engulfed.

Dat was a dark tragic figure now, so human and pitiful, somehow so unable. Mam, so small and helpless, shoved open the barnyard door.

With a cry and a yank, Dat released the cows from the iron locks around their necks, the lever opening them in perfect unison. Each cow backed over the gutter and turned, bawling, as Dat waved his arms. He yelled and yelled, the sound of his voice futile now, as the roaring and crackling became louder.

The horses! Oh, please!

The floor above them broke—the hissing, tearing sound a knell of doom.

"Priscilla! No!"

Sarah dashed after her sister, whose sole purpose was to reach her riding horse, Dutch. Grabbing her by the shoulders, Sarah screamed and pointed to the break in the floorboards, the sparks raining down on the dry hay stacked by the stone wall. Priscilla wrenched her body from Sarah's grasp, flung herself along the corridor, and wedged beside the horse, desperately searching for the chain fastened to his halter.

It was then that the dry hay burst into flames, the sparks turning into blazing flares. One landed on Dutch's back. He screamed and pawed the air, but he remained tethered to his death by the chain. Sarah fought to contain Priscilla, who was crying out and babbling like a mad person, her need to save her beloved horse dispelling all common sense and thoughts of her own safety.

Choking on the thick, black smoke, Sarah tripped and pitched headlong toward the concrete corridor, the eerie flames consuming the rolling, tumbling smoke above them. As wailing sirens broke through the night, she thought this surely must be the hell written about in the Bible.

Clutching Priscilla, her knees torn from falling, Sarah crawled out of the barn to the stoop beside the cow stable and fell sideways onto the dew-laden grass. The night hissed black and orange as

15

the menacing fire continued to swell. There was no time to rest.

"*Komm*, Priscilla!"

Jumping up, Sarah ran to safety—a sobbing, terrified Priscilla on her heels.

"Stay here. I'm going to help Dat!"

Sarah was vaguely aware of Suzie and Mervin huddled together on the porch of the farmhouse, their faces white in the glow of the fire. Red fire trucks were screaming their way toward the barn, silver flashing on the wheels and sides of the huge vehicles. As the men in fire gear jumped down and wielded hoses, Sarah knew her help was now completely useless.

She turned to go back but felt Mam beside her and reached out a hand as Mam's arm slid about her waist. The cries of the tortured animals pushed Sarah's hands to her ears, where she clamped them as though her life depended on ridding herself of the terrible sounds.

"It's awful, I know. Oh, it's terrible," Mam kept repeating, over and over, as if her banal speech could fix it all.

Sarah was glad when Mam went to the porch to comfort Mervin and Suzie. Dropping down beside Priscilla, she pulled the younger girl against her lap. Pricilla lowered her head and shuddered from the force of her sobs.

They both cried out in high-pitched despair when the diesel fuel tank exploded, sending rockets of flames roaring high into the night sky, increasing the heat and velocity of the fire. That was when the animals' cries ended, each creature mercilessly engulfed and burned to death.

Sarah lifted her face to the night sky and found friendly white stars shimmering in the heavens, as if nothing out of the ordinary was happening. She wondered if God cared that their barn had turned into a raging inferno and trapped the innocent animals in its fiery maw.

Cars arrived, some with blue lights flashing on their roofs. Neighbors—Amish and English— appeared in the line that separated the light from the dark. They were like creatures emerging from a strange other world, their faces grim, their straw hats and camouflage caps all pulled down as if to shield their minds from the horror of it.

Sarah watched the line of men, most in black wearing wide hats, a silhouette of sameness and brotherly love. As neighbors, they stood by Dat, not saying much, their silence a better comfort than words. Words would be about as useless as their blazing barn, Sarah reasoned, so that was how the men likely viewed the situation.

Great streams of water continued to shoot from the expertly controlled hoses. The trained firemen on duty went about their business saving what they could, which Sarah knew wasn't much. The flames hissed where the water rained down on them, sending up plumes of white steam that were immediately swallowed up by rolling billows of black smoke. And still sirens wailed as more fire trucks rumbled to the scene.

The flames crackled, hissed, and steamed. The fire engines idled, and pumps roared to life as firemen swarmed about. The police arrived wearing dark uniforms with pistols and gold braids and an air of authority. Dat looked old and a bit humpbacked, his homemade Amish clothes drab and ill-fitting, his beard wagging as he told the officers what he knew. Sarah guessed it probably wasn't much.

The night burned into a weariness after that. As Priscilla continued crying, everyone crowded around Dat, the darkness taking back some of the light as the water quenched a fraction of the flames.

Looking down at her sister, Sarah bent her head and whispered, "Hush, hush."

Priscilla nodded, rubbed a forearm across her face, and said, "Let's go in."

Together they walked across the yard and up to the porch, where Sarah thought she heard a soft sound, a calling, but she couldn't be sure. Opening the door, she heard Levi crying out for assistance. Mam had already heard him and, after putting the smaller children back to bed, was a step ahead of Sarah.

"I can't find my flashlight!" Levi said indignantly.

"It's under your pillow, Levi. You don't need it. The house is bright from the fire," Mam assured him.

The loss of his flashlight, coupled with his fever and pain and the terror of the fire, was the small frustration that threatened to send him into one of his seizures. They were frightening to watch, the way his eyes rolled back in his head and his body became rigid, his head jerking and flopping. It was then that he could slide out of bed and fall on the floor with a terrible crash. They always worried about a broken hip or shoulder.

"I want my flashlight!" Levi bellowed.

Sarah quickly thrust a hand deep under his pillow and sighed with relief when an object hit the floor on the other side. She retrieved it, handed it over, and Levi grasped it greedily to his chest. He immediately quieted himself, the object a solace to him and his safety.

He sat, a large lump of a man, his hair disheveled, his beard uncombed, his eyes watering with the fever. Morose but calmed, he watched the barn burn.

Sarah found Levi's glasses, washed them in hot running water, and dried them with a clean paper towel. She brought them back and placed them on his face gently so he wouldn't get upset.

"You know *an dumba monn* drove his car in here." He said it flatly, without expression, his voice gravelly with the infection in his throat.

Mam looked at Sarah and raised her eyebrows. "You were dreaming."

"Oh, no, I wasn't. I had to get up and take some pills. A car. It was white. He had all the lights off."

"Get the police," Mam whispered. She stroked Levi's shoulder and massaged his back while Sarah hesitated.

"I don't want to go out there—all those men."

"You have to. Priscilla won't. I think they need to hear what Levi has to say."

Obediently Sarah went, slowly calculating which group of men looked the most approachable. Good. There was Dat. Walking on, she tapped his arm and said, "Dat," very quietly. He didn't hear her, so she tugged at his sleeve.

He turned, smiled, and said, "Sarah."

"Dat, Levi—Mam thinks the police should talk to Levi."

"Why?"

"He said there was a white car in here. Without lights."

Immediately Dat left in search of the officers. Sarah went back inside, away from the hissing and crackling, the mud and blackness, and the stench of rolling smoke.

The propane lamp sent the orange glow of the fire away, its yellowish white light restoring a sense of normalcy to the farm kitchen. Levi shuffled gratefully into its warm circle and settled into the well-used brown rocking recliner with the cotton throw across its back. He looked up with fear and respect when the officers walked through the door.

He told them he was Levi Beiler and politely and quite solemnly shook hands with the officers, peering up at them through his thick lenses. As they introduced themselves, Sarah stood nearby knowing that Levi would never forget their names.

Chapter 2

As the fire continued to rage, the streams of water that spurted from the long, snaking hoses turned the barnyard and the macadamed drive-way into a brown sluice of debris and charcoal-laden liquid. Firemen in professional gear, their training now being put to use, aimed the nozzles for the greatest efficiency as the night wore on.

Inside the house, Levi gazed in wonder at the stern figures before him—Jake Mason and Brian O'Connell. Awed by the sheer splendor of their uniforms, he filed the men's names away in his sharp, efficient memory.

"How are you, Levi?" asked Jake, the older one, his hair graying at the sides, his stomach snuggly filling the heavy black shirt like a large sausage.

Levi watched the officer's stomach, noticing the absence of wrinkles in his shirt.

"Good. I have a sore neck, though."

He looked questioningly at Sarah for reassurance, knowing the English language remained elusive for him.

Sarah stood by Levi, put a hand on his pajama-clad shoulder, and bent to whisper, "Throat."

Squinting, looking at them, he pointed to his throat.

"Sorry to hear it. Now tell me what you saw."

Levi knew he was important and had an audience, so he played it for all it was worth.

"I need a drink," he said, waving his hand, a kingly motion that sent Sarah to his nightstand. Mam cast a knowing smile in Dat's direction.

He drank from the straw, grimacing mightily, rubbed his hands, pursed his lips, and said, "A white car drove past the house with no lights on it."

Giving no sign of acknowledgment, the officer scribbled on a pad and resumed questioning Levi.

Yes, he'd been awake.

No, he hadn't seen the car here before.

The only person he knew with a white car was Fred Dunkirk, the guy who sold Watkins products, and he hadn't been here since September twenty-third.

The officers shook Levi's hand, thanked him, and turned to Dat, leaving Levi with a beatific grin and stars in his eyes—to think he'd shaken the hands of real policemen.

"You have no reason to believe this was an act

of revenge, someone acting out against you? No past grudge, perhaps?" Jake asked.

Dat shook his head, bewildered.

Sarah watched his expression with love for her father flooding her heart. He was an ordained minister, carrying the burden of being a servant of the Lord, striving to keep peace and unity among his people—the small district of twenty-some families—protecting his flock from "the wolf," the ways of the world.

Yes, of course, he had not always said or done the right thing. But so far as he knew, he had no reason to believe anyone would take such hateful revenge, allowing innocent animals to meet horrible deaths like that.

In Sarah's eyes, at the tender age of nineteen, her father was a wise and godly man, temperate, slow to speak, and above all, kind and gentle. There was pain in her large gray-green eyes when she met Dat's, also the color of restless seawater, a distinct feature handed down from Grandfather Beiler.

"I certainly have no reason to believe someone would do this against me," he said quietly.

The policemen nodded.

Dat lowered his head and thought of Jonas Esh's Reuben, who'd been excommunicated for a time—for sins he had brought on himself by his own rebellion. But Reuben did not have the ability, the meanness of heart, to react in such a way. He believed in Reuben, knowing the Esh boys all went through their rebellious phases because of questionable parenting. But when treated with patience and kindness, they all came around to see the folly of it.

What had his father said? You can accomplish more with honey than vinegar.

So when he lifted his head to meet the eyes of the policemen, these thoughts had brought a softness, a peace, to his own.

"No," he said firmly. "No."

As one officer nodded, the other's hand went to his belt as a device chirped and crackled.

Sarah was startled and restrained a giggle, thinking how closely the sound resembled the chirp of a blue jay at the feeder. She mentally formed a picture of a large, aggressive bird attached to the policeman's glossy black belt.

For the remainder of the night, the family huddled on sofas and recliners, covered with various afghans and cotton throws. Levi was taken back to bed after the policemen left. There he mumbled and coughed, the light of the dying barn fire playing across his features.

Mam stood at the sink staring out the window at the horrible reality of the loss. The acceptance drew her shoulders forward in a hunch of despair, her hands clenching the Formica top as if she could fix everything as long as she stayed erect, watching.

Sarah sat by Levi's bed, where the windows were low. Her knees were drawn up, her hands clasping them, her head resting against the cushion of Levi's blue La-Z-Boy. She watched the silhouettes of Amish men and English ones, of firemen and fire trucks, the smoke and the steam and the mess. Wondering how they would ever recover from this completely insurmountable financial loss made her sick to her heart.

"Mam!" she called suddenly, the need to rescue her mother from her pitiful stance at the sink rising to her throat.

"What, Sarah?"

"Come sit down. You can't stop the fire by standing there hanging onto the countertop."

Mam turned her head, looked sheepish, and then sank into the nearest hickory rocker, murmuring and shaking her head in disbelief.

"Try and get some rest, Mam. Morning will come soon enough."

Mam nodded, but Sarah knew she would only shut her eyes and remain wide awake beneath the closed lids, her mind churning with questions tumbling over each other as she planned the upcoming day. The children needed to go to school. Their lunches needed to be packed. Mervin had brought home his arithmetic workbook with red check marks all over one page. Had he done the corrections?

There would be breakfast to prepare for these

men. She counted the dozens of eggs in the propane gas refrigerator in the *kesslehaus*, where she stored the extra eggs from her fine flock of laying hens.

As if she read her thoughts, Sarah called, "There are plenty of eggs, and we have canned turkey sausage."

"Yes, Sarah. Bless your heart."

Sarah was warmed and rejuvenated by the sound of her mother's voice. Dear, dear Mam. At a time like this, when tension ran high, she remembered to appreciate her daughter's help. By the light of the flickering flames, she smiled.

The Beiler farm, as always, had been immaculate, the level black-topped driveway lined with maple trees, the lush green grass beneath them mowed twice weekly, in the spring especially. The white fence beside it contained the herd of clean black and white Holsteins, the clipped and well-fed brown mules, Dutch, the riding horse, and George, Charlie, Pansy, and Otter, the driving horses. The stone farmhouse stood off to the left, a proud old house that had weathered centuries of rain and sunshine, arctic temperatures and tropical ones, humidity, drying winds, thunderstorms, and the dark of night.

Dat had just renovated the shingle roof, replacing it with more expensive standing seam metal that was pewter gray, almost black, and complemented the ageless gray and brown stone.

The porch had been expanded and stretched across the entire front, except for Levi's enclosure with its tall windows shaded by the maple trees and the boxwoods adding a thick, green skirt.

There was a new addition built on the side, a *kesslehaus*, the hub of Amish farm life. Against one wall stood the wringer washer and plastic rinse tubs. Against another wall were a deep sink, countertops, and cupboards containing canning supplies. The cupboards also held Sevin, Round-Up, insecticides, Miracle-Gro, Epsom salt, and pickling lime.

That was also where they stored the extra-large matches called barn burners used to light the fire for the *eisa kessle* (iron kettle). The huge cast-iron pot rested on the cast-iron top of a brick enclosure. Heavy pieces of wood, along with newspaper and kindling, were fed into the enclosure and lit with a barn burner through an opening on the front that was then sealed with a cast-iron door. The door was securely shut to contain the heat that was necessary to heat the water in the kettle for cold packing hundreds of jars of fruits and vegetables.

The floor was cemented and painted with at least three coats of a light brown oil-based paint—the color of mud. The man at the paint store had tried to persuade Mam that nowadays the water-based paint was as good. But she pursed her lips and shook her head. Her eyes flashed as she said,

27

no, it wasn't. She knew what held up under the countless comings and goings of a large family. Only her oil-based paint would protect the floor against kicked-off boots, endless baskets of laundry, bushels of corn, peaches, and apples, cardboard boxes, and stainless steel buckets.

Adjacent to the *kesslehaus*, the kitchen was large and homey. Golden oak cabinets were constructed along two walls in an L-shape. The large gas refrigerator, an EZ Freeze from Indiana, fit snugly beneath two small cabinets built above it. On the other side of the room were the gas stove and the canister set containing flour, sugar, tea, and coffee running along one countertop.

The kitchen table was large. Two leaves extended it to the required size for seating the seven of them. At one time, when the married boys had all been at home, they'd had as many as four leaves. The brawny sons had needed elbow room as they shoveled heaping mounds of mashed potatoes, beef, beans, and corn into their mouths to nourish their craving stomachs.

The seating area was like an extension of the kitchen, a circle of sofas and chairs, propane lamps housed in oak cabinets, magazine racks containing the *Die Botschaft*, the *Connection*, *Keepers at Home*, and the *Ladies Journal*—all periodicals about Plain life. Mam looked forward to reading them when Mervin brought in each day's mail on his scooter.

Levi's room was off to the left, facing the front lawn and the white dairy barn that was added on to the older barn structure in 1978 and now housed much of their livelihood. They'd added the cement manure pit, the new barnyard, and the large shop and implement shed the year after they remodeled the house.

Mam had been guilty, plain down guilty, when Ammon King's work crew started gutting the dear old house. What had been good enough for her mother-in-law all of her life should have been good enough for her. But Dat squeezed her shoulders and said they'd been blessed and were now financially able to make the renovations. Though she beamed and smiled and her eyes twinkled as she secretly anticipated her wonderful "new" house, she always kept her head bowed and tried to be humble—but she really wasn't.

They made do in the buggy shed during the renovations that summer. Now Mam grew pots of ferns and fig trees and African violets on the new wide oak-trimmed windowsills. She hung the required dark green window shades in the living room but made pretty cotton curtains in plain beige for the kitchen.

She was, after all, a minister's wife, and her house needed to be in the *ordnung* (within the rules) as befitted the wife of a leader in the church. But, oh, how she adored it! She scattered hand-woven rugs made from cast-off clothing, enjoying

29

the charm the vibrant colors added, and went about her days with a song in her heart, surrounded by the things she loved.

Sarah must have dozed. There was a knock on the door followed by a rustling sound. She realized that someone was in the house. Sitting up and squinting, she carefully lowered the footrest of the blue La-Z-Boy, glancing at Levi's form beneath the covers, and stood up.

"Hannah."

At the same time, Mam's head rolled across the back of the hickory rocker. She gasped, "*Ach* (oh), my!"

Hannah, the wife of Elam Stoltzfus and the mother of several married daughters and two boys, Chris and Matthew, was their closest neighbor. "Don't be scared. Stay there. *Ach*, Malinda!"

An old sweater was slung across her purple dress, a black apron pinned around her rotund form. Gathering Sarah and Malinda in a massive hug of sympathy, she bore enormous amounts of goodwill, kindness, and *an mit-leidich's g'feel* (understanding). She shed a few discreet tears as she spoke, trying in vain to contain them. Stepping back, she kept a large hand on each of their shoulders.

"Oh, I told Elam, of all the folks in Lancaster County, Daveys are the least deserving of this tragedy. Your whole barn! In one night? Do they

30

know what happened? Was it the diesel? *Gel* (right), that was probably where the fire started. You know, I would have come up, but to tell you the truth, I was afraid I'd get smashed flat by a fire truck. Those sirens give me the woolies. *Ach*, Davey."

Leaving Mam and Sarah, she went to greet Dat, his eyes red rimmed, his face streaked and blackened.

"Davey."

She shook his hand as firmly as a man might, then pulled her upper lip over her lower one, ducked her head, and blinked. In the morning light, her dark hair gleamed under her white covering, a shroud of motherliness.

"Good morning, Hannah."

"Oh, you look awful tired, Davey. What a night! What a dreadful night. Elam came up here right away. He said you got the cows out. That's good. But the horses. Oh, I can't think of the horses. I thought of Priscilla's Dutch."

Mam lifted a finger in warning, her eyes rolling to the couch where Priscilla lay sleeping, or appeared to be.

"Well."

Hannah turned to the cardboard box she'd been carrying and carefully extracted two large jelly-roll pans containing her famous breakfast pizza.

"*Gook mol* (look here), Malinda."

Where cooking was concerned, insecurity was

completely foreign to Hannah. There wasn't a shred of humility in her. She knew the firemen would be complimenting the huge pans of breakfast pizza as they reached for second helpings. She knew, and she was glad.

Hannah took charge, telling Mam and Sarah to freshen up as she had breakfast under control. Matthew was bringing French toast in her stainless steel roaster.

Mam looked as if she might cry. Instead she laughed with eyes that glistened too brightly.

Sarah went upstairs, her legs cramping with fatigue. She entered her room and held the curtains aside, watching the scene below. It looked like the end of the world—the apocalypse —only all in one spot. Twisted, blackened metal lay jumbled among horrible, charred timbers, once so strong and useful and sweet-smelling from centuries of supporting a roof with the harvest stored below. Now all was reduced to nothingness.

Patches of determined little flames kept breaking out, defiant and rebellious against the dousing torrents of water that had extinguished them. The smoke was unrelenting, groping its ghastly black way into nothingness. The very maw of hell, Sarah thought.

Dat had often expounded on heaven's wonders, but he also spoke of an awful place of fire and brimstone, where torment is never quenched. Well, this earthly fire was quenched. *Kaput* (done). All the power of the devil, and that's exactly what it was, could not prevail against the human spirit of kindness, sympathy, and the goodness that made a community pull together.

In her mind, Sarah pictured their whole church district with ropes held taut over their shoulders, their backs bent, pulling large cut stones to build a wondrous Egyptian pyramid, like the Israelite slaves in a Bible story book. As the knowledge that good triumphs over evil seeped through the fear and doubt, sealing off the conduits of worry and anxiety, Sarah knew she had nothing to worry about.

Hannah was the first one, lifting Mam's burden of breakfast. During the restless night, while they had dozed, uncomfortable, unable to sleep, Hannah had been mixing flour and yeast and sugar and oil, spreading the dough to each corner of the large pans, her heavy fingers repeating motions she'd done hundreds of times. Fried, shredded potatoes were next, then crumbled sausages and large bits of bacon that were applied with a liberal hand. The egg beater had been put to work mixing dozens of eggs that were then poured over it all with a flourish. After sprinkling shredded cheddar cheese on top, Hannah had popped the preparation into a hot oven before tackling the dishes.

She'd wake Matthew early. He was the cook.

Sarah smiled to herself. Matthew Stoltzfus.

Tall, dark, and built like a wrestler, and happily dating the sweetest, cutest girl in the group of Sarah's friends.

She shook herself and peered to the right as she heard the grinding of a tractor-trailer's gears. Surely they weren't bringing the bulldozers already.

Incredulous, her eyes popping in disbelief, she watched as the large truck bearing a yellow earth-moving machine came slowly up the drive. A line of buggies followed, the horses tossing their heads impatiently, champing bits in frustration.

"Sarah!"

"Yes?"

"You better hurry up."

She dashed to the bathroom, pulled out the steel hairpins, and ran a brush through her long, curly hair. Opening the silver faucet, Sarah cupped her hand beneath the streaming water and wet her hair. She used a fine-toothed comb to help tame the silken, brown curls and then applied hairspray liberally, her fingers working the pump of the lime green bottle of Fructis. Satisfied, she carefully placed a neat white covering on her head, sliding the straight pins along each side to hold it in place.

She decided to stay in the green dress she'd donned in a panic. It was the color of grass. She yanked a black apron from the closet, slid it over her head, and tied the strings behind her back. She pulled on warm socks and ran down the stairs.

She was surprised to see a line of weary men already waiting to fill their plates. Dat hurried by with clean towels as they washed up at the sink in the *kesslehaus*.

"Pour grape juice," Mam instructed curtly, the strain of the night showing in her eyes.

Quietly, Sarah opened the refrigerator door, found the gallon pitchers of chilled homemade juice, and began to pour, her eyes downcast.

"Matthew, what took you so long?" Hannah said, her voice rough with irritation.

"It takes a while, using up all that bread," was his jovial answer in the gravelly voice that amazed Sarah.

They'd gone to school together. All their years, they had stood in singing class and played baseball and volleyball and Prisoner's Base and King's Corner. He was in fourth grade when she entered first grade, a scared, sniveling little girl who cried every single morning that first week. She couldn't imagine her life without Matthew Stoltzfus in it, albeit in a detached way since he'd started dating Rose Zook.

They were the perfect match, and Sarah was happy for Matthew. So happy, in fact, that she cried great tears of happiness that puddled into a rushing river of misery. It wasn't safe to sit on its banks and observe the way the water took away all her peace and comfort and hope for the future.

But she was happy for Matthew. Really happy.

He stepped up to the table and set down a steaming hot roaster piled high with French toast, looked sideways at her, and said, "Hey, Sarah." She looked back at him, saw the sympathy in his eyes, and knew she'd be sitting by that rushing, roiling river again. Her voice came out a bit choked and shaky when she said, "Hey, Matthew," and she went right back to pouring grape juice as if her only interest in life was how accurately the liquid came to within an inch of the top of each glass.

Chapter 3

The men were ravenous, and the food disappeared as Hannah's stack of Great Value paper plates from Wal-Mart were filled one by one. English men with caps, mustaches, and long shoulder-length hair or no hair at all—their heads shaven cleanly, shining in the early morning light—lined up with Amish men, their straw hats removed, their hair and beards trimmed and cut in almost identical fashion.

The thing was—English people didn't have an *ordnung*. They could dress as they pleased. If they wanted to wear something, they could, and if they didn't want to, they didn't have to. Mentally, Sarah wondered what Elmer King would look like if he shaved his head like the one firefighter.

He'd probably look very English, at any rate.

How long would it take a whole head of hair to grow back?

"Good morning, Sarah."

She started, looked at Elmer King, smiled, and answered politely. She shouldn't think things like that, she told herself. But you couldn't help what you thought, could you? She'd never say what ran through her mind; she just thought it, which never hurt anyone.

She was aware of a wet smell—a stench, actually. It smelled like a campfire doused with water, sending up a stinking steam.

Eww. Someone smelled bad.

She saw Mam looking at the firemen's boots, the black ashes mixed with mud making great tracks on her clean kitchen floor. But she stayed quiet, of course.

Old Sam Stoltzfus was already in line, Sarah noticed. Bless him, so eager to help at an age when many men would have been glad to stay at home. Sarah knew, though, that his balding, gray-haired head housed vast knowledge about rebuilding barns, a veritable treasure of unforgotten skills honed by a lifetime of experience. Somehow, the sight of the well-known member of the community was an immense comfort.

Another comfort was the arrival of the women-folk who came before breakfast was over bearing casseroles and cake pans and Wal-Mart bags.

After the others were served, Sarah was fortunate enough to have a slice of the French toast for herself with a cup of good, strong coffee. The sweet toast was thick and spongy, heavy and perfect doused with maple syrup. How could a twenty-one-year-old guy cook like this? She shook her head and hoped Rose would appreciate him. Wow!

Sarah packed Suzie's and Mervin's lunches, making sandwiches with Kunzler sweet bologna and provolone cheese. She added chocolate whoopie pies, wrinkling her nose at the sticky Saran Wrap. The whoopie pies had to be a week old, but she guessed school children never really noticed what they ate. She grabbed a handful of stick pretzels from the bag of Tom Sturgis pretzels, added red, juicy apples, and snapped the lids closed.

Hurriedly, she pushed Suzie into the bathroom, wet her hair, and brushed out the tangles amid silent grimaces. Ignoring the ouching and complaining, Sarah wasted no time getting her sister ready for school.

"I don't know why we have to go if our barn burned down," Suzie said, unhappily adjusting a hairpin.

"You have perfect attendance, don't you?" Sarah asked.

"Yeah."

"Well, then. Careful on your way out."

Casting a worried look out the window of the *kesslehaus*, Sarah decided to walk to the road with them, grasping reluctant little Mervin's hand firmly in her own.

"Not so fast!" he protested.

"You always stalk along like a big old goose," Suzie added, still not quite accepting of the fact that she was being trundled off to ordinary school with all that excitement at home.

"Hey!"

"Well, I mean it."

"Think of the story you'll have to tell the other children!"

"Maybe Teacher Esther will let you come watch!" Mervin shouted.

Sarah watched them go, waved, and turned to go back to the kitchen. Suddenly, she noticed how strange the farm seemed without the big white barn beside the house where it belonged. Is that really how fast a barn can simply disintegrate into a jumbled, stinking mass of blackened timbers?

She couldn't think of the horses and hoped they were turned to ashes, the way bodies were when they were cremated. The calves had died, and a few of the heifers. The wagon parked in the haymow, the diesel and fuel tanks and bulk tank and milking machines—so many things she never thought of were gone.

The trucks and bulldozers and men swarmed around the remains of the barn as the smoke continued to billow, changing from black to gray to white before it was absorbed into nothingness by the atmosphere.

Suddenly she stopped, horrified. Oh, no! She couldn't watch, but she couldn't look away.

The men had found a great, black skeleton, or pieces of one, with large chunks of charred flesh dangling from it like a steak that had burnt on the grill too long. The men rolled, shoved, and then lifted it. When the head dangled, Sarah uttered a strangled cry, turned to lean across the white fence, and retched, heaving up her breakfast. Reeling and sliding to the bottom of a fence post, she willed herself not to faint.

Sarah had never seen anything so grisly, so unnerving. The smoke now appeared as a grinning specter of death, and she had to look away, unable to let her imagination conjure up the evil she felt.

When the insistent whining of the diesel engine in the dozer suddenly stopped, Sarah swiftly lifted her head to witness a sight that would remain locked in her mind forever. Priscilla, a blue wraith with her thin limbs flailing helplessly in the throes of her agony, pounded desperately on the great yellow monster that was taking away her beloved pet.

Sarah heard the screams, the wails of denial, through the film of her own tears. A black form, Dat surely, retrieved Priscilla gently as the dozer operator hopped off his machine and also went to her.

Sarah pressed her fist to her mouth. As tears streamed down her cheeks, her chest heaved painfully, the weight of her sister's grief squeezing the breath from her. She walked slowly, her head bent. When she reached the yard, she noticed the well-manicured lawn that had been so perfectly maintained now contained deep ruts where fire trucks and countless other vehicles had sunk their heavy tires into the sodden soil. Was there no end to the devastation?

Surely the fire had been an accident. If it wasn't, she thought she might not be able to deal with it. Who could be so ruthless, so completely lacking in mercy? She desperately hoped there had been a smoldering spark in the diesel shanty. Didn't that happen sometimes?

Sarah reached Priscilla and took her shaking form from Dat's arms where his filthy, smoke-blackened hands had held her as if he willed her to gain strength from him. Looking out over Priscilla's head, his eyes—dry but so filled with pain and devastation—appeared black.

Reaching out, Sarah said, "*Komm*, Priscilla."

As before, Priscilla went, obeying her sister's voice.

The bulldozer operator's brown Carhartt sleeve reached across Dat's back as they turned away, the English man's coat in stark contrast to Dat's homemade black one. It was human sympathy, man to man, English to Amish, with no difference at a time such as this.

When they reached the *kesslehaus*, Sarah supported Priscilla as she reached to open the door and then turned her to look squarely into her eyes.

"Priscilla?"

It was a question, but her sister knew the meaning of it. She nodded, met Sarah's eyes.

"Sarah, don't be mad, okay? I'm alright. I just knew it was Dutch, and—I shouldn't have acted that way. He just couldn't take him away. I know it's dumb."

Before Sarah could answer, the door opened, and Elmer King *sei* Lydia (his wife, Lydia), a young woman of the community, came out to the girls and wordlessly took Priscilla in her arms, caressing her back as the sobs returned.

"*Siss yusht net chide* (It just isn't right)," she kept saying. "Priscilla, don't cry."

Priscilla took a few deep breaths, steadied herself, and offered to help in the kitchen, bravely facing her loss. Dat came in repeatedly, his eyes soft with care, and inquired about his daughter's well-being without her being aware of it. Mam cried softly but soon lifted her gray apron, removed a rumpled Kleenex, and blew her nose in one hard snort. She sniffed again, put the Kleenex back, and resumed her organizing.

The food arrived steadily all forenoon: dough-nuts from the bake shop at Weis on Route 30, boxes of canned fruit, plastic bags of potatoes, cakes, puddings in plastic ice cream containers, stews in blue granite roasters, and endless amounts of meats and cheeses. Some went to the refrigerator in the basement after being carefully recorded on a notepad to help them remember who had brought what and where it was stored.

That was Mam. She was the best manager in Lancaster County, Hannah said.

Sarah watched, amazed at her mother's ability to deal with the responsibility of the day's demands after only a few hours of sleep.

Ruthie and Anna Mae arrived, shock and sympathy written all over their faces, carrying the little ones. Mam swooped in to extract her beloved grandchildren from her daughters' arms.

Ruthie had two children, Sarahann and Johnny, the baby. Anna Mae had little Justin, only three months old. Mam had had a fit when Roy and Anna Mae named their son Justin. She didn't know what they were thinking, she said, giving their son such a worldly name. But Dat smiled ruefully and said they'd better stay out of it before they stepped on toes they had no business stepping on. Anna Mae had always been inclined toward fanciness, Mam said. A real handful.

So they accepted and loved little Justin, and Sarah thought it was a nice name. She was glad

Anna Mae had a Justin, so she could have one, too. A namesake was never frowned upon.

After the food was mostly *fer-sarked* (taken care of), they planned dinner. Definitely the roaster full of beef stew. They'd do a sixteen-quart kettle of corn and one of green beans and potatoes. Three heads of cabbage would make *graut* (coleslaw).

The women bustled about. They sliced heads of cabbage with wide knives and energetically scraped them across hand-held graters, keeping time with talk punctuated by bouts of genuine laughter or teasing. The boys—Abner, Allen, and Johnny—arrived with their wives and a horde of little ones who raced around the house, running underfoot the way little cousins do, the excitement high when Doddy's barn burns to the ground.

When Dat was surrounded by his three married sons, his spirits were lifted, energized by their unfailing support. The boys had all chosen to buy homes and start their roofing and siding business in sister communities, where land prices were inexpensive. Now they had a nearly two-hour drive to their parents' farm. Nevertheless, Dat was encouraged by the presence of his sons and their families, greeting each one with a special light of welcome shining from his tired eyes.

The dinner was set up on plastic folding tables in the *kesslehaus*. Great platters of cakes and bars and cookies were placed on another table with lemon meringue, pumpkin, and cherry pies.

Sarah laughed when Hannah hid a particularly high chocolate shoofly pie in the pantry, saying she knew that was one of Amos *sei* Sylvia's (his wife, Sylvia's), and no one made them like her. What the men didn't know would never hurt them.

Sarah stood, her arms crossed, listening to the men as they sat on the porch, their heads bent as they ate hungrily. Talk had started, as Sarah knew it would. The speculation, the blame, the endless questioning.

David Beiler was a meticulous man. No greasy rags in his diesel shanty. Haying season hadn't started. It was too early for hot, green hay. The FBI would be coming. Just watch. Something like this isn't let go in this day and age. Arsonists don't get away with it. Too much technology. Too many smart people. Nobody can light a fire these days and get away with it.

Levi sat in the middle eating vast quantities of the good food, his black sweater gaping open at the front. While he insisted his sore throat was worse, he explained in great and vivid detail his night vigil before the fire.

The men listened kindly, laughing uproariously. Levi laughed with them, his small brown eyes alight with the happiness he felt at being one of them, knowing he had seen that white car and that the Watkins man hadn't been there since September twenty-third.

That really tickled his brothers, who roared

in unison, and Sarah laughed out loud, too.

Helping himself to another slice of pumpkin pie, Matthew Stoltzfus turned and watched Sarah laugh. She went to Levi and wiped his mouth tenderly, the light catching the blonde highlights of her glossy, rippling hair, and he wondered at it.

All day lumbering trucks carried away some of the wet debris, but many of the smoldering remains were simply pushed out of the way to prepare for the monumental task ahead. The cows had been dispersed to neighboring dairy farms, where helpful neighbors, who felt they were doing their duty, each took on a few extra ones.

Old Sam Stoltzfus and Levi's Abner sat in the shed beside the buggy with papers spread before them, making a drawing, sketching roughly. Sitting close to the telephone, they would soon be ordering lumber and metal.

In the house, Mam finally sank into Levi's blue recliner and slept for almost an hour.

The daughters-in-law, Maryann, Rachel, and Emma Mae, were all eagerly waiting for the van to take them to their parents' homes. Living so far away, they missed Lancaster County, their birthplace. They were glad to spend time with loved ones in spite of their in-laws' loss.

"Whew!" Priscilla sighed after the last noisy little people had followed their mothers out the door.

Sarah was already drawing water, to which she

added soap and a rag, preparing to get down on her hands and knees for the task of washing away the dirt that had been tracked all over the linoleum.

"This is the biggest mess we've ever had," Suzie complained from her place at the sink, where she was washing endless dishes. According to her, dishes multiplied while sitting on a counter, so you never really finished.

The girls worked together late into the evening and then sat at the table, so weary they hardly knew what they were saying but too tired to take their showers. The boys, Abner, Allen, and Johnny, had decided to stay to help Dat with the decisions about roofing and siding, offering to make phone calls, helping to calculate the vast amount of concrete that they would need to pour in the morning.

As they caught up on the news of the community and other concerns, the conversation was woven with tales of other barn fires in previous years. What about the barn fires in Belleville? Folk lore or truth?

As they spoke, a mist of unsettling sensations hovered in the air. Sarah tried to shake off a foreboding feeling of evil that meant to destroy them. Why them? Why a family of ordinary people who went about their everyday lives? Nothing in Sarah's memory had ever evoked this sense of uneasiness.

Before the fire, she had always gone to bed trusting, innocent, knowing that in the morning Dat would be at the bottom of the stairs calling her to do the milking. She'd never even thought of a fire destroying their barn. Now she could never return to that innocence.

The fire marshal had come, hadn't he? Suddenly, Sarah sat bolt upright and inquired loudly about the fire marshal's appearance. What was the verdict?

David Beiler lowered his head, a look of pain crossing his features yet again.

"I just hoped you would forget to ask," he said quietly.

Priscilla's eyes opened wide with fear, and Sarah was frightened for her as well as for herself.

"Was it—did someone light our barn on purpose?" she asked, gripping the arm of her chair.

"I wish I could spare you the truth, but I can't. We have to deal with this strange and troubling fact. It was the work of an arsonist."

"Really?" Sarah gasped.

"So Levi was right."

"Afraid so."

"There are about a million white cars in the state of Pennsylvania, so it doesn't seem to be very helpful—what Levi saw," Johnny said somberly.

"You mean he may as well have seen Santa Claus swooping out of the sky with his reindeer?" Allen asked.

They all laughed, which helped ease the fear. Sarah knew Priscilla had heard enough. It was time to go to bed.

Upstairs, she flicked the small pink lighter and lifted the glass chimney, holding it at an angle. Rewarded with a steady orange flame, she settled the chimney back on the head of the kerosene lamp.

Priscilla was rooting around in Sarah's drawers. That was strange.

"What are you doing?"

"May I wear your nightgown?"

"Why?"

"Oh, just because."

"Don't you want to take a shower?"

"No!"

"Priscilla, what's wrong? You're acting strangely. Why don't you go to your own room?"

"It's dark over there."

"You have a light."

Sarah stopped and looked at her sister, annoyed. She stood gripping a rumpled nightgown to her chest, as if the power of her clenched hands could hold the dark and the evil away from her body. Her eyes were large, too wide open, filled with a sort of wildness now.

When Sarah met her eyes, she dropped them, but her hands remained clenched. Going to her sister, Sarah held her hands in both of her own and whispered, "Priscilla, are you afraid?"

Instantly, Priscilla's pent-up sobs rose to the surface, the culmination of terror and loss and all-encompassing fright. Her innocence forever taken away, she was unprepared to deal with this new and awful thing that wedged its way into their life.

The crumpled nightgown fell to their feet and covered them as Sarah pulled her sister's shaking form into her arms and held her, willing her touch to comfort the girl and bolster her courage.

"It's okay," she murmured over and over.

Finally, Priscilla took a deep breath and nodded her head.

"It's just that . . . Sarah, if a person so intent on hurting animals did that, lit the barn, burned Dutch, what's going to keep him from lighting the house and killing us all? I'm afraid to go to bed."

Suddenly defiant, she reached for a Kleenex from the box on Sarah's nightstand and shook her head.

"Go ahead, say it. I know you think I'm *bupplish* (childish)."

Sarah sighed and assured Priscilla she was not *bupplish*. But Sarah also felt as if a giant hand was squashing her down so tightly that there was danger of her life's breath being taken away.

Was this just the beginning?

Chapter 4

It was only five o'clock when Mam whispered Sarah's name at the door of her room. Sarah moaned groggily and snuggled deeper into her pillow. But the sudden remembrance of the fire and what the day would bring quickly propelled her out of bed. Hurriedly, she dressed, instructing Priscilla to grab the sheets from her bed. There was lots of laundry to be washed before breakfast.

It seemed funny to hear only the soft swish-swish of the agitator. It made only a quiet hum instead of the usual sound of the air motor. The diesel tank, the air tank, and the fuel tank had all been rendered unusable by the heat of the flames, so they were using a generator and a Maytag wringer washer with an electric motor as a temporary set up.

The heaps of clothes at her feet were piles of everyday comfort, the smell of the Tide detergent and Downy fabric softener a solidifying thing. Their essence was something dear and familiar, and no arsonist could touch it.

While the first load of whites swirled in the sudsy water, Sarah went to the kitchen, sniffed, and smiled appreciatively.

"Mmm. Coffee ready?"

Mam nodded, her cup steaming on the table.

Pouring herself a cup, Sarah went to the refrigerator, bent to retrieve the Coffee-mate French vanilla creamer, and splashed a generous portion into the steaming brown brew. She took a sip and closed her eyes.

"Did you sleep well?" Mam asked.

"I did. But Priscilla slept with me. She's . . ."

"Is she alright?"

"I think so."

Mam smiled a sad, knowing smile, one that slid sideways and evaporated as her eyes clouded over with concern.

"Priscilla has always been so soft-hearted. She's so attached to her pets, has been all her life. We should have gotten Dutch out before any of the cows."

Blaming herself as always, Mam fretted about her daughter, who was at the tender age of fourteen.

"We'll just have to get another horse as soon as the barn is done. The sooner one appears, the faster she'll heal."

Mam nodded.

She admitted to Sarah, then, that she knew how Priscilla felt, having lain awake grappling with the onslaught of "why" and "whodunits," the fear of the unknown raising its ugly head. One couldn't escape it. Besides, she didn't really know what was expected of her on this day. Mam felt as if all her pillars of support had been knocked away during the fearful night.

How could she manage a meal if she wasn't sure who was bringing what, how many women would arrive to help cook and serve, and how on earth she'd ever get her laundry room floor clean again?

Sarah blinked, aghast. Her own mother! She always had a firm hold on every situation, a step ahead of her husband, fussing like a capable little biddy hen.

She told Sarah she'd prayed during the night, but her anxiety meter ran so high it seemed as if her prayers bounced off the ceiling. She was sure God was not happy with her for being so afraid.

Sarah pictured her mother lying flat in bed with a pressure gauge attached to her head, the red needle pointing all the way to the right as steam rose from her ears. She giggled, a hand over her mouth.

"What?" Mam asked, perturbed now.

Sarah told her, and Mam had a good laugh, then wiped her eyes and said that was better than a shot of vitamin B.

"You and your imagination, Sarah. Now you better get the washing done. You know Hannah's going to be up here first thing."

When Sarah stepped out with the first load of whites, she recoiled from the heavy, stagnant air, rife with a wet, smoking stench, the early morning darkness a reminder of what had occurred such a short time ago.

As she hung up tablecloths, pillowcases, sheets, and towels, she imagined the driver of the white car hunched over a small pile of newspapers and kindling with a lighter or a propane torch or a book of matches. What exactly did one use to bring down an entire beautiful Lancaster County barn?

As it had been, their barn had been special. The original section was built in 1805 with good limestone laid meticulously by their staunch German forefathers, who were hard working and smart, fiercely brave and determined to thrive in this new land. They certainly had done so, raising amazing crops in the Garden Spot of America with its fertile, productive soil bearing fruits and vegetables to feed their well-kept animals. They prospered beyond their imaginations.

Gott gibt reichlich (God giveth richly). They had laid the foundation of thankfulness, stressing gratitude with each load of hay, their faith as firm as the enduring stone walls of each family's barn. But now the seemingly indestructible stone was crumbled and blackened, severely damaged. Would their own faith withstand this ogre of evil intent?

Sarah shook her head, showers of foreboding ruining her day like a quick squall that hindered the drying of the laundry.

What did the man in the white car look like? Was he young? Old? Smart? Cunning? Rich or poor? Why had he done it? Perhaps he was mentally ill. If he drove a car, he was not physically handicapped, like Levi.

She shivered in the cool morning air, a vivid picture of the devil himself driving that car entering her mind. Enough now, she told herself, and stood, watching the shades of peach and pink and gray spread across the east. Another day was at hand. What would it bring? She did not have long to wait.

Men and boys began arriving in vans and buggies and on foot. Huge tractor-trailers carrying stacks of clean, raw-cut oak timbers, pine siding, and sheets of metal belched smoke from their exhaust pipes as the drivers throttled down to make the turn into their driveway.

The previous day, clacking yellow bulldozers had crawled and pushed while a knot of able men considered the damage to the concrete and stone. What was worth salvaging and what needed to be replaced?

Old Sam Stoltzfus, Dat at his side, had moved among the bulldozers, tablet and pen in hand. His gray and white beard moved gently as he spoke, his wide-brimmed straw hat pulled low over his eyes, his shoulders still held erect, even if his back remained bent.

The order had been placed as soon as possible.

Now the great saws bit into sturdy oak logs as they cut the stoutest beams for the new building.

They decided to replace the stones with modern poured cement walls. Dat's eyes had not remained dry as he watched the blackened stone and crumbled mortar being hauled away on whining dump trucks. They'd be used as fill somewhere, an unseen foundation for another hotspot where developers paid phenomenal prices for squares of valuable farmland that were sure to turn a hefty profit.

It was the way of the world, and the sadness of it brought a lump to Dat's throat. He thought of those stones, the heritage of hard work, simplicity, and a frugal lifestyle. It was all being encroached upon by the lust for profit and the promise of a softer, easier, better way of life, the goal being idleness and free time.

Was it a healthy objective by Amish standards? David Beiler knew the answer and concealed his own private mourning.

Would future generations know the fulfillment of a hard day's work, when sweat flowed from a brow that was content? Would they find peace in doing without earthly wants and desires? Would they recognize that true happiness springs from self-denial? Would the will to do for others motivate their days? Or would the Amish church eventually weaken with the fires of the world, seeking after earthly possessions?

As a minister, David Beiler made the comparison in his mind. He sent up a prayer asking God to give him strength for the work in the years ahead.

Then didn't that Samuel *sei* Emma and all her sisters, some from clear below Kirkwood in Chester County, get a driver and start making doughnuts at one o'clock that morning? She was something else, Mam said.

They carried in huge plastic trays of plain and cream-filled doughnuts, some covered with powdered sugar and some dunked in big, plastic Tupperware bowls of glaze (even some of the ones that had cream filling on the inside). The women all smiled and nodded, their coverings white and neat, their dark hair combed sleekly. Their dark brown eyes were alight with interest, looking as if they'd had a good night's sleep and hadn't worked at all.

Oh, it was a fine coffee break, and it bolstered Mam's spirits.

There was tray after tray of these doughnuts and containers of chocolate chip cookies and Reese's peanut butter bars and oatmeal bars with a white glaze crisscrossed over the top. There were blueberry muffins, pecan tarts, and fruit bars that oozed cherry-pie filling.

Hannah, of course, had breezed into the house soon after six o'clock. She came bearing a bag filled with milk filters containing coffee grounds that bulged comfortably after the ends had been sewed shut. She set huge stainless steel kettles of cold water on low burners, placed two filters of coffee grounds on top, and left them to brew. It shouldn't boil, just heat to a high, rich coffee temperature until shortly after nine o'clock, when the forenoon *schtick* (break) was served.

Henry Schmucker called to the men to take a break—the concrete crew, the men still cleaning up the blackened debris, and those building the oak walls on the ground. The rich odor of freshly cut wood was pleasant after the smell of the hovering, wet smoke.

Henry was Mam's brother and a good foreman at a time such as this. Dat said he was a mover and a shaker. Things got done when Henry was around, he said.

The men filed past the long, folding tables picking up large Styrofoam cups of good, black coffee, grabbing napkins with a doughnut or two plus perhaps a bar or a cookie. They stood in jovial groups, talking and laughing, the air permeated with the purpose of the day.

A barn raising was something, now, wasn't it? English men wearing jeans, T-shirts, and baseball caps worked alongside Amish men wearing varying yellow straw hats.

The dreaded photographers, the bane of every Amish barn raising, arrived with their large black and gray instruments of intrusion slung jauntily over their shoulders or around their necks. Sarah knew their air of assured professionalism and superiority raised the ire of peace-loving folks.

She was the first to see them as she walked to the mailbox with the letter for the gas company Mam had given her. How could she know the cameras would instantly begin whirring and clicking? The photographers eagerly captured the long, easy stride of the tall, young Amish girl clad in a rich shade of blue. The black of her apron, the green maple trees as a lush background, the white letter in her hand, the early morning light a natural wonder—it was irresistible. Sarah was an added bonus to the barn raising.

Returning to the break area where the food was being served, she helped herself to a filled doughnut, bit into it, leaning forward as the powdered sugar rained down. Even with a napkin, eating a powdered doughnut required a certain skill, especially when wearing black. A small breeze could waft the airy sugar straight onto an apron, where it would cling and then multiply by five as it was wiped off.

"Mmm," she said around a mouthful of doughnut.

Samuel *sei* Emma caught the praise, acknowledged it with raised eyebrows, and then laughed good-naturedly.

More women arrived bearing dishes of food. They hurried to place it in the kitchen before moving swiftly toward the coffee and doughnuts. There was plenty to go around, and the women rolled their eyes with guilt as they tried to be delicate while procuring a second doughnut.

Aaron *sei* Lydia told Sarah there is only one way to eat a filled doughnut—in two bites while letting the filling go squooshing off wherever it wants.

Outside, the noise and yells of the men began in earnest when they began to set the massive timbers in place.

"*Noch an tzoll* (Another inch)."

Men heaved, their brawny strength pushing and pulling the oak beams and posts into place. When the first wall was finished being assembled on the ground, they attached heavy nylon ropes to either side of it. With strength provided by sheer numbers, black-clad men swarmed across the timbers and pulled the wall up and onto the new foundation. They fastened the structure with massive bolts, and dozens of hammers rang out as they pounded heavy nails into place to secure the huge oak six by sixes.

On the ground, the other walls were already finished and ready to be put into place. Sam Stoltzfus and Henry Schmucker were the captains of the great endeavor called a barn raising. It was literally that. A barn being raised in front of your eyes, Sarah thought.

"If you blink, there's another wall in place,"

she told Priscilla, who was standing beside her. Priscilla laughed, and there was a joy in her laugh.

The raising of those walls boosted their spirits in a way that was hard to explain. It just seemed secure and safe and hopeful all at the same time, this coming together of all these good folks to help lift David Beiler's family out of its fear and sadness.

Sarah watched warily as a photographer approached her. He was of average height, with sandy hair cut close to his head and glasses with thick lenses, which made his eyes appear smaller than they actually were.

"Hello," he offered.

The greeting wasn't spoken with a Lancaster County accent. It was spoken more like a "Hel-loo" as in "loop."

His smile was genuine, and Sarah had no reason to dislike him as long as he kept that camera lowered.

Sarah smiled. "Hi."

"Can I ask you a few questions?"

Sarah nodded carefully.

"Why can't I have a doughnut?"

The question was so surprising, so not what she was expecting, that she burst out laughing in her musical way. His sandy eyebrows went up, and he laughed with her.

"Maybe if you'd say 'may I,' " Sarah said shyly.

"May I?"

"Yes, of course."

"May I take a picture?"

"Of the doughnuts?"

"No, you."

"Oh, no. It's not allowed. I'd get in trouble."

"Why?"

Just in time, Sarah saw Matthew Stoltzfus walking across the yard with Rose Zook beside him. In broad daylight! At a barn raising!

Sarah was surprised but glad to see them and excused herself from the impertinent questioning. She turned away and missed seeing the puzzled photographer shrug his shoulders in resignation, then help himself to three glazed doughnuts.

Rose Zook wiggled her fingers prettily and trilled, "Hey, Sarah!"

Sarah greeted them warmly.

"Boy, I'm glad to see you. I was ready to get away from the photographer."

"Was he nosy?"

"Just a bit."

"Rose, I'm going to help now. I'll be ready to leave about three this afternoon. See ya. Good to see you, Sarah."

"See you, Matt."

Rose looked at him, and they exchanged an intimate look, one that excluded Sarah completely. She said nothing, waiting until Rose was ready to go. They stood together, watching the great walls being hammered into place.

It was a true visual feast. Men in black and navy-blue broadfall trousers topped by shirts of every color of the rainbow, wearing golden yellow straw hats, black felt hats, or no hats at all. They were set against the yellowish brown of the fresh cut timbers with the blue sky in the background, the verdant growth of trees and pastures, the dark loamy soil tilled and waiting for crops to be planted.

To Sarah, it was more than visual. It was a feast for the heart as well. Nothing could chase away the gloom of fear and uneasiness like this picture before her. It was the sunshine of brotherly love and caring, standing together through anything and everything that God handed to them.

Like the soaked but still smoking pile of black debris, the dread had to sit on the sidelines like an injured player as the game went on, played out by the goodwill of all these men who had come because of their caring, heartfelt willingness to help.

When the first rafter went up and was fastened in the way of the forefathers, with mortise and tenon, Sarah swallowed. How often had she seen the wooden pegs firmly pounded into the holes drilled into the heavy beams?

They were holes and pegs, so solid and indestructible. But to Sarah, it was a part of her life, her childhood. When she and her siblings had swung from the great old rafters, sitting on the black rubber tire attached to the heavy jute rope, it had never once entered their minds that the centuries-old beams joined by those wooden pegs would give way.

As a teenager, Sarah had helped stack the heavy, prickly bales of hay, so pungent and sweet smelling, clear up to the rafters. She'd reached out a hand and touched the mortise and tenon, wondering at the craftsmanship.

Who had built this great barn? Did the people in the 1700s and 1800s look just like us? Was there, perhaps, a handsome young man, married to his first love, who had pounded the peg into place?

It was enticing, this imagining and wondering. Somehow, the hay stacked so tightly, the alfalfa rich in nutrients for the milk cows below, spoke of the agelessness of this great old barn, housing the fruits of the earth, the animals, a way of life.

The barn had held through the howling winds and snows of winter and the claps of thunder and sizzling lightning during welcome summer thunderstorms that sent them to seek shelter. They threw open the great doors to let the moist, cool air rejuvenate their tired and sweating bodies. The elements were friendly, even in their extremes. Who could know that one tiny flick of a lighter would bring this majestic barn to its destruction?

So Sarah was thrilled as each rafter was firmly pegged in the old way. She was comforted by the sight and gathered hope to her heart.

Rose sighed, a dramatic expression intended to evoke questions. "Oh, that Matthew is something else. He's so cute!"

She clasped her hands rapturously as she watched him, steadily keeping her eyes on his dark, muscular figure. "Look at him, just hanging onto that timber, pounding away! Supposing he'd fall? Oh, I can't stand it!"

Clearly, Rose did not see the barn or the men or feel the emotions Sarah felt. But then, Rose hadn't experienced the night of horror and the ghoulish fear threatening to overtake common sense.

"It does look like he's barely hanging on," Sarah agreed, laughing.

"I hate barn raisings. They're so dangerous."

Sarah bit down on her lower lip, staying mercifully quiet. She watched the men, heard their shouts, observed their willingness to obey, and marveled at the scene before her.

Chainsaws whined and buzzed, their biting teeth sending fountains of sawdust spraying upward. Tape rules snapped as men measured and then set into place another heavy beam, an accurate piece of the huge jigsaw puzzle unfolding before their eyes.

It would be nice to have a special friend in her life like Rose did, Sarah thought. She yearned to have the sense of belonging Rose had. Sometimes she felt as if, at age nineteen, there was a void in her heart that only a true love could fill.

Yes, Mam had warned her. Go slow. God comes first. He's most important.

So she yearned, said nothing, spoke of a love only to herself, and hoped someday, somewhere, God would have mercy and fulfill the want she harbored.

Chapter 5

Inside the house, Sarah decided that Mam might as well forget about a clean floor, today or any time soon. She walked delicately around boxes of food, toys, and mashed doughnuts and Cheerios.

A baby screamed from the old high chair Mam kept for feeding the grandchildren. Usually there were two or three babies who needed a high chair, so one of the mothers had to hold her infant while she spooned yogurt into its mouth.

What a gigantic beehive! Sarah stood, uncertain. What to do?

Mam was everywhere, and so was Hannah, barking orders, opening oven doors, checking huge kettles of bubbling food. There were women breading chicken, rolling it in beaten eggs, then seasoned flour and bread crumbs, arranging it on trays to be taken to the neighbors to bake in their electric ovens.

An oversized woman Sarah didn't know was

slicing a ham at the table, and by the alacrity with which the woman kept sampling the succulent slices, Sarah felt she'd be fortunate to taste any herself.

She jumped when the woman said, "Hi! *Bisht die Sare, gel?* (You're Sarah, right?)"

"*Ya.*"

"*Vitt dale? Siss hesslich goot* (You want some? It's really good)."

"Thank you."

Sarah reached for the steaming portion, popped it into her mouth, and said appreciatively, "Mmm."

"*Gel? Gel?*"

She was so delighted with Sarah's verdict that she laughed heartily and clapped a pink, greasy hand on Sarah's forearm.

"We could just simply eat it all, you and me!" she chortled, her round face shining with happiness.

Sarah still didn't know the woman's name, but she felt a definite kinship. The woman's goodwill and happy chortling came from the heart, showering Sarah with blessings that rained down like jewels. She'd never need to be afraid again, ever.

That's what happened when people helped each other in times of need. Love multiplied and grew so fast you couldn't even begin to count the vast supply.

All over the kitchen, the women were smiling,

patting backs, and supporting one another's decisions about how much butter to brown for the noodles, when the browning process was finished, when to mash the potatoes, and which was better —sour cream, cream cheese, or just plain butter.

There were lima beans and peas and corn, macaroni salad and potato salad, cole slaw and three-bean salad, deviled eggs and red beet eggs, and tiny, dark green, seven-day sweet pickles.

The women put Sarah and Rose to work, carrying the food to the trestle tables covered with heavy white tablecloths. Loud groans from the sink caught their attention. The women had become enveloped in steam as they struggled to mash the potatoes with the hand masher.

"We need the air drill. Sarah, go get Matthew," said Hannah, who was keeping one eye on the clock.

Rose stepped forward.

"I'll go."

Hannah nodded assent.

Sarah continued her work, carrying out great plastic bags of Styrofoam trays, plastic cups, plastic utensils, napkins, and salt and pepper, as well as applesauce and dishes of fruit. She looked up to see Rose with Matthew in tow, dragging an air hose and a drill.

The beaters were soon attached, and a loud whirring sound followed as the potatoes were whipped into a frenzy. Hands were raised in the air amid cries of "*Geb acht*! (Be careful!)"

Matthew grinned, his dark hair falling over his eyes as the loud noise continued from the whirring of the air motor. Mam threw in the cream cheese, Hannah the butter, and Elam Zook *sei* Ruth insisted on the sour cream.

They gathered round, teasing Matthew, then Rose, who blushed as pretty as the flower she was named for. The boiled potatoes turned into a great vat of whipped mounds laced with so much butter and varieties of cream that the women all proclaimed them better than wedding potatoes! In short order, two more kettles were done in the same manner and were also fussed and talked and exclaimed over.

"*Ach*, my gravy! Somebody get the gravy!" Mam called, waving a hand as the rich ham gravy bubbled over the top of the kettle and all over the gas stove.

Sarah reached it first, flicked the burner off, and moved the kettle off the burner in one fluid motion, spilling a substantial amount of gravy across the top of her hand.

She yelped, flew to the cold water spigot, and let it run across the now flaming burn. Instantly, a row of faces peered into the sink, clucking, asking for B & W salve.

"Comfrey salve," said one.

"Oh, no. You can't beat B & W. Specially with burdock. Do you have burdock?"

"I'd put chickweed salve on it."

"Flour and honey."

"No, not flour and honey. That leaves infection."

"Not in my book."

Sarah was in pain, the babble of voices a sea of irritation, but she tried not to let it show.

No one could seem to agree. Mam did have a jar of B & W on hand but no burdock leaves.

"You likely don't have any weeds," someone said.

"Burdock? Oh, I'm sure there is burdock in a fence row somewhere."

Matthew offered to go, Rose accompanying him, as the women returned to their work stations, finishing the final preparations for the huge dinner that would be set out under the maple trees.

The pain was unbearable when Sarah lifted her hand from the cold water, so she let the water run across it, wondering how it would ever heal. Why now, of all times? She berated herself, gritting her teeth to keep from crying out.

When Matthew returned with the burdock with its large velvety leaves and firm spines in the middle that reach across the leaf diagonally as well, Sarah instantly recognized them.

"That's what I'm supposed to use?"

"Yeah, I'll steam one. I've done burn dressings before."

"There's a stainless steel saucepan to the right of the sink. Here. Bottom drawer."

Matthew found it. She moved over so he could add a small amount of water and set it on the stove.

"It has to boil."

Sarah nodded.

There was no sound except the running water on Sarah's hand until the lid rattled on the saucepan. Matthew lifted it and plunked the heavy leaf into it.

"Are you sure about that burdock leaf?" Sarah asked.

"Course."

"It's not poisonous?"

"No."

"Where's Rose?"

"She wanted to help outside."

"Oh."

Matthew lifted the now limp, brightly colored leaf from the boiling water, laid it carefully on a clean paper towel, then brought the jar of B & W salve, a homemade herb-infused aid for healing.

Standing by the sink, he reached out and turned off the cold water.

"How does it feel?"

Sarah didn't say what she wanted to say. She just nodded her head grimly and kept her eyes averted, desperately trying to keep from shivering because of the pain.

Gently, he patted her hand dry, watching her face, and asked if she was okay.

Again, she nodded, her mouth a determined slash across her white face as she moved to sit on the couch.

"You sure?"

"Yes."

He swabbed some ointment on a piece of paper towel. Then he smoothed it gently onto the burn.

Matthew was bent over, concentrating, extremely intent on his job, so Sarah's eyes wandered across the contours of his face, his eyebrows like two dark wings above his down-cast eyes, the nose with a wide bridge, straight and chiseled, perfection. He straightened.

"Does it hurt?"

She looked up, the sting clouding her vision, as he looked down into her pain-filled eyes. It wasn't her fault that he didn't look away, she chided herself later when she felt so guilty and brash and so bold and so . . .well, stupid.

It wasn't her fault that as he had laid the burdock leaf across her hand, his hands were shaking more than a little. When he wound the sterile white gauze around it to ensure the air could not reach the burn, she couldn't help it that he gazed at her hand. She wondered why.

When she stood up, he was much too close, and she wished he'd move away. When he didn't, she sat down right away, and he looked at her hand again, and said he'd better go on out or he wouldn't get anything to eat.

She said, yes, he'd better.

"Thanks," she added, in a strangled voice full of misery and want and denial.

He blinked. He clenched his lips, opened his mouth, closed it again, and looked at her. Then he went outside, quickly, leaving Sarah sitting in an abandoned kitchen filled with open oven doors and empty kettles, sticky aluminum foil, flies, and dirty dishes.

She guessed this was how it was before you found a person who would be your special friend. You were just too vulnerable. Well, it wasn't right. Matthew was just her neighbor, dating Rose, the perfect couple. Rose was so sweet, blonde, and so right for him.

Deep shame crept across her features, misery so intense on its heels that she lowered her face into her hands and stayed that way until Mam bustled in for a few large spoons. She was so intent on her mission that she failed to see Sarah huddled on the couch.

The burdock leaf miraculously took the pain away. If only there were a plant she could pluck from a field or fence row and tape it across that mysterious region of the heart, she thought ruefully. Stepping outside, she walked slowly to the huge maples with the kaleidoscope of activity beneath them.

There was plenty of food, as Mam figured there would be. Hungry men piled their plates high.

They sat together on folding chairs or benches or cross-legged on the ground, their heads bare now, having removed their hats for silent prayer before the meal. Children raced around the perimeter of the trees. Some upset plastic cups of water as mothers hurried to correct their behavior.

Sarah stood uncertainly, hungry but reluctant. Why did she feel as if she had done something wrong? She wanted to walk out the field lane and just walk and walk and walk, across highways and around houses and places of business and people's gardens and keep walking until she was rid of this senseless thing that had happened in the kitchen.

She hoped Matthew and Rose would be married in the fall, and she'd find a special friend and begin her dating life right after that.

"Hey, Sarah!"

It was Levi, sitting on a folding chair, holding court as usual, his brothers teasing him unmercifully.

"I want cake and vanilla pudding and strawberry tapioca," Levi called loudly.

Heads were raised, smiles given generously, as Sarah waved, hurried to the food table, and began to fill his order.

"Not quite so much," Mam whispered, and Sarah nodded, removing some of the vanilla pudding.

Levi's weight was an ongoing battle they never overcame. His love for food filled his days with joy and anticipation. Sarah just never quite had the heart to deprive him of dessert in spite of his widening girth.

What else did Levi have to look forward to, besides his cards—the football and baseball cards he shuffled constantly?

Carefully she walked to Levi with the loaded plate, setting it on the small folding table directly in front of him.

"There you are, Levi."

There were no words of gratitude, just a suspicious look and a concentrated narrowing of his eyes as he held his head to one side. A remarkable amount of time passed as he examined the plate of desserts, leaving Sarah a bit uncomfortable, standing in full view of so many men and boys, who were politely averting their eyes, busying themselves with their own plates of food.

Pressing his lips in a thin line, Levi decided to speak. "You took some of the cornstarch pudding off."

"Just some."

"Why?"

"Levi."

Embarrassed, Sarah bent and said, soft and low, "Mam said."

"Why?"

"Just because. Shhh, Levi."

Clearly upset, Levi's eyes turned dark with pain and disappointment. He opened his mouth, choked, and started wailing loud sobs of hurt. Many faces turned to watch. Tender looks of pity followed before heads bent to their plates.

David Beiler, masterful in the art of comforting his oldest son, stepped over, laid a hand on the heaving, overweight form, and told him softly that Sarah would put more cornstarch pudding on his plate, his eyes telling Sarah how much—a minimal amount.

Her face turning a shade of pink, her discomfort painfully obvious, she stepped up to the dessert table and waited her turn behind a tall, wide-shouldered youth she didn't recognize. His hair was blond, cut in English style. But he wore broadfall denims and a pair of gray suspenders, his shirt a decided plaid pattern, not the usual plain fabric that was in the *ordnung*.

She thought nothing of this. The "worldly" haircut was common among the liberal youth. The years of *rumspringa* (running around) produced young men who tried their wings—experimenting in fashion, sometimes driving cars, as well as being active in organized sports. Experimentation in forbidden "things of the world" like alcohol and tobacco was not uncommon, resulting in a certain sadness as parental authority was undermined by the lusts of the flesh and the eyes holding court over a young soul.

Families bore it with *gaduld* (patience) and always with the expectation that the young people would eventually tire of these things and seek a more lasting peace—a way of life that spoke of obedience, sameness, a love for parents and God, and a return to the fold. This return was hopefully followed by dating, marriage, and raising a family in the same way their parents had.

It was always a joy to behold when a "wild" youth made the decision to start the instruction class in the church. Heads would be bent, and furtive tears would be wiped away. Fathers and mothers were grateful that the sleepless nights, the anxiety and fear, had brought this reward, one they were not worthy of, their spiritual humility a beautiful thing.

Parents of a youth who did not conform, meanwhile, carried a certain shame buried deep in the heart, an uncomfortable thorn that varied in its ability to cause pain but always there.

The line moved forward. Sarah watched as this unknown youth bent to lift a slice of chocolate cake, promptly dropped it, and watched helplessly as it rolled beneath the plastic table.

"Shoot."

"Don't worry about it," Sarah said.

He turned and smiled easily, unself-consciously. The humor on his open face was genuine, a magnet that drew her eyes to his. The smile on her lips reached her eyes, turning the gray green seawater color to one flecked with gold.

His eyes were very blue. She wasn't aware of it

until later, though, when she recalled their inter-action.

He plunked a larger slice onto his plate. Sarah added a small amount of pudding onto Levi's plate, caught Mam's eye, who smiled ruefully and shook her head, only a bit, then followed the tall blond youth until she came to Levi.

"There. Now eat."

Levi looked up at Sarah and drew a deep breath—one that quivered, like a small child.

"Are you angry with me, Sarah?"

"Of course not."

She reached out to ruffle his hair. Dat smiled at her, and Levi beamed as he lifted his spoon, happiness and anticipation shining from his florid face.

"*Ich gleich dich* (I love you)."

"I love you, too, Levi."

This exchange was not lost on the blond youth, who watched Sarah and forgot to eat his cake. He'd never seen eyes that color. They reminded him of the ocean but only when it was stormy, not when it was calm. When she moved, he thought of the antelope that roamed the plains of Wyoming. Why had he never seen her? Who was she? He never did eat his cake.

After the plates of food were consumed, large garbage bags were filled and taken to the pile of smoking debris, where they disappeared, the intense heat consuming the plastic.

Women and girls moved from table to kitchen, *fer-sarking* leftovers, planning tomorrow's meal, complimenting. They were relaxed now, the crowning point of the day achieved.

And it had gone well, hadn't it? It surely had.

Hannah sat smack down in the middle of the riotous mess and folded a fresh slice of whole wheat bread around a large portion of the succulent ham. She poured a glass of ice cold meadow tea and said the young generation could do dishes, which drew a mixed response.

Out in the *kesslehaus*, Mamie Stoltzfus said Hannah sure hadn't changed now, had she? Always running the show, being the boss, and then the minute the real chores started, she sat there in all her glory. It just irked Mamie.

Barbara Zook agreed, but shrugged her shoulders and said that was just Hannah's way.

But still, Mamie said.

Sarah moved to the sink where Rose had begun scrubbing the pans with dried food clinging to their sides. As Rose finished with the pans, Sarah took them and dried each one as if her life depended on it. In reality, her thoughts were far away.

Through the kitchen window, she watched the beams being put into place. Agile men clung to the precisely cut lumber, the hammers flailing. But she was not really seeing anything. What was wrong with her?

She felt guilt about Matthew, and the stone in her heart was now an unbearable thing. There was Rose, beside her, washing dishes at a rapid speed, chattering happily, her blonde hair and beautiful blue eyes adding another stone marked "Shame" to the one that had "Guilt" inscribed on it.

Who did she think she was? Why had Matthew been the one to dress her hand? Why not Mam, or Hannah, or anyone else?

Silently groaning, she half-heard Rose. The men on the new yellow lumber swam together like colorful fish, but her unfocused gaze obscured the sunlight-infused picture before her.

"Sarah, you're not listening to me!"

Rose was emphatic and then looked perplexed as Sarah's hands—bandages and all—stopped their motion and tightly gripped the edge of a large roaster.

"What's wrong with you?" she asked, her bright blue eyes inquisitive, innocent.

Everything's wrong with me. Your boyfriend, Matthew, is an elusive rainbow in my life. I want him. I'm terribly guilty, my mind is so jumbled I can't see straight. How can I get out of this?

"Nothing," she said.

"Well, Sarah, of course there is. You've been through a lot. It can't be easy, knowing someone lit your barn on purpose. It would really give me the creeps."

"It does."

"Of course it does.

Sarah met her friend's eyes in a sort of half-slant. Seeing the blue gaze of love and concern, the childlike honesty and trust, only multiplied her guilt.

It was time for everyone to go home. Then she could sit in a clean, quiet kitchen and have a genuine old-fashioned talk with Mam.

She needed advice. She needed Mam.

How desperately now she wanted Mam to tell her that it was alright to let yourself love your best friend. No. Mam would never.

Sarah dried the roaster viciously and avoided Rose's eyes.

Chapter 6

The new barn stood like a beacon of renewal, a proud sentry of fellowship, caring, and love administered to those in need. Yet the weeks following the barn raising taxed the good humor and energy of the whole family.

It was the rain. The constantly scudding gray clouds containing inch after inch of rain persistently rolled in from the east, slowly eroding the optimism of even the most encouraging member of the family.

Even Mam, who usually refused to spend needless money to dry clothes, gave in and hired a driver to take the mounds of laundry to the Laundromat over along Route 30. She muttered to herself as she dumped out the gallon jug with its heavy accumulation of loose change and counted her quarters feeling as blameworthy as someone who had just committed a crime.

The thing was, those great, gleaming washers that spun her towels and tablecloths and the broadfall pants and dresses would simply disintegrate her clothes one of these times. She placed no trust in anything electric. Who knew if she wouldn't be shocked—simply sizzled to death the moment she reached out to grasp that handle to extricate what was rightfully hers? Sitting and sewing all those clothes wasn't just anything, after all.

And how many times had she pressed the wrong button accidentally, setting the heat on the dryer to high, ruining her good dresses and capes and aprons, wrinkled completely beyond repair? It was risky, going to the Laundromat.

Sarah adjusted the white covering on her head, hurriedly sticking the straight pins through the thin organdy. She ran down the stairs when Jim Harper, the driver, tooted his horn, jangling her nerves the way it always did. He was the only driver who did that. All the others sat in the driveway, waiting patiently if the family wasn't immediately aware of their arrival, although they turned their heads occasionally, to see if anyone was coming out the door. But they didn't put the palms of their hands on the center of the steering wheel to let their impatience be known.

Sarah helped Mam lug the heavy plastic hampers and totes to the small navy blue van. She arranged them in the back, slammed the door, and went around to the side.

Mam said hello, but Jim just grunted and said, "Seat belts."

They complied, and he moved off, complaining about the weather and that he couldn't see what was wrong with driving a horse and buggy to the Laundromat. He was clearly unhappy with the few miles he would be able to charge.

Mam humored him, saying with a choking sound in her voice that the horses had burned. Jim placed a hand on Mam's shoulder and apologized profusely, saying he didn't know. He was sorry, he said.

Mam assured him and told him she wouldn't drive a buggy to Route 30 and through all the stoplights, even with the safest horse. Too much traffic, too many tourists gawking.

Sarah groaned aloud when she saw the occupants at the Laundromat. Oh, no.

"Mam, look!"

"Oh, we'll be busy. She'll let us go."

Sarah knew better about Fannie Kauffman, the most inquisitive, anxious woman in at least a fifty-mile radius.

They had no sooner settled themselves after

filling the hungry machines with Mam's precious quarters than she bustled over, the pleats in her ill-fitting black apron shelving over her hips, pinned much too tightly between layers of over-eating.

"Malinda!"

"Fannie."

"It just rains, doesn't it? I told Elam that if it doesn't stop raining, we won't get the tobacco in until June, which will just make it late for market, and we won't get our price. But then, who am I to complain? You losing your barn and having that loss. My goodness. I said to Elam, I guess the Lord chastens whom He loveth, *gel*? *Gel*? You have to wonder what you did to deserve this, *gel*? David likely did nothing. He's such a perfect man."

There was really no nice way to answer that hailstorm of words, Sarah thought, so when Mam smiled a bit rigidly but made no comment, it only increased Fannie's velocity.

"But then, you have Levi too, you know. A retarded boy. Well, you do good, though, you do good. You know I wasn't at the barn raising, not that I didn't want to, but my sciatica was acting up. Pain! Oh, Malinda, I was in mortal pain. My lower back, down the back of my legs. I had Davey's Rachel to do my work every day that week."

There was a shrill beep, and Fannie erupted from her chair and lunged across the gleaming

84

waxed tiles to reach the stopped dryer. She grabbed the handle of the large machine and gave it a tug before extracting the armfuls of clothing.

Mam sighed, a deep, tired, very relieved sound. She cast a weary look at Sarah when Fannie wheeled her cart over to the plastic table beside them and started shoving hangers into the shoulders of Elam's shirts.

"How's the barn coming? Are you milking yet? Are you? Good. That's good. But you know how much your cows will drop back in production? Way far. I told Elam that family has no idea how great their loss will be yet, even if you have Amish fire insurance. It never covers it all."

She stopped for breath and then bent to pick up a stray dryer sheet, holding it to her nose for a quick sniff.

"These dryer sheets don't work."

Mam raised an eyebrow, enough of a reply for Fannie to keep up her verbal onslaught.

"Have you heard about Junior's Melvin? Our Junior? He had such a stomach ache. . . ."

Sarah watched a young girl slumped in a blue plastic chair near the door, her legs sprawled in front of her. Her light brown hair fell over her cheeks like a curtain of privacy, a signal, along with her drooping shoulders, to leave her alone. She was thin, almost painfully so, and her hands picked restlessly at a thread along the bottom of her beige shirt.

Sarah felt a tinge of pity, then concern, when a small white vehicle pulled up to the front window. A young man hopped out and tore open the steel framed door, almost colliding with the girl in his haste.

She pulled her legs in and wrapped her arms around her middle. Her shoulders squared as she turned to face him with large, dark, defiant eyes. She recoiled as he lowered his head and hissed something quiet but deafening with a menacing force.

Sarah turned away. This was none of her concern. She watched though, unable to turn her eyes away as he hooked a hand beneath the girl's elbow and clawed at it, forcing her to stand and follow him, her head bent, the fine brown hair falling over her cheeks.

A white vehicle.

Well, no sense in making the comparison. There was none. Who could ever find the person in a white vehicle that supposedly lit their barn a few weeks earlier?

Sarah half-heartedly listened to Fannie and watched the small red light on the washer, the suds banging up against the glass and churning the clothes inside to a clean maelstrom.

The rain fell relentlessly as lines of traffic hissed past, water streaming off them. The stop-lights, signs, store fronts—everything was wet and shimmery with water.

Sarah tried to imagine Noah's flood in Bible times. It would have rained a hundred times harder. Then the springs of the earth would have opened, water gushing from the ground in a way no one had ever seen before and wouldn't again, ever. The water would have covered the streets, then the vehicles, the signs, the stores, the stop-lights. People would be drowned by then, or clinging to treetops or high buildings. She shivered, thinking of it. Water everywhere.

Fire was the opposite of water but just as destructive.

Already, Sarah missed the barn. It was on days just like this that, as a child, she had played in the haymow with her brothers, the clamorous rain drumming down and sometimes drowning out their voices. The only thing between them and the sound of it was the old sheet metal and a few wide lathes.

It was safe and cozy and crunchy with hay. They piled bales to make perfect houses, brought lunch and had dinner in it, spitting out the prickly hay seeds if they dropped onto their sweet bologna sandwiches.

Allen claimed people could eat hay if they chewed it long enough and then promptly inserted a long strand into his mouth and chewed furiously. Abner told him to get that out and quit it—cows had two stomachs, humans had only one and weren't supposed to eat hay.

The washer clunked and then stopped. The red light went off, so Sarah got up, opened the door, raked the wet laundry into a large, wheeled basket, and pushed it to a dryer.

Fannie came rolling over. Rolling was the only way to describe her—rounded and tipping from side to side, like a child's plastic ball that bounced along.

"Sarah, don't you have a *chappy* (boyfriend) yet?"

From behind the door of the dryer, Sarah shook her head, "No, I don't."

"What are you? Twenty? Twenty-one?"

"Soon twenty."

"My girls all married before twenty. What are you waiting on?"

Fannie snapped a dishcloth and folded it meticulously, without looking at her.

"There's no hurry."

"Sure there is. A girl blooms like a rose at age sixteen, and it's all downhill from there." She laughed ridiculously, becoming hysterical at her own joke.

Sarah smiled weakly, and decided one ill-mannered person could erase weeks of gratitude for the wonder of human companionship. She decided to stand her ground.

"I have dreams of becoming an old maid and having my own dry goods store."

Her words carried well, reaching Mam's ears as

she ducked behind a washer to conceal her wide grin and jiggling shoulders.

Fannie finished and left hastily, splashing clumsily through the rain in her large black Skechers, her bonnet stuck haphazardly on her head, no doubt flattening the questionably white covering beneath it.

Inside, Mam shook a finger at Sarah.

"Now, Sarah!"

"Well. She could have stayed quiet. She's simply so nosy. It's ridiculous."

"Her heart's in the right place, though."

"You sure?"

Mam didn't bother answering but asked Sarah if she really wanted to be an old maid.

"You should say 'single girl.' "

"Or leftover blessing? No. I don't want to be alone all my life. Of course not. I want my own house and yard and garden. Just like you. But . . . well, Mam, you know how it is."

"Is it still?"

Sarah nodded, which produced a drooping of Mam's kind features.

"You do try and let him go? Out of your thoughts?"

"Yes, Mam. I do. Seriously, the harder I try, the worse it gets."

Sarah launched into a colorful account of her burned hand, the way Matthew reacted, Rose's innocence, her guilt. But she stopped the story there, reserving the attractive blond young man and hiding him from her mother's scrutiny, knowing disapproval was forthcoming.

They folded soft towels, the clean-smelling linens, and were careful to test the heat in the dryers containing the dresses and black aprons.

"Well, Sarah, you know I'll always tell you the same thing. This time is no different. Pray, pray, pray. Always. You will discern God's will for your life once you have given up your own will, and I'm afraid Matthew is simply that. Your own will—wanting something you can't have. You know how much human nature tends to run along those lines. Just like Aesop's fables. Remember the story of the fox who wanted the grapes that were out of his reach?"

"And when he finally acquired them, they were sour, and he wondered why he'd wanted them in the first place," Sarah finished for her mother, nodding good-naturedly.

Jim, the driver, was gruff and short with them on the way home. He required a twenty-dollar payment, saying he had insurance to pay, and he sure wasn't making any money hauling people to the Laundromat.

Mam handed over the twenty-dollar bill, but her eyes sparkled too brightly, and she slammed the front door with plenty of muscle behind it.

Sarah ducked her head and splashed through the rain with the hampers of laundry, happy to put it all away in the drawers and closets, thankful to have clean, dry clothes, for now.

Surely the rain would stop soon. She paused by the window of her room and saw the muddy churning waters of the lower Pequea Creek had risen way beyond its banks. She shivered, a foreboding clutching her reason.

The new barn was stately, built solidly in the old pattern. The exterior's new ribbed metal siding was white, the color of the old barn. New cupolas proudly straddled the peak of the roof, the weather vanes turning as the wind changed direction, guarding the Beiler farm with their resilience. Look at us, they seemed to say. We're new and better, here for the next hundred years.

Sarah smiled and was glad.

The old stones and timbers were gone, but good had come of it as well, Dat said. The new barn was better. The ventilation design, the materials—everything was better, especially the diesel and the air system. It was the sadness of lost history that kept him humble, the ruined painstaking work of his forefathers.

He said the Amish church had seen changes in the past two hundred years, and they weren't all bad, same as the new barn. Some things were good, like milkers and bulk tanks and pneumatics, battery lamps and fiberglass carriages and nylon harnesses that were lighter and more durable. Better.

And still it rained, day and night.

Dat slogged through the mud to accomplish even the smallest task. Mud was everywhere from the way things had been churned up around the barn by the dozers and lifts and other equipment. Dat said if it continued raining, the roads would be closed due to the high water. He hoped no one would try to cross the creek where it overflowed; that was downright dangerous.

Priscilla stood by the window in Levi's room, chewing alternately on the inside of each cheek. Or she chewed the nails of her right hand, her eyebrows rising taut above her large, anxious eyes, watching the green maple leaves dripping water.

Levi sat at his card table, laying out the football cards, the sequence in his head followed to perfection. He looked up, considering his sister.

"Go away, Priscilla. You bother me."

"Hush, Levi."

"I mean it."

Dat looked up from the German *Schrift* (scripture) he was reading. His glasses were perched on his nose, allowing him to peer over them, and he smiled. This would be interesting, he thought.

Priscilla didn't answer. She just reached out to ruffle a few cards.

Instantly, Levi's hand came up, his eyebrows came down, his shoulders straightened, and his voice burst out in one big bellow.

"*Ich tzell dich schimacka*! (I will smack you!)"

Calmly, Priscilla bent over to retrieve the stack of football cards, holding them at arm's length, a smile teasing him.

"Give them."

"Say, 'Please.' "

"No."

Priscilla walked away, holding the cards, still teasing.

Levi didn't feel like getting out of his chair, so he yelled at the top of his lungs for help from Dat.

Dat looked up.

"What, Levi?"

"Priscilla has my cards!"

"She does? Well, I guess you'll have to come get them."

"I don't want to."

"Why not?"

"I'm tired."

Dat thought he heard the wail of sirens in the distance. On a night like this? Surely a fire would not survive this deluge.

When Levi continued his howling, Dat hushed him and curtly told Priscilla to give him his cards. Then he told everyone to listen. He thought he'd heard sirens.

The cards forgotten, Priscilla stood, a statue of fright, the color draining from her face, remembering the fire. She moved slowly, as if in a trance, and placed the cards on Levi's table, never hearing his resounding "*Denke* (Thank you)."

In her mind, the barn would soon be burning.

Dat saw Priscilla's fear, slowly laid his German Bible aside, and went to her. Gripping her arms, he looked into her terror-stricken eyes and gave her a small shake.

"Priscilla!" His voice was kind but firm.

As if roused from a faint, she blinked, looked at Dat, then fell against him. As she sobbed out her pain and anguish, his arms came around her, his head laid on her hair. He sent a prayer to the Father to protect his vulnerable daughter.

Mam came, lifted a hand, and caressed her back, saying the siren was likely only the medic for someone who needed assistance because of the high water.

After she cried, Priscilla could always pull herself together and talk about her fear. Tonight her words came fast and low. She said she missed Dutch so much, she hardly knew what to do. Would she be allowed to get a job some-where—to save up money for a new horse? She knew it was too much to ask.

"See, Dutch was important to me in a way that even people aren't. With a pet, like dogs and cats and ducks and chickens, it's different. They need you. People don't really, because they have other people."

Dat listened and nodded, deeply moved.

Then the high insistent wailing grew closer and much more resounding.

Sarah was reading the cousin circle letter, one that circulated among her cousins and kept them all in touch with the news in each other's lives. She heard the sounds around her in an absent-minded way as she sat away from the others. But when the siren's wails became louder, she laid the circle letter aside, rose to her feet, and asked hurriedly if there was another fire.

"It's only the twelve o'clock *pife* (whistle)!" Levi shouted.

Dat said, no, it was after suppertime.

The light was gray, the day heading into evening. The chores were done and the dishes washed. It was the time of day when every member of the family wound down and relaxed.

Mervin and Suzie were playing shuffleboard in the basement, obviously having heard nothing as the game continued with the sound of the thumps from below.

Everyone was ill at ease. Dat put his Bible away, and Mam gripped the countertop as she watched the dreary evening through the kitchen window, wondering, hoping.

Sarah merely paced, slowly moving from window to window, stopping to pick up a magazine, dusting a bookshelf with the hem of her bib apron, filling Levi's water pitcher for the night—anything to keep from holding still. The wailing, that rising and falling sound, always meant something was wrong—a person was hurt or a building was burning. Or now, with the rain and the creeks overflowing their banks, was someone injured, lost, or worst of all, drowned in the brown roiling, rushing water? At times like this, Sarah wished for a telephone in the house.

Mam was listening by Priscilla's side again, and Dat joined her, concern mapping out the love he so plainly felt for his troubled daughter.

The sirens came to an abrupt stop. Should they sigh with relief or hold their breaths for the bad news that might follow?

"We didn't used to be like this," Sarah said suddenly.

"What do you mean?" Mam asked.

"Well, look at us! Priscilla crying, Dat too nervous to study, me unable to hold still. We're just a family of nervous wrecks."

Dat nodded soberly. "With good reason, Sarah. We've just come through a terrifying night, followed by unanswered questions in the weeks that have followed. Now when a vehicle pulls up to the barn, I'm instantly on edge, wondering if the driver will bring harm. I'm suspicious, always alert to unexpected danger. Before the barn burned, it never crossed my mind to be afraid. We have lost an innocence."

Mam nodded, her agreement evident in her eyes.

"Are you alright, Priscilla?" she asked, her arm sliding across her younger daughter's shoulders.

"Not as okay as I will be a year from now," she answered, wisely recognizing her own ability to rise above the frightening circumstances that had assailed her life.

Sarah hoped she was right.

Chapter 7

In the morning, low clouds hung like dreary curtains, hiding any chance of happy sunshine. The Beiler family woke and went about the morning chores, slogging through the slippery mud and rivulets of water, carrying feed and water to the calves, feeding the rowdy heifers that bounced around stiff-legged, splattering mud and water as they vied for dominance.

In the new cow stable, the cows had created a wet path from the wide, rolling door to their separate stalls, their hides slick from the night's rain, their legs caked with the slop from the barnyard.

It was Sarah's turn to milk, so she moved among the cows changing the heavy milkers, listening to the rhythmic chukka-chukka sound from the compressed air pulling the milk from the cows' udders.

Everything was so new, yet so much the same.

The windows tilted open to allow the misty air to circulate. The firm contours of the new cement permitted the brand new feed cart to be pushed around with ease.

Not everything was finished. Some doorways still didn't have their wooden doors. Some of those that had doors needed a doorknob here or a few hinges there. But all in all, it was over-whelming that, even with the amount of labor involved, so much had been accomplished in such a short time.

Dat lifted an especially heavy milker from one of his best milk cows, his eyes wide with surprise, his muscles bulging against his shirt sleeves. He looked at Sarah and said, "Well, goodness! Looks as if the cows are feeling right at home again. She's really producing."

And then, because David Beiler was a man filled with gratitude in all things, his eyes watered and ran over behind his glasses. His mouth wobbled just enough for Sarah to see he was filled with emotion. And she was glad.

In all things, Dat would say, good can come of tragedy, to those that love God. Loving God was elusive, since you couldn't see Him. You could love God best by loving other people, and this was the one virtue Dat stressed, his family being recipients of his own love and forbearance to his fellow man.

If you point a finger in accusation, three more

on your own hand point straight back at you, he'd say.

No question, God sent disappointments and setbacks to each person, and of all the undeserving people in the world, Dat was the one. But Sarah also knew that His ways are not our ways; His thoughts are not our thoughts.

As he poured the good, rich milk into the gleaming new Sputnik, a stainless steel vat on wheels, he blinked back tears at this undeserved blessing. David Beiler knew his view of God and the church had been illuminated by a higher and better light.

Surely, God had dug, mulched, and applied fertilizer so his fruits would multiply. This barn fire had been painful, indeed. But hadn't He designed the agony that separates the dross from the gold?

The family sat at the breakfast table. The propane gas lamp, hissing softly, cast a cozy light into every corner of the kitchen in spite of the low-hanging clouds outside. The rain had stopped for now, but as the water drained from hills and slopes, the creeks and rivers continued to rise, filling them with a brown, butterscotch color, swirling and churning, murky and threatening.

Mam brought a platter of fried eggs and set it between her plate and her husband's. She sighed and looked to Dat. He nodded, and they all bowed their heads for the silent prayer, Levi's loud whispers rising and falling as he thanked God for what he was about to receive.

They lifted their heads after Dat. Some reached for their glasses of orange juice, and a few began buttering toast as they passed the egg plate from one to the other. They spooned stewed saltine crackers, slathered with generous portions of homemade ketchup, onto their plates alongside small sections of rich sausage. It was a bountiful breakfast for a hungry family that had already done a few hours of work.

Mam's eyes twinkled as she set a cake pan in the middle of the table, waiting for the praise that would surely come.

"Overnight French toast!" Levi yelled, his eyes alight with anticipation.

"Yum!" Mervin shouted simultaneously.

Levi turned to his youngest brother, lifted a heavy hand, and cocked his head to one side like an overgrown bird. Mervin caught his eye, grinned, and slammed Levi's hand with one of his own in a cracking high five. Levi laughed out loud. His day was starting out right.

Dat said it was getting late to plant corn, but he guessed it would clear up and dry out. It always did.

Mam poured his coffee and asked what his plans were. Dat smiled and said he'd been thinking during the night that a very important thing had not yet been accomplished since the fire. When

Dat said something in that tone of voice, everyone listened, knowing it would be good.

Looking at Priscilla, he announced, "I think it's time we replace Dutch, if you're willing to accompany me."

The only way she knew to express herself was to clap her hands and let her eyes shine into the light of Dat's.

"Can I go?" Suzie asked, hopefully, already knowing the answer.

"Sorry, Suzie. You have school."

Mervin cried and kicked his chair. Levi told him he could go along, but in the end he had to go to school. However, he went with the promise of a waterer for his rabbit pen, which was sold with other pet supplies at the New Holland Sales Stables.

"A good day to go!" Sarah said, enthusiastic as ever. She loved a good horse sale, and today's would be doubly exciting, helping Priscilla try to bond with another horse.

Mam opted to stay home, saying an empty house and her sewing machine were a wonderful way to relax and catch up on her much needed sewing.

Levi didn't ask if he could go. He just took for granted that he would. He hurried to his room to choose a brightly colored shirt, so he wouldn't get lost. His muttering was punctuated by loud bursts of happy laughter, followed by serious admonishments to himself.

"Now Levi, you are not allowed to have ice cream first. You have to eat a cheeseburger. Or maybe a hoagie. See what Dat says."

When Dat brought the carriage and the new horse, named Fred, to the sidewalk, Sarah was ready and helping Levi into his "gumshoes." Priscilla dashed out and clambered into the back seat, a flash of blue and black and a whirl of eagerness after the fear and heartache of losing her beloved pet.

Levi needed help to get into the buggy, so they tilted the front seat forward the whole way, allowing easy access to the back one.

Dat helped Levi, steadying him, encouraging, as Sarah held the bridle. The new horse had a good look about him. His eyes were calm and sensible, with no white showing in them. A steady flicking of his ears was the only sign of his mindfulness.

The buggy tilted to the side as Levi lifted his bulk up one step, with Dat supporting his waist. He lifted the other leg up and into the buggy, gripping the silver handle on the side.

He plunked down heavily beside Priscilla and said loudly, "Cheez Whiz!"

"You're too fat, Levi!" Priscilla said, laughing at his expression.

"I am not. I'm a big man."

"Yes, you are, Levi. You're a big man," Dat said, grinning.

"I can smack hard too, Priscilla," Levi said soberly.

"You better not."

"Then you have to be nice to me."

"Come on, Fred," Dat said as he clucked and pulled gently on the reins. The new horse moved off as if he'd done this thousands of times, trotting nicely past the maple trees dripping wet with morning moisture. He turned left on the macadam road, perfectly obedient, the picture of a good sensible horse.

"Boy, must be that Samuel Zook knows his driving horses. I think we got ourselves a winner."

Dat closed the front window carefully over the nylon reins, protecting them from the cold, swirling mists. He had no more than clicked it into place when a feed truck came around a bend in the road with its slick blue tarp flapping on top and its engine revving after maneuvering the turn.

Down went Fred's haunches, and up came his head. With a swift, fluid motion borne of raw fear, the horse reared, shied to the right, came down running, and galloped off across a neighbor's soggy alfalfa field. The buggy swayed and teetered as Dat fought for control. Levi yelled and yelled and wouldn't stop, increasing the horse's fear.

They came to a stop in the middle of the squishy alfalfa field with Fred snorting and quivering.

Everyone was thoroughly shaken up. Levi's yells changed to incoherent babbles of fear.

"Well, here we are," Dat said calmly. They all burst out laughing except Levi, who said it wasn't one bit funny and Dat should not be so *schputlich* (mocking).

So there they sat, the steel wheels of the buggy firmly entrenched in the sodden earth. Fred decided this was the end of his journey and refused to move.

Patiently, Dat shook out the reins, clucked, chirped, and spoke in well-modulated tones. It did absolutely no good. The horse stood as firm as a statue carved in stone, the only sign of life the flicking of his ears and an occasional lifting or lowering of his head.

Dat opened the door of the buggy and leaned out to evaluate the situation. The wheels were partially sunken into the muck and sprouting alfalfa.

"He's probably balking because it's hard to pull if he lunges against the collar. It could be too tight."

Sarah glanced down at Dat's shoes.

"No boots?"

"So we just sit here?" asked Priscilla.

"Probably."

Levi said they wanted to go to the horse sale, not sit here, and Dat better start smacking this crazy horse.

Dat said, "No, Levi, sometimes that only makes it worse. He'll go when he's ready. Horses that balk are often confused."

Priscilla made no comment but then said, "Let me out, Dat."

"It's too muddy, Priscilla."

"I can clean my shoes when we get there."

"Alright."

Dat got out and stood tentatively in the soft field. Sarah sat forward, allowing the back of her seat to lower, so Priscilla could scramble over it.

Going to Fred's head, Priscilla rubbed his nose and spoke to him like a petulant child. She told Dat to get in, then tugged lightly on the bit. Her answer was an angry toss of Fred's head. She kept up the repetitive stroking, adjusted the collar, and loosened a buckle on one side of the bridle, her fingers searching expertly for any discomfort from the harness or the bridle.

"Alright, Fred. Come on now. We have to buy a horse to live with you."

Priscilla coaxed, tugging gently, and Fred decided it was time to go. He veered to the left, almost knocking her off her feet, before gathering his hind legs into a lunge and taking off in great leaps, mud flying from his hooves as well as the buggy wheels.

Inside the buggy, Dat lifted a forearm to protect himself from the chunks of mud that found their way through the window as he struggled to control the horse. Then he slid back the door of the buggy to see what had happened to Priscilla. He was rewarded by the sight of her dashing across the soggy alfalfa field.

Sarah breathed a sigh of relief when the buggy clunked over a small embankment and down onto the welcome macadam where Dat pulled Fred off to the side, waiting for Priscilla. She lost no time running to the parked buggy, her breath coming in gasps.

Pricilla's hair curled every which way from the moisture in the air. Her covering sagged and slid off the back of her head. She didn't look at her shoes; she just slid them off, put them under the front seat, and plopped down beside Levi.

"You're wet!" he yelped.

Priscilla grinned, gasped for breath, and rubbed a wet hand against Levi's cheek. She was rewarded with a resounding smack, his favorite way of dealing with life's outrages.

His famous smacks were never hard, never hurtful. His nature was much too affable to be taken seriously, so they were accepted without reprimand and just considered a part of their good-humored Levi.

Fred stepped out and trotted willingly the remainder of the way to New Holland, stopping at the one red light obediently, stepping out when asked.

When they arrived, Sarah helped Priscilla clean

up in the large well-lit bathroom, supplying a fine toothed comb for her hair, pressing and shaping her organdy covering as best she could.

A few English girls gave them a not-so-friendly glance when they cleaned Priscilla's gray Nikes with wet paper towels, but there was nothing to say, so Sarah averted her eyes while the other girls washed their hands and rolled their eyes at each other. Well, they'd just have to think what they wanted. Not everyone had a car that always did exactly what was required of it. Especially not the Amish.

Priscilla glared after them, sensitive to these things at her age.

"They were mean."

"Not really. It isn't very sanitary, cleaning your shoes in here."

"You want to go back and sit in the field again?"

Laughing, Sarah clapped an arm around her younger sister's shoulders and thanked her for saving all of them.

"Thanks. Dat is so—well, he just doesn't have it," she answered.

The large arena where the horses were sold was filled with a solid wall of people stacked in diagonal layers in the stands. Every color imaginable reflected from the electric lights against the white walls, the metal railing, and swirls of dust. Far below the cavernous roof, an auctioneer and two seated clerks took up positions at a podium. A horse was brought in, pawing the sawdust, his eyes rolling with fear.

"We need to find Dat," Sarah said loudly above the din.

"That will be a job."

"Let's go to the pens."

Priscilla hesitated.

"Why not?"

"There's so many men."

"Come on!"

They ran down the steps and through the alleyways until they arrived at the long row of riding horses tethered to a board fence, patiently switching their tails. Some of them appeared high strung, others docile. Others were too thin and misshapen, their coats scraggly.

"They'll go for killers."

"Likely."

As Sarah had guessed, Priscilla found no extraordinary horses and finally said they may as well go back.

Men in plaid shirts with seed-company logos across the fronts of their caps lounged along the fence, respectfully dipping their heads. Children ran and shouted, weaving through alleyways and much too close to the horses' hind feet. They dashed about chattering like excited little squirrels, eating Skittles and Starbursts and M&M's. It was great fun to be at a horse sale.

The girls said hello to Reuben King and Lamar

Stoltzfus, two boys from Sarah's youth group, and then moved on to find seats, with Dat and Levi, if possible.

So many straw hats and black coats! They simply stood, their eyes searching the crowd as the auctioneer prepared to open the sale.

Priscilla's eyes darted from row to row, but Sarah's had stopped, resting on Matthew Stoltzfus sitting with his brother, Chris.

Ah. He was here. Why hadn't she dressed better? She should have worn the new rose-colored dress. She hated the sweater she was wearing. It would look better on Mam. And here she was, her covering gone all flat and frumpy because of the morning's heavy fog and humidity, even if it wasn't actually raining.

Oh, he looked so good. His already tanned face and dark hair set him apart, way apart, from the rest of the crowd. Her heart was hammering in her chest. Her mouth went completely dry. She swallowed, choked, and tried desperately to hide all this from Priscilla.

"There! Right there they are."

Of course—the opposite end of the arena.

Sarah turned, her sense of loss so complete the whole crowd may as well have been stripped of color as her world changed to black and gray. She followed her sister numbly, looking neither left nor right.

Dat looked up, grateful to see them arrive, and

patted the seat beside him. Priscilla bounced into it, a rapturous smile lighting up her pretty face. Sarah sat down on the remaining seat, apologizing to the large woman next to her who was wearing an inexpensive pink cowboy hat and brilliant red boots, her belt completely hidden between her jeans and too-tight shirt.

"That's okay, honey. You make yourself comfortable."

She leaned sideways to accommodate Sarah and smiled, a genuine wish of good humor on her painted red lips. Sarah smiled back and settled in, the smile sliding off her face as she glumly assessed her situation.

Here she was, still in the hold of whatever in the world you called the emotion that controlled her whenever she caught sight of Matthew Stoltzfus, and he was happily dating her best friend. Since the barn raising, her river of misery had grown simultaneously with the rising creeks. Her mental agony, like the non-stop rain, was almost unbear-able at times.

This had been going on since she was fourteen and in vocational class. Only when Matthew spoke to her was her day colored with a vibrant shade of yellow, like the sun or a rose—the flower of love—or blue, like the great clean wondrous sky. It was always Matthew, in her dreams, in her waking hours. How could he deny her now, after what happened at the barn raising?

Then guilt and shame intensified the hovering shapes of depressive thinking, and Sarah knew for certain this had to stop. With great effort, she turned to the sight before her, the horses, the men and boys riding them. Occasionally, a lithe English girl rode one, too.

The loud voice of the auctioneer rose and fell, its staccato rhythm giving her an intense headache. Sarah wished she hadn't come.

Just when she thought she couldn't sit there one more minute, a rider entered the ring on a black and white paint. The horse had a fine small head and curved ears, the flowing mane and tail neatly brushed, the coat sleek and gleaming from good grooming. His rider sat with easy grace, bareback, holding the reins loosely.

The horse didn't really trot or gallop—he flowed. His hooves lifted and set down easily, as if there were springs in his legs that moved them without effort.

Priscilla leaned forward, the knuckles on her hands white as she clenched the armrests of her seat.

"Dat!" she whispered.

Dat saw and winked broadly at Sarah. He knew.

Sarah winked back. Then a strange hiccup jumped in her chest, and she realized she was crying. What a precious father! She knew that he wouldn't stop bidding until he had procured the one object that would successfully erase the hurt and the pain the arsonist had inflicted with a small rasp of his lighter.

The bidding started at five hundred dollars. Priscilla sat back, her hands gripped in her lap.

"Five hundred! Five! Five! Who'll gimme fifty? Five hundred fifty! Yes! Six hundred!"

Sarah watched Priscilla, whose pulse was beating against the side of her neck where her sweater had fallen away. The pupils in her large green eyes dilated as she gripped her hands more tightly.

When the bidding escalated to one thousand, she put her hand on Dat's arm and said it was okay to let him go. Then she turned confused eyes to Sarah, pleading, unsure.

The horse pranced and stepped lightly, tossing his head in excitement, and still the rider sat easily, a tall, blond youth who appeared to have been riding horses since he was six years old.

Levi sat on Dat's right side, a can of Mountain Dew in one hand, a large bag of buttered popcorn in the other. His face shone with happiness. He was completely unaware of Dat's subtle nodding of his head. The popcorn was more important.

The bidding escalated. The rider pulled the horse to a stop and then cantered him slowly around the ring.

Dat paid eighteen hundred dollars for Priscilla's horse, and not one person at the New Holland Sales Stables thought it was a penny too much.

The poor girl had suffered plenty at the hand of that arsonist, who still ran loose, they said.

When Dat smiled at Priscilla and said, "Let's go!" she burst into tears. Sarah had to help her find her way out between the seats, apologizing with multiple soft expressions of "Excuse me" and "I'm sorry." They finally made it out the side door. When they led Priscilla to the horse, he lowered his head. Priscilla cupped her hand beneath his nose and laid her forehead against his. The tears dropped off her face and ran in little wet rivulets down the horse's face. She whispered brokenly, "Hello, Dutch."

Dat got out his red handkerchief and blew his nose hard, then dried his eyes, and squeezed Priscilla's shoulders.

Levi reached deep into the popcorn bag for another handful and slowly blinked his eyes.

Chapter 8

Sarah stood in the middle of the garden and leaned on a hoe watching Priscilla ride Dutch, circling the pasture. They were in perfect tune with one another, a sight to behold. Sarah never tired of it.

It was the middle of May. The rains had stopped, and the soil had dried. The warm bright sun shone from a blue sky alive with scudding white puffs of clouds. Sighing, she turned, picked out a few cucumber seeds from the small packet in her hand, and dropped them in the hole she had made with the hoe.

With all the rains and the flooding, the planting had been late this year. Sarah was grateful to be able to plant the "late" seeds—corn, cucumbers, lima beans—crops that wouldn't push their way up from the soil if the earth was not properly warmed by the sun.

Chattering barn swallows, daring little acrobats of the air, wheeled and turned, grabbing insects as they executed their aerial show. From a distance, she heard the clanking and squeaking of Dat's corn planter, the mules walking at a rapid pace, their nodding heads and flopping ears never quite in harmony.

She knew Dat would be on the cart, watching the planter, his thoughts on his sermons, the congregation, the troubles and concerns as well as the joys. Last night, though, he'd talked plenty, for Dat. He wasn't a person of excessive speech, but he needed a listening ear, he'd said.

The barn fire had occurred, yes. Someone had lit it, with intent to destroy, provoke, excite, whatever. Who knew for what reason they did this? And now the men were sidling up to him at church and saying that he needed to do something about this. Some seemed to think he was not doing his duty as a minister to let this all go on as if nothing happened. He could at least cooperate with the prosecutors. The church members thought Dat was too compliant and said he had to do what he could.

Every Sunday, Dat would develop a headache and a tic in one eye. Apparently, no one in the congregation had gotten a decent night's sleep since the fire.

Take Amos Fisher. He said he slept in his own bed, or tried to, until all kinds of images encroached on his thoughts. Here he was, with forty head of cattle, beef cows, all housed in his new ventilated barn. What if someone snuck in and just got a big bonfire going?

He'd taken to sleeping on the couch in his kitchen, so that he could at least hear a car if it drove by. The sleeplessness was making him groggy, and his arthritis was flaring up in his thumbs. It would be different if Sylvia cared. She just rolled over on her good ear and slept like a rock. Amos didn't know what would happen if his new barn burned.

Dat tried to explain to Amos how difficult it was to pin down this arsonist, and the police weren't even completely sure it was an arsonist. He didn't get very far after that, the way Amos flew off. So what could he do?

Softly, Mam asked what his own personal feelings were.

Dat gravely stroked his beard and shook his

head from side to side as he contemplated the question. Arriving at a decision, he sat up straight, his far-seeing eyes not really aware of his surroundings.

He said he looked on the situation as a spiritual chastening, a call to be a better person. In the Bible, hadn't Job suffered tremendously? For Dat to poison his own life with unforgiveness was unthinkable. Yes, the loss had been great, but the aftermath had been rich in blessings.

The sight of those caravans of men arriving to help was one blessing. He'd simply wanted to kneel before them all and wash their feet as a sign of humility, the way Abraham did in the Old Testament.

In view of the tremendous caring and love poured out on his family, who could stand if he didn't forgive?

Suddenly, Dat's face took on a silly grin. "And besides, now my cow stable has plenty of new and modern things, for an old preacher."

Mam laughed with him, knowing how happy he was with the new barn and appreciating his resilience.

So, Sarah had thought, no matter how overwhelming the flood of kindness had been, someone always managed to insert a prickly note of dissension. Like Fannie Kauffman.

In the garden, Sarah tramped down the last of the soil, straightened her back, and went to find a small wooden stake for the cucumber-seed packet to mark where they'd been planted.

She reached up to the top shelf in the garden shed, her hand searching for a stake. Something smooth and round came into contact with her fingertips. A lighter. Hmm. Why was a white Bic lighter on the top shelf in the garden shed? Slipping it into her pocket, she decided to tell the family. It was extremely odd.

She found a stake, attached the seed packet with a thumbtack, and stuck the marker into the ground. That was really cute.

Mam hurried out to the garden, saying it was time for the pea wire to be put up. Those pea vines were growing faster every time she checked them.

Sarah had just emerged from the garden shed with an armload of stakes when a gray car came slowly up the driveway and rolled to a stop beside the garden.

Two policemen extricated themselves from the unmarked car as Mam dropped her roll of wire and went to greet them. They exchanged pleasantries, Mam's voice low and careful, the way she was with strangers.

"This the new barn?"

"Yes."

"No information? Nothing unusual? No sightings? No media?"

"Um, excuse me. What is media?" Mam asked, clearly ashamed that she didn't know.

"Photographers? People asking questions? Reporters?"

Mam shook her head.

Sarah's heart pounded. Should she come forward with the lighter? But it had been in the garden shed and likely had nothing to do with the fire at all.

She decided to keep her peace and went back to pound stakes into the loose soil.

The policemen asked for Dat, and Mam pointed to the team of mules pulling the corn planter.

Quite suddenly, the white lighter felt red hot, like a small plastic conscience burning a hole in Sarah's pocket. Stumbling across the garden, she was surprised that her hand wasn't burning, that the lighter was smooth and cool.

The officers looked up.

"H . . . hello," she stammered.

"Yes, young lady?"

She held up the lighter, explained how uncommon it was to find a lighter on the top shelf in the garden shed.

The tall, heavy officer asked quickly if there were more children around. Was there a possibility that one of the younger children had hidden the lighter?

It was terrible to see the color drain from Mam's face and the raw dread in her eyes. Surely not Mervin or Suzie? "Get Dat," she ordered, her voice quivering.

Sarah handed the lighter to the police and ran swiftly past the strawberry patch, white with blossoms, past the raspberries, the compost pile, the woodpile, and over the small wooden bridge built over a cement drain pipe. She stood at the edge of the field, waving her arms, although she remained quiet, until he came closer.

"*Komm*! *Komm rei*! (Come in!)"

Dat waved in acknowledgment, finished the row, and then turned the mules toward the house. He left them standing by the garden without tying them and went to greet the officers, tipping back his straw hat to wipe the dirt from his brow.

"Yes. Mr. Beiler."

"Hello. Good to meet you."

"I'm supposing each member of the family has been thoroughly questioned?"

"As far as I know."

"You have no reason to believe any of your children would have been playing with this lighter?"

The officer held it up, and Dat's face blanched, quiet confidence replaced with confusion.

"Well . . ."

"Your daughter found it."

Sarah answered Dat's questions and turned to find Suzie and Mervin scootering home from school.

"Here are the little ones."

119

Dat's voice tried to be confident, but the bravado held a tinge of doubt.

What if? Sarah thought.

What if Mervin had been playing with the lighter, became afraid, and hid it? Or Suzie? It was unthinkable, Suzie being so timid, so conscientious. Still, one never knew.

The children were called to join them. Priscilla came from the barn, her face glowing from her ride, but she swallowed, wrapped her arms about her waist, and scuffed her sneaker into the dirt.

The police questioned them, not unkindly, but so seriously it seemed as if they were threatening.

Mervin shook his head no. So did Suzie, pure innocence shining from her untroubled gaze, a clear testimony of her genuine goodness, a repeat of Priscilla.

Then Mervin began to cry. Dat looked sharply at Mam, questions clouding his eyes.

Speaking in hiccups, his English broken and mixed with Pennsylvania Dutch, the way little Amish children do, Mervin said he'd found it.

"When?" the officer asked intently, bending low.

"When the barn burned."

"Which side of the barn?"

"Over there. Where the heifer pen was."

"You're absolutely sure you weren't playing with the lighter?" Dat asked, his face stern and serious.

Mervin nodded, his blond hair wagging over his ears. His guileless eyes stared straight into Dat's, which was not lost on the officers, who were acquainted with every trick humankind could imagine, and then some.

"Then why did you hide it?"

"You mean, in there?" Mervin pointed to the garden shed. "I was afraid you would think I started the fire, and I didn't."

Mervin lowered his head, the silky blond, brownish hair falling over his eyes, a curtain to allow him time to compose himself, to decide to be forthright.

"Dat, I just crumpled some old newspapers and—I wanted to see how high the fire goes, how fast it spreads."

Lifting his head, he stared wild-eyed at the officer standing closest to him.

"I didn't do it," he burst out.

The officer nodded, his eyes liquid and kind.

"Well, we could take the lighter, get the finger-prints," said the other, "but I doubt if it would tell us much. Arsonists always wear gloves of some sort. Or almost always."

"Is there anything we can do to make the community safer? Members of the congregation are sleeping very little, if at all, imagining this arsonist on the loose, afraid they'll be the next victim."

"As far as you personally doing something to

help? No. If someone has an old, especially prized barn, or lives close to the road with the house a good distance away from the barn, yes, there is something they can do. They can always sleep in the barn. It's the only sure way to hear anything. Or get an extremely good watchdog, trained to bite intruders, which is questionable. What if a person stops and gets out of a car during the night for reasons other than lighting a fire?"

Dat nodded soberly. "So we'll have patience. Wait. See how it goes, right?"

"About the only thing we can do at this point."

Priscilla turned to go back to Dutch, but Mam called her back. Pea wire was cumbersome, unhandy, and Dat had corn planting to do. It was late in the season.

Sarah smiled and said goodbye to the officers.

No one like Mam to bring you straight back to reality, plunk you down in the middle of it, and put you to work.

Dat was the kindhearted one, the dreamer who colored your days with different shades of jokes, laughter, smiles, little sayings, or poems. Mam was a hard-core realist.

Grumbling to herself, Priscilla walked slowly to the roll of pea wire. With her foot, she sent it rolling slowly across one of Mam's prized geraniums.

"Priscilla Beiler! Now look what you did!"

Mam almost never shouted. When she did, it

was stentorian, fierce in its power to bring the offender straight to their knees in repentance.

"Sorry, Mam."

"I should think so."

Bending, Mam plucked off pieces of the broken geranium, held them tenderly in her cupped hands, and scuttled to the house. An air of righteous indignation hovered over her white covering, its wide strings flapping behind her.

Sarah stood, her hands on her hips, surveying the damage.

"One geranium gone," she said, wryly.

"Boy, she got mad."

"Well, you need to be careful."

"I didn't try to roll that wire over the geranium."

"Dat spoils you, Priscilla."

"I know. I love my Dat."

Sarah smiled and continued pounding wooden stakes into the ground, remembering when she was fourteen years old, riding horses, swimming in the creek, going to Raystown Lake during the summer at Uncle Elam's. Life was one happy chunk of solid uncomplication, as sturdy as a cement block, and as simple. And it was supposed to stay that way.

Turn sixteen, date Matthew Stoltzfus, marry him, and live in a small white house under a maple tree—a house with a porch, two small dormers on the roof, and ruffled white curtains at the upstairs windows. She'd grow zinnias and lavender and daisies in the garden, and Matthew would help her pull ears of corn that they'd freeze in small bags tied with red twisties.

They'd go to an island somewhere, to a beach, and swim. She had never seen the ocean, and she planned to some day. With Matthew.

She had turned sixteen, alright, but everything had gone wrong after that. Everything. Matthew treated her the same way he had always treated her. He just didn't seem to think there was anything wrong with that. He liked her a lot. She was his friend, Sarah, still as easy to get along with as always.

It was Rose who bowled him over eventually. Sarah remembered exactly where she was standing when Allen told her Matthew had asked Rose Zook. She had almost fainted from an acute sense of shock, followed by a gloom as thick and impenetrable as the hide of an elephant.

Mam had stood by her side. They'd talked, reasoned, shared their feelings, and grew close. But at the end of the day, she still had to sit on the slippery banks of the muddy river called misery —and simply deal with it.

Every weekend, she saw him. Them. Sometimes on Saturday evening if there was a volleyball game or a skating party or a hockey game. Always on Sunday evening at the supper, when the Amish youth groups gathered at designated homes of parents or siblings, and a large supper was served to as many as a hundred or two hundred of them.

Volleyball games, or baseball for the boys, were often in action at the suppers, followed by hymn singing. They'd all assemble along lengthy tables, the girls on one side, the boys on the other, hymn books scattered along the tables with pitchers of water and plastic cups, dishes of mints.

They sang many hymns, and sang well, the parents chiming in as they sat along the walls on folding chairs.

And always, there was Matthew. He would smile at her, genuinely pleased to see her each weekend. She lived for his smiles. They were like a benediction, a scepter held out for her to touch, blessing the week that stretched out empty and arid without them.

Eventually, when Rose became his constant companion, Sarah had given up in a way. But only sort of. The thing was, he'd single her out, go out of his way to say, "Hey, Sarah. How's it going?"

Or the funny, "S'up?"

He knew she'd laugh when he said that. So many reasons to believe that someday, somehow, they'd be together.

Until they weren't. Now he'd been with Rose for a year. A whole year and they'd grown closer and closer. Rose beamed and smiled and related every incident of their personal conversations to Sarah, including the times she loved him best. Sarah had hidden all of her own feelings securely away, despising the dishonest person she'd become. The incident at the barn raising had been her undoing, again.

Well, life went on, and that was that. But just thinking about it made her so angry that she pounded the wooden stakes for the pea wire so hard that she sank them in too far into the ground, and Priscilla had to pull them up a bit.

"Stop being so *rausich* (aggressive)."

"Get the job done!" Sarah grinned.

"Why don't we just let the pea vines crawl around on the ground, and pick the peas from there?"

"They don't produce as many peas. The sunlight can't reach them very well."

"Who says?"

"I don't know. I guess Mam."

Sarah straightened her back and gazed at the horizon, where storm clouds were gathering at a rapid rate. To the east, the white light of the brilliant late spring sun was being chased away by a threatening darkness rolling steadily along the horizon.

A rumbling, soft and low, brought the uneasiness that accompanied an approaching storm, so Sarah increased the pounding, wanting the pea rows to be finished before a spring deluge turned the soil into a quagmire.

The cows in the pasture lifted their heads. Crows flapped their dreary way across the sky, their hoarse caws preceding them. Sarah stopped pounding and watched the straight line of the crows. She shivered.

"I hate crows."

"Whatever for?"

"They're evil, like a premonition of something bad."

"No, they aren't. Duh, Sarah. My favorite book in third grade was *Blacky the Crow*. Shame on you. You know what? It's your imagination going way overboard again. I never saw anyone who could imagine stuff the way you do."

Sarah laughed and brought the mallet up and over her shoulder in a mock stance. Priscilla shielded her face with her hands and begged for mercy, laughing.

The crows wheeled back, their sizable black wings flapping faster as they lowered themselves into an oak tree behind the shed, their garbled crowing accompanying them.

Sarah watched as the mighty, dark birds shuffled from branch to branch, quarrelsome as they vied for position. The leader raised his wings, flapped them ominously, then settled down, a strangled caw his last attempt at frightening them.

Sarah turned to watch the approaching storm and heard the distant rumbling. As the air around them became quiet, only the crows' squabbling broke the humid eeriness.

She became rigid with—what was it? Apprehension? Leftover fear? For reassurance, she turned to the new barn, a large, well-built monument of hope and goodwill, evidence of what a band of men could accomplish in the face of evil.

Still, she shivered.

Priscilla pounded in the remaining stakes. Together they stretched the wire between them, then pulled up a few spring onions, peeled off the outer layers, broke off the hard growth along the bottoms, and crunched them between their teeth without bothering to wash them.

Next Sarah pulled gently on the prickly radish tops, exclaiming at the size of the large, red orb attached to it. She rubbed it across the black bib apron she wore, twisted off the top and the small root growing on the underside, and popped it into her mouth.

Her eyes watering, Sarah exclaimed loudly and ran for the water hose wound on the bracket by the *kesslehaus* door. As she bent over gulping large mouthfuls of water to cool her fiery mouth, Priscilla howled with glee.

The crows squawked their sinister calls of warning. Sarah stood, the hose in her hand, water spurting unnoticed, as they flapped their wings, exploding from the tree and wheeling on the still air. The rolling black clouds moved and changed their appearance in the background.

Chapter 9

The storm bent the enormous maple trees, the wind whipping the branches into helpless, skinny arms, flailing and twisting madly. A plastic bucket went skidding drunkenly across the porch floor, banged into a ceramic flower pot, and fell off the porch into the newly planted petunias below. The wooden porch swing creaked on its chain, pushed by the force of the approaching storm. Barn cats ran stiff-legged, their tails aloft like furled sails, slipping to safety through the small hole cut along the bottom of the barn door.

Dat came clattering up to the forebay, the brown mules leaning back to stop the corn planter after they trotted through the door. Dat's eyes were wide beneath the flopping brim of his straw hat. Just in time, he yanked down the wide garage door, lowering it behind him, before lunging to the windows to watch the fury of the wind. He'd never seen darker clouds or ones that churned like these. He hoped the rest of the family was all safely in the house.

The two maple trees bent and twisted, the small leaves whipped furiously, and the hail began to pound on the metal roof with a deafening clatter. Inside, the girls huddled by the windows, recoiling as the darkness exploded into a blueish slash of sizzling lightning, followed immediately by an earsplitting crack of thunder.

"Get away from the window," Mam warned.

Obediently, they stepped back, gasping as the hail pelted down, bouncing around in the green grass like cold, icy toads, hopping and careening all over the place.

"*Siss an schlossa*! (It's hailing!)" yelled Levi from his swiveling desk chair by the row of windows.

"Good thing Dat made it to the barn," Mam said, so grateful her mouth quavered with emotion.

Then she asked, "Where are Suzie and Mervin?"

Sarah wheeled, wide eyed.

"They're . . . they were right here in the kitchen. They came in with us."

"No, they didn't. They went to the barn."

"They came in when it became windy, I thought," Sarah said, suddenly alert, searching the dark kitchen for any sign of them, their shoes, a tossed head scarf, Mervin's little straw hat.

"They're in the barn," Priscilla said again.

The rain followed the pelting hail, coming down in gray sheets of windblown water. It sluiced down the driveway, poured out of the downspouts, and ran down the windowpanes, obliterating the barn and outbuildings in its force.

Mam's eyes became large with anxiety, and she chewed her lower lip without realizing it.

"I just wish Suzie and Mervin were here."

"Mam, it's okay. I'm pretty sure they're in the barn."

"I hope."

Sarah went to the door leading to the upstairs and called their names, receiving no answer. She went to the basement, searching, knowing they would be in the kitchen with Mam and Priscilla if they were in the house. But she searched anyway to ease her mind.

The lightning flashed through the small rectangular window, illuminating the whitewashed stone of the old part of the cellar. Sarah winced as the intense clap of thunder followed.

They had to be in the barn.

Upstairs, Levi whimpered with fear. He told Priscilla that God was mad at them, for sure. The barn burned, and now this.

It was raining too hard. It rained five inches in an hour and thirty minutes. Ninety minutes of water dumping and blowing from the sky, the likes of which they had never seen.

Dat remained in the barn, helpless but glad everyone was safely in the house. He fed the mules and horses and swept the loose hay and dirt from the forebay, frequently going to the window to watch the rain in disbelief.

The small creeks and waterways of Lancaster County were already running full. The butterscotch-colored water had returned to its normal gray-green, but it was still rushing swift and high even before the storm struck.

An alarming amount of water rode in on the great gray wings of the storm, releasing the deluge in a thirty-mile-wide swath of wind and moisture. The creeks rose at an alarming rate, churning and bubbling over the banks into pastures, flooding newly planted cornfields and new alfalfa pushing its way into a hearty growth of verdant strands of nutrition for the many herds of Holstein cows scattered throughout the county.

In a few hours' time, many motorists became stranded. Cows bawled from the safety of higher ground, as small meandering creeks turned into vicious, dangerous torrents that swept away anything in their paths.

When Dat bent his head and splashed his way into the house, he found Mam white-faced and bordering on hysteria. Her rapid words pelted him, and he felt anxiety rising within him.

"Where are Suzie and Mervin?"

"Aren't they with you? In here?"

Sarah didn't think anything out of the ordinary could possibly happen. Their barn had burned so recently. They'd spent one night in pure terror and now lived in fear and uncertainty. God didn't do things like this. Not tragedies in pairs.

"They're probably in a shed somewhere—the garden shed," Mam said, her voice only an octave lighter than anger.

Dat wheeled without a word and went out through the rain, searching everywhere as Mam breathed rapidly, brokenly. She put up her hands and took out the pins in her covering. She pulled it off, put the pins back in it, and laid it carefully on the countertop. She tied on a navy blue head-scarf and a black sweater and left the house without another word.

Sarah and Priscilla were mute with fear.

"*Selly glaenie hausa*! (Those little rabbits!)" Levi growled. "Always making trouble." He bent his head, shaking it from side to side, making clucking noises, as if that alone could bring them safely into the house.

The rain still came down steadily but with less force, as Dat and Mam splashed from haymow to implement shed, garden shed to corncrib and back to the garage, calling, calling.

When Sarah could not stand another minute of waiting, she joined her parents, dashing sense-lessly after them shouting, "Suzie! Mervin!"

There is nothing emptier than the emptiness of a missing person. The very atmosphere is depleted of rationality when someone cannot be found.

Sarah's mind absorbed this emptiness, this wet, watery world without Mervin and Suzie in it. She imagined them, soaking wet, stranded behind the Stoltzfus barn where the road turned sharply upward. She imagined them sitting beneath Hannah's porch roof, safe and warm and dry.

She'd give them a cupcake with white frosting on top. She imagined the small winding stream of water between them, so small it didn't even have a name. Surely they wouldn't have tried to go to the Stoltzfus place in that rain?

After searching every corner of every building, there was nothing to do but huddle under the porch roof and begin meaningless suggestions born of raw fear.

No, not the police. They didn't need to know.

There was a certain unwillingness to let their neighbors find out. Not us, again. It's embarrassing.

These words were not spoken, only thought, but they were thought together—a bond of understanding encircling them. As long as they didn't know for sure, why trouble anyone?

It was when Mam began to cry that Dat sprang back to reality, put a hand on her shoulder, and said everything would be alright. Mam jerked her shoulder away and yelled at him in a voice tinged with craziness.

"We have to find them, Davey!"

Sarah thought of the crows cawing from the oak tree and felt the hopelessness, the first slice of dread cutting into her heart.

Suddenly, a thought sprang into her mind. Why had God kept the knowledge of the fishing poles from them? She knew before she went to see, the fishing poles would not be there.

They had told only Levi. Levi remembered everything, didn't he?

Sarah rushed at him, grabbed his shirt front, hauled his big head around, and glowered at him.

"Why didn't you tell us?" she hissed, overcome with dread.

"I couldn't remember. I couldn't say if I forgot." Levi cried. He begged Sarah for mercy.

Sarah stormed to the porch, a weeping Priscilla in tow, and in a terrible, hoarse voice told Mam and Dat.

"No! No!"

Mam sank to her knees pleading to her God to spare her little ones, please, please. Dat looked across the porch, seeing nothing, his straw hat dripping dirty water, his beard beaded with rain. And then they moved as one, back out into the rain, knowing their search must go on.

As Sarah opened the gate, she saw the slippery mud and the fullness of the cow's udders as they stood patiently by the barnyard. She knew they should be milking. But she and Priscilla, Mam and Dat followed the cow path in the dripping aftermath of the storm, stumbling over tufts of grass as they spread out, unwilling to see, unable not to.

Ah. The creek had risen to a heart-stopping muddy flood that tumbled and churned behind the wild rose bushes and tall weeds immersed by the rising waters. They ran up and down its length, calling, calling, calling.

"Mervin! Suzie!"

They were wet, their shoes sucking the mud, their throats dry with apprehension, and still they called. Finally they stopped and looked at each other.

"We need help," Dat said calmly.

They cried together but differently now, a sort of acceptance settling itself over the hysteria, quenching it. Their heads bent, they walked back to the house. Dat moved to the phone shanty like an old man, bearing the weight of his missing children.

The medics were the first to arrive in their red and white vehicle equipped to save people's lives and a driver and an assistant blessed with helpful knowledge to relieve the pain of people in accidents, old people in cardiac arrest, or stroke victims. In this situation, they could only wait and talk into squawking devices or cell phones.

Many vehicles followed. Large green SUVs with blue lights rotating on their roofs, fire trucks, black and white police cars. Again.

Amish folks arrived, on scooters, walking, with umbrellas. Elam Stoltzfus and Omar Zook from across the pasture. Hannah came, sloshing through the rain, her flowered umbrella a bright spot of color in the gray evening.

Someone started the Lister diesel, its slow

chugging a comfort of normalcy. Men were milking, doing Dat's chores, as others formed an organized search party.

The light was gray as the storm wore itself out in small showers and slivers of light to the west. It seemed the world had been scrubbed and tossed about, then righted and patted dry, as if the countryside had emerged from a huge washer.

Sarah stood with Priscilla, numbly watching the scene with eyes that were still clouded with refusal to believe. They couldn't have been swept away. That creek was not high enough. Suzie could swim. She was quite good at diving and swimming at their cousins' pond. She would have made her way safely across, even if the creek was rising fast.

All that evening they searched. So many men. Why couldn't they find anything? At least a fishing pole, a tackle box.

Panic became a constant foe, successfully fought back only to advance again with reinforcements of alarm, trepidation, and horror.

It was the failure to know for sure, the overwhelming doubt, that was hardest.

Hannah, her daughters, Matthew and Rose, women from neighboring homes and businesses —all came and went, their voices reassuring the family with genuine kindness.

Mam remained in her hickory rocker by the stove, a figure bent with restrained panic, her eyes wild, showing white. The frightened look stung Sarah's heart.

In the gloom, they sat. Mam's lips moved as she prayed. Someone wiped a furtive tear.

Hannah brought her forest green container of coffee. Sylvia Esh contributed a stack of Styrofoam cups, a tall plastic container of creamer, a glass sugar shaker, and some plastic spoons. An English woman dressed in a pants suit brought a large white cardboard box containing doughnuts from the bakery in Bird-In-Hand. Hannah promptly opened the lid, chose a custard-filled one, cupped her hand underneath it, and turned her back to take the first bite.

She should turn her back, Sarah thought. Then because she was guilty of spiteful feelings, she began to weep softly, wiping her nose furtively when no one was looking.

Priscilla glanced at her sister, bowed her head, and wept quietly with her.

Outside the commotion heightened with those milling about on the porch, an increased flurry of activity, and Mam shot out of the hickory rocker, her mouth open as if to cry out, but no sound emerged. The hand she lifted to her mouth was shaking so badly she could not keep it there, so she clenched both hands at her waist, the nails digging into each palm.

What was it?

Sarah got up and moved stiffly to the screen

door. In the near darkness, a great shout went up, an exultation of humankind, a victory over fear and anxiety.

A burly fireman, his brown canvas raincoat dripping, his large face wreathed in smiles, carried a form wrapped in an orange blanket.

Suzie!

Sarah rushed to her, clawed at the blanket, and found a white-faced, wild-eyed Suzie, her hair matted to her head with silt and mud and water.

Mam grabbed Sarah by the sleeve, pushed her aside, and murmured incoherently as she tore the child from the fireman's arms with a wild possessiveness. She sat down on the porch chair and let the blanket fall away, touching Suzie's face and dirty hair as she checked for injuries.

"Suzie. Oh Suzie," she said over and over.

Dat and Priscilla and Sarah crowded around, reached out, touching, reassuring, as Suzie burrowed her head into the rough, orange blanket against her mother's shoulder. She cried and cried, then said she was thirsty.

Thirsty! And all this water.

Only forty-five minutes later, they found little Mervin's lifeless form washed up against the large culvert that went beneath Abbot Road, about a mile downstream.

He had been carried to an eddy, where dead leaves and stalks swirled and caught against the side of the large, concrete culvert that was normally more than sufficient to let the meandering little stream run through.

With Suzie on her mother's lap, sipping hot mint tea with sugar, and the women crowding around the scene of deliverance, the arrival of Mervin's body was a hard blow of cruelty.

Another fireman, another orange blanket. But this time, no cry of victory, no shouting, only a solemn handing of the small still form to his father, who lowered his face, his straw hat hiding it, the only sound a paroxysm of loss and love for his small young son.

Mam bore it stoically, although her tears would not stop flowing all through the evening.

Dat carried Mervin in and laid him tenderly on the kitchen sofa. Slowly, reverently, they folded the blanket away, revealing the face of their beloved Mervin, his features perfect, showing no signs of suffering or struggle. Sarah gazed on the sweet face of her brother, so angelic in death. She cried as if her heart would break.

Why? Always the questioning, the constant chipping away of faith.

When Suzie was strong enough, she began to talk. She and Mervin had told Levi but left quickly, knowing it was soon chore time. They'd only wanted to catch a few of the fallfish that swam in small creeks in spring.

They had waded to the other side, then decided to follow the bend in the creek. They probably went farther than they thought, catching fish. When the storm came, they were scared. Afraid Dat would be angry, they had waited too long. They hid beneath some trees, then panicked, and tried to cross. A wall of water caught them, tumbling them about.

She did have Mervin's hand. When she realized the situation was dire and the brown water had much more power than she expected, she struggled to save herself and her brother. When she crashed into an overhanging tree and Mervin was whirled away, she figured she'd probably drown, even though she so badly wanted to live.

She had caught the low branch of the tree, but she didn't know she'd have to cling to it as long as she did. The water rose fast. She had to continually creep her hands up the branch to keep her head from going under.

She knew Mervin had been torn from her grasp, but hope kept her outlook bright. She talked to herself, telling herself to hang on, another five minutes, then another, and when the huge spotlight shone on her face, she thought she yelled. But in reality, she could only make weak mewling sounds, like a kitten. Her hands were scratched and broken open, her fingers stiff with cold and fatigue, but she was alive.

The coroner came, a small portly man who gravely performed his duty, nodded, and left.

They took Mervin away, still in the orange

blanket, wearing his black trousers and gray suspenders over the blue shirt with two buttons missing. Dat and Mam felt him all over, as if to remember every inch of him. They kissed his beautiful, cold face.

"Goodbye, Mervin," they said and then turned away to hide their faces, their shoulders shaking with the force of their sobs.

Quietly, Hannah produced a box of Kleenex from the light stand, letting her hand rest on Mam's shoulder.

The boys came again from Dauphin County with their wives and children, crying, hugging, saying, "Thy will be done."

They sat around the kitchen table and talked, while Mam, seemingly stabilized by these motherly duties, helped organize blankets and air mattresses, extra pillows.

Suzie had a hot bath, shampooed her hair, and reappeared, dressed in a clean flannel nightgown, her eyes still wide with fright. They plied her with chicken corn soup and a toasted cheese sandwich.

Hot chocolate? Shoofly pie? No, she could not eat.

Finally, she asked if God could forgive her for letting Mervin drown in that awful brown water. Everyone shook with sobs.

Mam gathered her up in her arms and held her as if she would never let her go. Dat hovered over her and said she was not responsible, little Mervin's time to go had come, all designed by the Master's hand.

She cried then, in great, shuddering sobs, a tremendous healing balm for a young child of ten.

"Well," Dat said, blowing his nose. "Well, there's no use asking why these things happen. It seems harsh, one chastening gone and another bitter one arriving so soon after. But we want to accept, examine our hearts, and repent of any wrongdoing. Hopefully, from this we will learn lessons, have our views and values widened, and our spiritual needs fulfilled. In all things, there is a purpose, and we don't question."

Sarah listened, frustrated. We don't question? How could he say that?

Dat was a good, kind person, and so was Mam. They lived righteously and worked diligently at home and in the church, striving to secure the love that binds. And this was their reward?

Nothing went right, not one thing. How could God look down from his throne and call this fair? He must be strict, she thought. And besides, she prayed and prayed and prayed for Matthew, and He never answered her. Her yearning heart was now filled with grief.

Chapter 10

In the manner of the Amish, the help began to arrive immediately the next morning. Neighbors came to do chores at five o'clock, just as Dat was holding a lighter to the propane lamp.

It was Elam, wishing him a good morning, inquiring about his night's sleep. Yes, he'd slept, Dat assured him but didn't elaborate about the long sleepless hours when his heart had cried out with the voice of Job. "For the thing I greatly feared has come upon me. . . . I have no rest, for trouble comes."

Oh, he could exhort, lift up the weak, talk of reason and reward. But in the still of the night, he'd wrestled with his own personal angel. Where have I failed that all this trouble comes upon me? he silently asked. Where have I gone wrong? Perhaps I am puffed up, self-righteous. I have not given to the poor as I should have.

"Those poor Daveys," they all said. "And him a minister, yet. You'd think he'd have enough on his mind, *gel*?"

Hannah was in charge, producing a breakfast casserole made with eggs, bread, cheese, and ham. She'd added parsley, peppers, and onion.

The men cleaned the barn and prepared the machine shed for funeral services, moving equipment and power washing. Dat and Mam sat with the *fore-gayer* (managers), the three couples from their church district who were chosen to organize everything over the next few days.

Elam and Hannah, of course. John and Sylvia Esh, and Reuben and Bena King. They were all in their forties or fifties and had experience with funerals. They would do well, Dat knew.

They sat together at the kitchen table and made a list of those they would "give word" to come to the funeral. Who would carry the coffin?

Grandfather Beiler arrived, leaning heavily on his walker, his knees wobbling as he let go of it to place a kind hand on his grieving son's back. He knew well the throes of grief, having lost Suvilla two years prior.

Grandfather Kings, Mam's parents, arrived, white-haired, thin, and capable for their age. Mommy King went to her daughter, her arms embracing the grieving form. They stood weeping, the one a solace to the other, as mothers tend to be.

Levi sat in his chair and told their neighbor, Elam, that Mervin had drowned in all that water. He told him people drown when they breathe water instead of air. It rained too much, but not quite as much as Noah's flood.

Elam nodded and gave Levi a York peppermint patty. Levi asked if that was all he had; he wasn't so *schlim* (fond) of peppermint patties.

In the new part of the basement, the women cleaned and scoured, washed windows and arranged long tables. The men set up gas stoves, and other women arrived bearing boxes of food. The fire company donated the sliced roast beef, the meat traditionally served on the day of a funeral. Dat said it was too much, and Mam shook her head and said that was for sure, but they wiped their eyes.

Aunt Rebecca sewed new black dresses for Suzie and Priscilla in one day. Mam said she was so talented on the sewing machine.

They all had to wear black now for a year, whenever they put on their Sunday best. It was a sign of mourning, of respect and tradition, and it was taken seriously. They did it gladly.

Aunt Rebecca sewed the black dresses, capes, and aprons with the summer's heat in mind. She chose the fabric wisely, using lightweight rippled fabric that had a bit of body. Priscilla was very happy to wear the dress, as Aunt Rebecca was a bit fancier than Mam.

Sarah had two black dresses, one almost new, so she wore it on the first day of preparation. Since there was not much for her to do, she wandered to the basement, eager to see who was causing all the friendly chatter, the sounds of much needed fellowship.

Hannah grabbed her in a firm hug, shed a few tears with her, and asked how she was doing.

"Okay, I guess. As okay as I can be," she answered.

Sylvia and Bena gripped her hands, patted her shoulders in the motherly fashion of older women, and then began asking questions, their eyes friendly, without guile, bright with curiosity.

Sarah related the drowning in Suzie's words, while they clucked and sympathized.

"I never saw anything like that storm!"

"I hope I never have to experience one like it again!"

"It wasn't *chide* (right)."

A large woman Sarah did not know brought two cake pans covered with aluminum foil. Hannah reached for the cakes, thanked her, and then wrinkled her nose in distaste when she saw all the horsehair clinging to the aluminum foil.

"You almost have to put your food in a plastic garbage bag. You know, the kind you pull shut. These hairs get into everything. Especially in spring, like now," Sylvia complained.

Bending her head, Sarah huffed, breathing out sharply, trying to rid the aluminum foil of the offending hair.

"Ick," Sylvia said.

"A little horse hair won't hurt you," Bena laughed.

"Amish people grow up on it!" Sarah said, smiling widely.

The women planned lunch, preparing a kettle

of chicken corn soup with homemade noodles that Bena had brought and canned chicken pieces from Omar *sei* Ruth.

Someone had brought ground beef; another had brought sausages. There was plenty of bread and applesauce and pickles, so that was what they prepared for the family, the relatives, and the many people who came to help.

In the late afternoon, the men from the funeral home brought the small, embalmed body back to the house. Tears flowed afresh as they prepared the little body for burial. They sewed a white shirt, vest, and trousers, a sort of half garment, draped over the body, appearing neat and very, very white. Mervin's blond hair was so clean, his skin so perfect, his eyes small half-moons of dark lashes laid permanently on his cheeks.

Sarah choked, thinking of the hateful, clawing flood waters reaching up and over his sweet face, squeezing the warm loving life completely away from him at such a tender age.

How could God allow it? She cried silently with Priscilla.

She couldn't bear to watch Mam lovingly dress her small son one last time, caressing the sweet face before tearing herself away and slumping against Dat, her grief almost more than she could bear.

The vanloads of people arrived then as the viewing was being held that evening. Relatives and friends, both English and Amish, came to grieve with David Beilers.

Da Davey und die Malinda. Sie hen so feel kott. (Davey and Malinda. They had so much.)

Parents brought Mervin's little classmates, all dressed in black except for the light blues and greens of the boys' shirts. Their faces paled with various stages of anxiety, wondering if Mervin would look different when he was dead. They peered into the plain wooden coffin set on wooden trestles in the emptied bedroom and were too scared to cry, except for the older girls, who sobbed quietly into their handkerchiefs.

And except little Alan. He and Mervin weren't just friends. They were real buddies. They scootered to school together, traded half their lunches with each other, and shared every bit of accumulated wisdom they had learned in each of their six years. They both thought the teacher was fat and grouchy, but they weren't allowed to talk about it at home, so they talked plenty to each other.

Children were supposed to respect the teacher, whatever that meant. They just knew that it was no fun to color the best you could and then still get scolded for going out of the lines when you barely did ever. Or have your ear pulled if you got out of line at singing class, which wasn't one bit your own fault either, the way Mandy pulled the songbook in her own direction.

Poor little Alan stood there in his lime-green shirt and black vest and trousers and his black Sunday shoes and blinked his eyes rapidly. And then because Mervin really was dead, he turned his face into his father's side and cried and hiccupped with pain. His mother handed him a Kleenex and patted his thin, heaving shoulders. Death was very real, then, for six-year-old Alan.

Sarah sat with the family, shook hands solemnly with countless well-wishers. She held the grandchildren, helped her sisters-in-law with their rowdy little ones and crying babies, and shook yet more hands as the rooms became steadily warmer.

She was tired, her eyes red with fatigue and emotion, and she thought the night would never end.

Then Matthew and Rose appeared, dressed in the traditional black. Rose's hair gleamed blonde beneath the propane lamps, and Matthew stood tall and dark and attentive behind her, his face already so tanned by the May sun.

And here I am wrinkled and tired and sweaty, holding this fussy baby. And here he comes, of course.

She received Rose's hug graciously, their tears mingling. Sarah was truly in awe of her sweet, beautiful friend. When Matthew gripped her hand, she looked down at his vest and refused to meet his eyes.

The contact with his hand meant nothing at all.

It was merely a handshake, same as everyone else. Then why did her eyes follow him as he moved across the room, the yearning in them unknown to him? She could tell herself anything she wanted, but her yearning was there, always.

She longed to get away alone, sink into a soft bed, and sleep for a whole long night and part of the following day. She longed to get away from here, this community, these people. Somewhere far away. Away from Matthew and the river of hopelessness. Maybe, just maybe after the funeral, she would.

The day of the funeral service dawned a perfect day, the kind where the humidity has been lifted by the force of a storm, the air so clear it intensifies the green of trees, hills, and crops to a heartbreaking hue. Now it reminded Sarah so intensely of heaven. Purple and lavender irises took on a brilliant new color, the light of the sun coaxing all of God's majesty from them. The late tulips waved their red and yellow banners of comfort and encouragement to the mourners who attended the services.

The driveway and surrounding areas were covered with gray and black buggies, horses of black and brown obeying their drivers, stopping when asked, and moving on when it was time. Young men from David Beiler's church district moved among the teams, numbering the sides of relatives' buggies with a piece of white chalk.

It would all be done in order, the parents riding in the first buggy behind the specially built carriage that would carry the plain wooden coffin. The remaining family members would follow in buggies marked with the number 2, then 3, and so on, until the cousins, uncles, and grandparents were all in line, moving slowly to the graveyard.

But first, hundreds of people gathered in the clean implement shed, squares of carpeting laid on top of the stained concrete, the glossy benches in neat, parallel rows. The mourners were directed to their allotted spaces by the kindly *fore-gayer*.

In the house, a close relative led a special service for the immediate family. It was an hour spent grieving together, the coffin in their midst, before the actual service.

After that, they filed solemnly behind the pall-bearers into the large shed containing hundreds of their friends and relatives, all dressed in black except for the men's white shirts and the women's white coverings. The clothing was an outward sign of inner peace and love, the weaving of lives in a simple black and white bond of unity. They were all there together, all believing in the same God, their souls redeemed by the same Jesus, their views and values not always identical but always tempered by the fires of surrendering to one another, bending to each other, acquiring a level of unity by love.

The sea of black and white spoke to Sarah's

heart, the tremendous impact of generations of a people who strove to live together. They believed firmly in holding their neighbors in high esteem, in loving their neighbors as they loved themselves. This love was built on the foundation of Jesus Christ.

Oh, it wasn't perfect, she knew. Views and values were often solitary, each individual deciding what was right and wrong for them, shifting like sand. The winds of change and self-will constantly worked against this solid foundation. But the *ordnung* provided a guideline, a coming together, a rope on life's pathway to heaven.

When Isaac Stoltzfus, an uncle to the family and a minister, stood up, the funeral became starkly real. Sarah bowed her head. Isaac spoke of heaven's joy at receiving a small child who was innocent and had not yet trod life's sin-cluttered path. In her mind, Sarah saw Mervin with a small white robe around his heavenly body and wings of sparkling gossamer. He would have lovely blue eyes, his open mouth smiling, singing, his hair as gold, as heavenly as anyone could imagine. Happiness was all about him, a giant bubble of perfect love that no one on earth could begin to fathom.

Sarah cried. It was the parting, the agony of his death, the way he had died, the murky brown water entering his nose and mouth. How terrified he must have been. How alone. That was the hard part.

A second minister spoke of God's love, the love He had for Mervin, and how much further along he was now. Meanwhile, those left behind battled on, courageously meeting Satan and his allies on life's road to heaven.

When the service was over, each person filed past the open coffin. Many shed discreet tears, then left the family to view the beloved face of its youngest member before the lid of the small wooden coffin was closed.

Sarah looked at Mervin one last time and etched his features in her heart. She lifted the soaked Kleenexes to her nose one more time, her head bent, and told him goodbye.

In the buggy that was marked by a 7, there was a plastic bottle of water and two sandwiches in a Ziploc bag. She rode with her cousin, Melvin, with Priscilla and Suzie in the back seat, the youngest in the family, riding behind their parents and older brothers and sisters and their wives and husbands.

Melvin took up the reins, and thanked Dan, the young husband of her friend, Anna, who had tended the horses. Melvin looked at Sarah, grinned, and asked if she trusted him to drive.

"Of course," Sarah said, grinning back.

Bending, she retrieved the bottled water and the sandwiches. She asked her sisters if they were hungry, then handed them a sandwich to share.

Melvin watched out of the corner of his eye. Sarah handed the remaining sandwich to him.

"You take half."

"I'm not hungry."

"It'll be really late, Sarah."

"That's okay. You eat it."

"You sure?"

Sarah nodded.

Appreciatively, Melvin ate half of the diagonally cut sandwich in two bites. He reached for the other half before noticing the line of buggies was moving.

"Oops. Better mind my business."

He stuffed the remaining bread into his mouth, his cheeks bulging. Unable to cluck, his mouth filled with bread the way it was, he took up the reins and shook them.

Melvin was already twenty-five years old, a member of the church, his hair sort of cut in the *ordnung*. But he was a bit of a rebel, a free thinker who did things by his own standards. When he could get away with his antics, he would.

He was Mam's oldest brother's son, tall, powerfully built, a hard worker who was a foreman on his older brother's roofing crew. He had a pleasant, if not handsome face, brown eyes that could be as sincere as a puppy's and sparkle with his own ribald humor or flash with anger.

Mam said he was sadly spoiled, but Sarah

always said if spoiling did that to a person, then she hoped all of her children would be spoiled. Melvin was by far her favorite cousin. He never failed to lift her spirits and encourage her.

The sandwiches were a special favor from the *fore-gayer*, a kindness for the burial and return trip to tide them over till the actual meal was served after the services.

Swallowing, Melvin clucked now, his horse still waiting for that certain sound before stepping out. It pulled impatiently on the bit and bumped into the back of the buggy ahead of them.

"Boy, this is going to be a real pain," he muttered.

"Why?"

"Oh, this crazy Buster."

"Well, maybe if you didn't name your horse Buster, he'd behave," Priscilla said from the back seat, where she was watching the line of teams snake slowly up the road.

"What's wrong with Buster?"

"It's a dog's name."

"Nah."

Sarah loved Melvin, watching his profile now —the way his nose looked as if he'd banged it against a wall, and it had stayed that way ever after. She loved him more as he launched into an entertaining account of a dog's name, the one he'd given his German shepherd, which certainly did not look like a Buster. His horse resembled a Buster. Sarah smiled.

When they neared the graveyard, the white fence gleamed in the sun around the plain gray gravestones that dotted the well-manicured lawn inside it. The mound of fresh earth beside the rectangular hole in the ground, surrounded by the trees and fields of Lancaster County in spring-time, brought the onslaught of unaccustomed grief once more.

Would they actually lower poor, drowned little Mervin into that gaping hole?

Melvin said it didn't seem real. His brown eyes filled with tears as he ran a forefinger beneath his crooked nose.

He leaned over in Sarah's direction, pulled out a white Sunday handkerchief, and honked his nose loudly.

"He'll make a real cute angel," he said, sniffing.

Sarah wanted to hug him, hard, but she knew it would only embarrass him, so she didn't.

They opened the coffin at the graveyard, giving them all one last opportunity to view little Mervin, his face so waxen in the sun, his hair so white blond. When they closed the lid that last time, Mam seemed to shrink into herself, the black bonnet on her head hiding the intense sadness of the moment.

The young men worked hard to fill the opening, their shovels scooping the soil over the small coffin after it was lowered. As they worked, a resignation, a softening, moved across Dat's features. He knew and accepted that one of his own was safely at Home, and in this he rejoiced, the spiritual side of him winning as always.

Back at the farm, everyone sat at the long tables, where the thinly sliced roast beef was layered on platters, accompanied by Longhorn and Colby Jack cheese. Bowls of mashed potatoes, thick brown gravy, and coleslaw completed the funeral meal. Dessert was simple canned fruit and platters of cake with coffee. It was good, sustaining the entire family in a tradition kept for generations.

The kindly folks stayed until everything was spotlessly cleaned and put back in order, the leftover food *fer-sarked*, benches and carpeting hauled away, and the milking done. They gave their final condolences, and the family was alone.

"Alone, but not alone," Dat said. God was right there with them, and He would stay in the days and weeks ahead.

They had weathered the fire, hadn't they? They'd come through this together as well.

Chapter 11

Suzie went back to school all by herself and cried her heartache to Priscilla when she got home.

Company began to arrive, the living room filled with well-wishers every evening and every Sunday. It was another tradition, a gesture of love and caring, a kindness that even Mam finally admitted was a bit overwhelming.

Her garden was becoming overgrown with weeds, and no one was weeding it. The yard looked hairy, she said. The radishes and onions needed to be pulled. The things that had been damaged by the hail and rain needed to be replanted. But always, there was company, and Mam sat politely, said the right thing, and cried quietly while her eyes darted longingly to the garden or to the sewing machine as she tried not to think of the piles of fabric that needed to be cut and sewn.

They went to Mervin's room and packed his clothes in boxes and then carried them reverently to the guest room and the cedar chest, where moths wouldn't enter and the heat of the attic would not fade the colors. Mam cried when she found a pair of underwear and two filthy socks in his drawer. He would change clothes fast and furiously, the clothes hamper against the wall completely forgotten as he dashed down the stairs again. He was not allowed to chuck the dirty clothes under his bed, so throwing them back in a drawer was not really disobeying.

They found a blue jay feather, two rocks, some fishing line, a red and white bobber, three birthday cards, and five dimes in the little chest on top of his dresser. Bits of paper, scotch tape, and markers sat on his desk. A picture of Jesus stuck on his mirror beside one of Donald Duck and Goofy, cut from a birthday card.

So typical of a six-year-old boy. So Mervin. And so final.

Time moved on. The Beiler family accepted and did not question, courageously going about their lives in the traditional Amish fashion. There were moments when the memory of the storm, the disappearance, the horror overtook them, sinking its claws of discouragement deeply into their shoulders. But with time, the despair became less and less.

Among her people, Sarah knew accepting death was another way of accepting what God had wrought. To question it, to become bitter, to fight or rail against His will was wrong. They believed death was His will, no matter how hard it was to understand. And so the healing process began, the wonder of each new day emerging once more.

It was in August, the month when everything in the garden seemed to ripen at once, that Sarah noticed a change in Levi. He lacked his usual good humor and often displayed fits of temper. It was surprising because he had been perfectly manageable at the time of Mervin's death, the funeral service, and the weeks after.

Sarah was in the garden with a plastic bucket of ripe tomatoes half full at her side. She bent over to grasp another sun-ripened red orb, wondering if they wouldn't have an entire bushel basket full today. The sun was already hot, the intense heat warm against her back, as she picked tomatoes.

Glancing at the lima beans, she noticed the heavy pods bulging where the ripened beans pushed against the sides. She straightened her back and sighed. So much for asking Mam if she was allowed to get a job. As long as there was Levi to look after, cows to milk, and the large farmhouse, garden, and lawn to care for, she'd be here.

She was increasingly restless and unsure if that Levi wasn't terribly spoiled. She wondered if she would ever get over Matthew. She was completely sick of going to Saturday night volleyball games and Sunday suppers and hymn sings when always—always, like a gigantic fly buzzing on her shoulder—his presence agitated her.

She knew when he arrived with the beautiful Rose, and when they left. She knew where he stood on the volleyball team. She knew when he filled his plate, where he stood in line, and where he sat at the singing table.

She knew when he was happy, hilarious, or quiet. She watched the features on his face like the captain of an ocean liner follows his computer—carefully watching the display to chart her own happiness.

If he appeared moody, her spirits rose. Yes! There was a chance that he wasn't happy and wanted to break up with Rose. Perhaps, oh, just perhaps, please God, let it be, he was becoming bored with her perfect beauty, her immaculate ways.

If he was bubbling over with smiles, his face lit with an inner happiness, her spirits plummeted to the depths, hope quenched, the "ztt" of a tiny flame plunged into water.

Every Monday morning, she showed Mam her plastic mask of untruth, happily talking of Rose and her other friends, Lydiann and Rebecca, and Josh and Abram. She told Mam all about them having had a good weekend.

She had no idea Mam knew. Mam saw the strained smile and the increasing despair, but she decided to let Sarah busily weave her web of unhappiness until she was ready to talk.

As Sarah suspected, there was more than a bushel of tomatoes to pick. The lima beans were ready, and the peach peddler had come the day before with a bargain Mam could not turn down: twenty-two dollars a bushel. My. Oh, my, she said.

Abner's wife, Rachel, was not well, so Sarah left her a message and offered to do a few bushels for her. That was why the *kesslehaus* floor was covered in newspaper, piled with ripening peaches. Sarah quartered tomatoes, digging out the green tops with a vengeance. Her mood was as black as the dresses flapping tiredly in the tepid breeze with the rest of the day's laundry hanging on the wheel line.

"Sarah!" Levi's loud, whining voice sent an arrow of impatience straight through her.

"What do you want?"

"I want pretzels and Swiss cheese."

Sarah looked at the clock.

9:37.

It was time for his snack, but he'd eaten three eggs for breakfast.

"No."

"You're being mean, Sarah."

"You're too fat."

When Levi began to cry, Mam scolded her, drops of sweat beading her upper lip, her face red from the heat.

"You sure are not yourself these days, Sarah. Why would you talk like that to Levi? Bless his heart," she chided quietly.

"He is too fat."

"Sarah, he's always been that way. What is wrong with you?"

"Nothing."

Dutifully, she laid down her knife, went to the refrigerator, and searched for the cheese. Taking up a block of the fine cheese made in Ohio, she shaved off a few thin slices, put it on a napkin, and added a small mound of Tom Sturgis pretzels.

"He'll need a drink," Mam instructed.

Woodenly, her anger just below the surface, she yanked out a two-liter bottle of Diet Pepsi, poured a glassful, added three ice cubes, and took it over to his card table, where another puzzle was half finished.

"You have to help shell lima beans later this afternoon," she informed him curtly.

Levi looked up at Sarah, his beady, brown eyes as sharp as a hawk's. "You old grouch."

Sarah smiled in spite of herself. Her lips widened into a genuine laugh, and she clapped a hand on his shoulder.

"You're the one who's a grouch."

"You know why? I don't feel good. My stomach hurts. You're a grouch because you can't marry Matthew. He likes Rose, and you can't hardly stand it."

"Now watch it, Levi," Mam said. She was not smiling.

As the tomatoes bubbled on the stove, sending their aroma throughout the house, Sarah got down the Victoria strainer and prepared to attach it. She adjusted the part that clamped onto the countertop and held the bowl. She attached the roller and handle, checking to make sure it was properly fastened. Then she turned to her mother and said, "Mam, why can't I get a job the way the other girls do?"

"Oh, Sarah."

It seemed as if that statement alone punctured Mam's sense of well-being as efficiently as a pin stuck in a balloon.

"Mam, I'm always here, working. I don't get to

experience the outside world the way my friends do. I need a break. Why can't I get a market job? Or a cleaning job? Anything to get out a bit."

"You should help Anna Mae more. She has her hands so full."

"So does Ruth. If Anna Mae would stay home instead of running to every Tupperware and Princess House party, she'd get her work done. Ruth has two little ones and quilts!"

Sarah's voice rose to a frustrated squeak. The tomatoes bubbled over, turning the blue gas flame to orange, so Mam flicked it off with a quick twist of her wrist. Then she turned, put her hands on her hips, and said firmly, "Sarah."

"What?"

Sarah looked up, her eyes pools of misery, and Mam knew the time had come.

Carefully, she laid her dishcloth on the countertop and said quietly, "Sit down."

"No. The tomatoes are ready."

Sarah knew Mam was very serious, so she obeyed, her heart beating rapidly as she sat down.

"Sarah, I know how desperately unhappy you are. You can't always be so false on Mondays."

Gathering her last fortress of defense, her last hope of regaining her pride, she burst out, "I'm not!"

There was a decided snort from Levi, who sat at his card table, observing all of this.

"Levi, now you be good, and stay out of this."

"Yes, you are, Sarah. And I know it's Matthew. You have never once let him go the way you should. He is dating Rose, and hopefully he will marry her."

Sarah shot a look of complete disbelief at her mother.

"How can you say that?"

"What do you care if you don't want him?" her mother countered. "Sarah, it's very wrong of you to want him. Thou shalt not covet. Matthew is Rose's boyfriend. You are not a part of his life, Sarah. He loves Rose very much. You can easily see that. You see, often when we are blinded by our own will, we see only what we want to see, not what is reality. Your frustration is making your life miserable. Just miserable. You try to keep that happy face on, and it's not working. Accept God's will, Sarah. Let Matthew go. Pray for God's guidance in your life. We had to do that over and over when Mervin drowned."

Sarah bent her head, hid them in her hands.

"I can't," she whispered brokenly.

"You can."

"It would be easier if he died," she said with so much misery that Mam's heart quaked with the fullness of her motherly love.

"Sarah, I want to promise you Matthew. I want to promise you many things that would make you happy. That's a mother's instinct—to keep her children happy. Dat and I want to give you your heart's desires, always. But sometimes it isn't possible, and we realize life is made up of choices and difficulties. The greatest gift we can give our children is courage, the will to do what is right in the face of adversity."

"Matthew isn't always happy." Tenaciously, a bulldog of resolve, Sarah clung to her love, to the terrible, hopeless yearning, the river of misery she chose to visit far too often.

"Well, Sarah, if you're going to be stubborn, we'll just give this a rest, okay? I can talk, but you are the one who needs to see. Let's get started with the tomatoes."

"But Mam, listen to this."

Shamefacedly, her eyes blinking back tears, Sarah related the incident at the barn raising, the intense feeling of love, and the way Matthew had reacted to the bandaging of her burned hand.

Mam held very still, her white covering well over her ears, her hair falling away on each side of her *schaedle* (part) and smoothed back firmly in the way of a minister's wife. Finally, as Sarah stumbled to a halt, she reached out a hand and placed it on Sarah's forearm.

"And that, Sarah, is precisely why I hope he marries Rose." Puzzled now, Sarah lifted her eyes to her mother's. "Matthew had no business bandaging your hand. He does that with more girls than you. Half of Lancaster County's girls want him, and he knows it."

Sarah was shocked as Mam's nostrils flared. Mam's voice carried a certain quality she had never heard. Her own humble mother, speaking in this manner!

"Seriously, Sarah, you have to listen to me. We all like to think that we're good Christians who don't decide our love by a handsome face, but we both know that is often the case. Almost always the first attraction. And Matthew has held you in his gaze seemingly always. I wouldn't trust him farther than I could throw him."

Mam's words were firm and rock solid with meaning.

Wow. Sarah mouthed the word silently, then slid down in her chair, and gazed at the ceiling.

"Do you want me to tell you another motherly quality? We want the best for our children, and we're secretly proud if our sons and daughters have 'a catch.' You know what I mean? But it's all pride, the world's way, even if we get caught up in it at times. We're painfully human, and not so perfect."

"So what should I do to change things?" Sarah asked.

"Stop thinking he wants you. He doesn't. He's dating Rose. He's a flirt."

Like rocks thrown at her, Mam's words hurt, and Sarah winced, now painfully aware of her mother's honesty. This was so unlike her soft-spoken mother.

Mam lifted the lid of the tomato kettle, and Sarah's life stretched out in front of her, a long, dry, windblown desert without a road or a map to guide her survival without Matthew. Or the hope of him.

With fresh resolve, Sarah dressed carelessly in the usual black that Sunday afternoon. Melvin would be by to pick her up with, of course, the trusted Buster. He was almost an hour late, and in the heat of August, her hair would not stay in place, springing from the hold of the hairspray, free to look awful, she thought.

Well, who cared? She had pondered Mam's words carefully, or so she chose to believe. No more Matthew for her.

When Melvin finally did arrive, he tied Buster to the hitching pole, went to talk to Dat, and had a glass of mint tea and a handful of pretzels. Eventually he got up, poured himself a drink of water from the pitcher in the refrigerator, took a long look at himself in the mirror over the sink in the *kesslehaus*, and told Sarah he was ready.

The crickets, katydids, grasshoppers, and cicadas were all trying to outdo each other, their symphony reaching a deafening crescendo in the tired dusty weeds by the roadside as Buster walked slowly up the hill.

"I love the sounds of the insects at the end of summer," Sarah said suddenly.

"Why?"

Melvin's brown eyes searched her face, his serious expression a magnet for the humor his face always evoked.

"Oh, I don't know. I love fall and winter. Weddings coming up, Christmas, cooler weather."

"Why would you look forward to weddings? I only go for the roast and mashed potatoes."

"And taking a girl to the table in the evening?"

"No, Sarah. You are so mistaken. You are so mistaken it's not even funny. I do not enjoy taking a girl to the table. You know why? Because I'm old and a member of the church, and the brides are always so glad I'm there. Then they can pan off any homely, unpopular girl on me, because they know I'll be agreeable and talk to them. Usually they're my age or older, fat or . . ."

Melvin's eyes became sincere, liquid with goodwill.

"Sarah, you know I don't think I have to have some beauty queen to take to the table, but last year about took the cake. I was given every odd-looking girl in Lancaster. I'm sure they're all precious in God's sight, and every one of them would make me a good wife. But give me a break. That last wedding at Jonas Esh's, I hardly knew what to do. I don't even remember her name, but every time she said something, she sort of shifted and banged her shoulder against mine. She'd go, 'Yes, me, too!' Bang! Or she'd say, 'Did you know Davey Beilers? The ones whose barn burned?' Bang! It went on and on all evening. I was never so glad to leave the table in all my life. I'm not sure she was all there."

By then, Sarah was laughing, silently shaking with mirth, listening to Melvin's one-of-a-kind description.

"But, Melvin, maybe she just liked to be close to you."

"Evidently."

After that, Melvin launched into a colorful description of the place they were re-roofing—the shrubs, the lawn, the swimming pool, the gated community—until Sarah realized they had already arrived at the home of her friend, Rachel.

Would she ever forget that evening when Matthew and Rose arrived happier than she'd ever seen them? Could she ever remember a time when they had arrived and she didn't bother wondering if they were happy in their relationship, or if they were having a weekend together that was not so good?

She ate the meatballs with barbeque sauce, the scalloped potatoes with cheese, the salad, and the corn but tasted nothing at all. She smiled and talked and went through the movements of every Sunday. And she hurt so badly somewhere in the region of her heart, or wherever it is that emotions are kept, that she thought she surely could not go on.

When a tall, dark, good-looking figure stopped and lowered himself down on the grass beside her, looked into her eyes, and said openly and unself-consciously, "Hey, Sarah! S'up?" she looked into Matthew's eyes and laughed with a happiness so intense she thought she couldn't handle it. She knew she hadn't even started to take Mam's advice.

Over by the volleyball net, a tall blond youth with his hair cut in the English fashion leaned against a buggy wheel. He quietly watched that girl whose curly hair always invoked in him a desire to smooth it back with his hand. He thought her eyes were like a restless sea.

So. That was how it was with her. This Matthew guy.

He'd bide his time. There was no hurry. He had checked the Fisher book, that thick manual of Amish people's names, birthdates, and addresses. He'd asked his mother.

Yes, she had said, she believed that was the minister David Beiler's girl. They lived near Gordonville. She knew her mother's family. Why did he ask?

He had shrugged his shoulders and left the room.

After supper, Sarah leapt like an agile cat and spiked the heavy volleyball as solidly as any guy, winning the game point. She turned, graceful, her eyes alight with the competition, holding up a slender brown hand to receive the high fives of her teammates, but he didn't have the nerve to push his way through.

When the guy named Matthew ducked under the net and teased her, the look of raw adoration she gave him cemented his resolve to stay in the background.

How, then, could he explain what soon followed? She was yelling, "I got it," and moving quickly toward the sideline, her hands together in perfect volleyball form. Suddenly she tripped over her feet and collided with him, her weight slamming him to the ground, the volleyball bouncing off as the opposing team sent up a great whoop of victory.

Blushing furiously, the seawater eyes stormy with defeat, Sarah looked at him and apologized. Before she had a chance to leap to her feet, he was on his, extending a hand.

"Sorry. I really slammed into you," she said before accepting his proffered hand.

Close up, the wonderful eyes were rimmed with thick dark lashes that accentuated their myriad of colors. Her skin was so tan and flawless, the hand so slim, yet bearing a certain power. Her black dress only served to remind him she'd lost her little brother, making her vulnerable still. He wanted to hold her in his arms and smooth her rebellious hair.

But what he did was say, "It's okay."

She certainly had slammed into him, both physically and emotionally. Maybe even miserably.

Chapter 12

The August night was unusually hot. A sound woke Sarah from a deep slumber, the aftermath of a restless tossing earlier, the heat making the night unbearable. It was either that or her thoughts.

Hadn't she impressed Matthew with that spike! He'd shown in his eyes how much he admired her, the way they had glistened with approval. So close he had been, too, standing right there in front of Rose, and he didn't care.

Now if that didn't mean something, she didn't know what did.

But then what a klutz she'd been, falling over that blond guy. He was nice, but she could never date someone who wasn't, well . . . Matthew. She wondered if that was the reason no one ever asked her for a date. Perhaps it was as if she walked around with a sign on her back that said, "Don't touch me. I'm waiting for someone else. Still."

The blond guy had jumped up and offered his hand to help her up. Not very many boys were so thoughtful. He was also very good-looking, in a blond, non-Matthew way.

A sound broke through her deep sleep, and her eyelids quivered, shaking her dark lashes. When the wail of fire sirens hit a high note, her eyes flew open. In one flash, her hand raked back the thin sheet, her feet hit the floor, and she flew to the window, her heart pumping, her teeth already chattering with fear.

Thank God.

The barn stood in the hot August night, a great white sentry of safety, the silver roof gleaming in the waning moonlight, the cows scattered like black dots across the undulating green pasture, now grayish-silver, their shadows black strips.

No flames leaping. No smell of choking black smoke. But the siren's wails drew closer.

Grabbing a robe, she felt her way down the stairs, finding Dat awake, wearing only trousers. His arms and shoulders gleamed white and strangely unprotected in the moonlight. She had hardly ever seen her father without a shirt. He seemed younger and more vulnerable.

"Dat."

Turning, he said, "Sarah."

He went to the bedroom, where she heard a drawer opening and closing. He reappeared wearing a white T-shirt with Mam following close behind. Together they went out on the porch, their eyes searching the horizon for any sign of a fire.

The night was still, the leaves hanging as quietly as if they were in the house. The only noise was the tired trilling of the insects, having now rasped and rubbed and sung their way to exhaustion. The stars hung from the blackness of night, winking and twinkling, the moon's dim light casting over the earth in shades of dull gray and white.

Dat paced the lawn, lifting his head to watch in all directions, the memory of his own barn fire still fresh in his mind. Mam was the first to see, gasping as the small pink glow turned to orange.

"Dat!" she called. "Look to the east."

Sarah looked, a dagger of fright following as she watched. Dat leaped up on the porch, his eyes wide as the orange light intensified.

"It has to be close to Ben Zook's," he said. "I'm going over."

"Walking?" Mam called, not expecting an answer the way Dat ran, hatless and wearing only his T-shirt and trousers. And him—a minister.

There was no use going back to bed. It was just after two o'clock. Mam and Sarah sat together on the wooden glider listening to the sirens, watching the night sky, and waiting anxiously for Dat's return.

After a few hours, they went to the living room and stretched out on the recliners. They knew there would be lots of work ahead of them, and they needed to rest. Finally they dozed off but slept only fitfully.

When Dat had not returned at five o'clock, they dressed, tied men's handkerchiefs over their hair and called the cows in. Sarah washed their udders with a disinfecting solution while Mam began to attach the milking machines. The friendly hissing of the gas lanterns that hung from nails on the walls was comforting, but they watched them warily now with, presumably, a barn burning somewhere.

When dawn broke across the farm, the rooster in the henhouse crowed raucously, the hens began their silly "be-gawks," the heifers mooed hungrily, and still Dat had not returned.

Priscilla woke then stumbled wide-eyed to the barn looking for Sarah, Mam, anyone. She said Levi was crying of a stomach ache. Mam hurried back to the house while Sarah and Priscilla finished milking. They fed the horses and chickens, poured milk in the cats' dish, washed the milkers, swept the milk house, and still Dat had not returned.

Sarah decided to check the messages on their voice mail and was relieved to hear his voice.

"Mam, this is David. The barn at Ben's burned to the ground. They didn't save anything. They think it was an explosion. I'll be home soon."

Mam's eyes filled with quick tears. She shook her head in thought, murmuring as she broke eggs into a bowl.

"It's awful. Just awful, girls. What a loss! It's unbelievable. How long can this go on before someone catches up with these people?"

Her words fell in a hard rhythm as she beat the eggs with a fork. Still muttering and shaking her head, she added chunks of fresh tomato, parsley, peppers, and onion, throwing in bits of leftover cheese and sausage.

Sarah fried potatoes and poured juice, while Priscilla hunkered on the floor, waiting until the toast was finished in the broiler. Suzie stumbled sleepily down the stairs, but Levi wouldn't leave his bed, saying his stomach pain was so bad he hadn't slept all night.

They told him about Ben Zook's barn, and he became so excited he forgot all about his stomach. He hurried, shuffling to the table, exclaiming that the man in the white car was at it again. He ate three slices of toast with butter and peach jelly and fried potatoes with homemade ketchup spread liberally all over them. Then he asked for shoofly pie to dip in his coffee. He burned his tongue on the coffee and said it was Sarah's fault. She should remember to add cold water.

Mam told Levi quite firmly that Sarah had nothing to do with it and to stop being so quarrelsome. Levi said that if he had to go to the hospital for his stomach ache, Mam wasn't allowed to go along.

When Dat finally arrived, his face was gray with black streaks where sweat had mingled with the ashes and smoke. His eyes gave away his feelings of helplessness in the face of another monstrous fire, flames crackling and leaping, destroying the centuries-old handiwork of another Lancaster County barn.

He sank into his chair, lowered his elbows to his knees, and hung his head, a gesture so unlike Dat. A dart of quiet fear pierced Sarah's mind. It was the defeat, the undoing of one who had always been so brave and capable of meeting adversity head on.

His gray hair was matted, stringy, the scalp showing on top where the hair had grown thin. The odor of smoke clung to him—a bad vapor of premonition.

No one spoke. The clock on the wall ticked away, unaware of the scene around the kitchen table. Levi slurped his coffee and drained it, carefully swallowing the last of the shoofly crumbs. Then he rubbed his face across an extended sleeve.

Sarah silently handed him a napkin, raised her eyebrows, and smiled. He returned the smile and punched her forearm with affection.

Dat lifted his head then, and met Mam's searching eyes. He found the caring and support he sought, his own eyes conveying gratitude without words. Then he began to talk, quietly at first.

"It's a mess. It's just a horrible thing—the cows tearing at their stanchions, bawling out their terror, the desperate bleating turning into cries that were intolerable, the hay that burned as swiftly as any flammable substance, the shrill, high shrieks of the horses as they banged around in their stalls. The fire engulfing them was actually merciful. We tried. We tried to loosen a few cows, but I've never seen a fire like that. It was like a cannon blasting through the barn."

Dat shook his head.

"Not that I've ever seen a cannon. I imagine the ball of fire to be like one."

"Ball of fire? Was it lightning?" Priscilla asked, her face ashen with memories still vivid.

"No. It wasn't lightning. They're all talking, talking, on and on."

He lowered his head into his hands, the work roughened hands now streaked with the soot and ashes of his neighbor's barn. A stupendous burden weighed on her father, and Sarah knew it was not the fire, not entirely. He sat up suddenly, his eyes weary but filled with a solid light of knowing.

"It's so hard to take. Ben is so angry. He is demanding that something be done now. They're like a clamoring mob. They say, Amish or not, we can't sit on our hands and take this. Someone started this fire, and he needs to be brought to justice."

"But . . . ," Mam began.

"That's just it, Malinda. It's not our way. It's not. We are a nonresistant people. Or used to be. To my way of thinking, we do not fight back. God allowed the arsonist to accomplish this. He could have stopped him, but He didn't. It is a chastening, and in everything, some good can come of it. We need to adhere to our way of forgiveness. But Ben is like a madman. He's stomping around, making threats, shaking his fist."

"But for him to have to listen to those innocent animals' suffering . . ." Sarah said gently.

"Oh, I know. I know. It's almost more than any man can handle. And Ben's barn was rich in history, valuable way beyond mere dollars. It was an old German bank barn, built in the late 1700s. You can't replace that workmanship. It's just . . . well, sickening. They're bringing in trained dogs to sniff out certain chemicals. And the media will go wild about this. With Ben's anger, we will not be a light to the world. I shudder to think of what he'll tell reporters. It'll be a real jolt to the community. I hope all of you stay home as much as possible. We don't want our pictures in any newspaper or magazine."

Quietly, Mam got up from her chair. She broke a few eggs into a bowl, turned on the gas burner beneath her frying pan, and added a dot of butter. She took Dat a cup of steaming hot coffee and then laid a gentle hand on his shoulder.

"You'll feel better after you eat," she said softly.

Dat reached across and patted the hand on his shoulder, saying quietly, "*Ach*, Mam. What would I do without you?"

The day was bright and hot and humid. In spite of the heat, Mam kicked into high gear, urging everyone else along. They would pull the corn they had planned on freezing and take it to Ben's, along with the lima beans.

"Sarah, take Priscilla with you. Pull the sweet corn in the garden, the early patch of Incredible. Keep it in the shade. Pick the lima beans. We'll take them over to shell them. Suzie, is your breakfast eaten? Hurry up. You can pick tea. I'll make concentrate. Get the woolly tea and all the spearmint. David, what time are you going back?"

"I need a shower and some clean clothes. Girls, now please don't forget. Watch out for the cameras. Don't talk to the reporters. Keep your faces hidden if they try to take your picture."

In the garden, Sarah and Priscilla bent their backs obediently, holding the heavy lima bean bushes aside as their hands searched for the ripening pods. There was no sound except the dull thunk of the hard pods hitting the plastic buckets. The sun was already on their backs like a giant toaster, showing no mercy for the girls' comfort level.

Sarah straightened and wiped the back of her hand across her forehead, where beads of sweat had accumulated.

Priscilla groaned. "Whose idea was this—to plant these endless rows of beans? Nobody likes them, except Dat."

"Levi."

"I could easily live without lima beans."

Sarah shrugged her shoulders. "You know how Mam is. A garden without lima beans is just unthinkable. It would be like making a dress with a *leppley* (the small fold of fabric sewn into the waist on the back of the dress)."

Priscilla giggled. Then she said seriously, "I think Ben Zook has every right to be angry. I hope the same person lit his barn that lit ours and that the police catch him, and he dies in jail."

Sarah gasped.

"Priscilla! Seriously. We are not allowed to talk like that. Not even think it."

To Sarah's disbelief, Priscilla began to sob hoarsely. A sort of feral anguish tore from her throat in great heaves, a sound Sarah had never heard from her sister.

As Sarah placed a hand on her sister's heaving back, Priscilla moved away quickly saying, "Don't. Don't." Sarah stood helpless, holding the corner of her bib apron, pleating it with her fingers, not knowing what else to do.

Priscilla sank to the soil between the lima bean bushes. She lifted her tormented face, her eyes streaming, and shuddered before catching her voice.

"Sarah, you don't know how it is to lose a horse. You were never like me. I know Dat meant well, and my new Dutch is all I could ever dream of. But that arsonist took away my real Dutch, and I'll never love another horse the same way. It's not just the barns burning—it's the loss of heartfelt love for the animals. They didn't ask for some . . . some . . ."

Priscilla was at loss for the proper word to describe the total disgust she felt.

"Don't say it. Priscilla. Don't. You can't hate. It will consume you, and you'll become spiritually unhealthy."

Viciously, Priscilla yanked off a lima bean and threw it angrily into the bucket. With a sneer, she said, "What do you know about it, Sarah? Huh? Nothing. Not one thing."

Sarah blinked. She started to say something but just looked off across the garden and down to the orchard, where barn swallows wheeled in the sky, their sharp jabbering a sound of home.

No, she didn't know. Or did she? Did she hate Rose deep down inside? Did she just frost her hate with a sweet icing of falsehood, going about her life intensely longing for the one thing she couldn't have? Could she stand here and show her sister the path of righteousness, when in truth she was decaying spiritually by the power of her own obsession?

She imagined herself covered with sticky, sweet, cream-cheese frosting, her stomach a carrot cake, spoiled, the gray-green mold growing, growing, taking over her health and happiness.

Was she hating? Did she wish Rose well? And her impatience with Levi. She'd always loved her handicapped brother. But of late . . .

Dear God. You have to help me. I can't do this alone. Oh, I can't. I love Matthew, helplessly, hopelessly. I can't get away from it by myself. Give me courage. Give me strength.

It took her breath away, knowing the truth. Roughly, Priscilla brought her back to reality.

"Come on, pick beans. Don't just stand there as if there was a spook in the orchard."

Numbly, like a manipulated marionette, Sarah bent her back and started to pull off the lima beans, a mighty battle beginning in her heart.

Her love for Matthew Stoltzfus was as all-consuming as the fires that had devoured the barns. He ravaged her whole life, like a disease that would eventually annihilate her.

Well, obviously, the fires were being started by a person who meant evil, who wanted to harm someone or something, who possibly held a grudge against the Amish and their Plain way of life.

Her love for Matthew was from God, pure, cleansing, bringing happiness. Or was it? Mam's warning flashed through her mind. Well, another obvious thing—what did she know? Mam wasn't at the suppers and singings, the volleyball games. She didn't know how Matthew admired her, talked to her, made her laugh. He didn't do that to the other girls at all. She was the only one.

Soon they'd break up. Soon. Rose was too

beautiful, too perfect. He'd tire of her, and he'd be all Sarah's.

And so her thoughts tumbled and twisted, first in one direction, then in another. But always, tenaciously, she clung to the love of her life.

Priscilla attached herself just as firmly to a total disdain of the person who had taken her precious Dutch from her. The barn fires had spawned the works of the devil in all their masked forms.

Upstairs, the girls showered and then dressed in the customary black, with dear little Mervin gone only a short time. They wore no capes, it being the middle of the week, but they pinned their black aprons neatly around their small waists. Leaning over their dressers, they combed their hair back sleekly, adding mousse or hairspray, anything to tame the unruly hair.

As always, Sarah dressed for Matthew. He was sure to be there, as were all the able-bodied men of the community. So she combed, patted, combed again, sprayed, stood back, frowned, then took it all down and began again.

"What is wrong with you? Your eyebrows are arched straight up, and you look as if you could explode or something."

Priscilla was ready to go, covering pinned neatly, her blonde-brownish hair pulled sleekly back, her flawless face tanned, her eyes, well, yes, she was turning into a very pretty young girl.

"It's my curly, crazy, dumb hair!"

"You always did have that."

"It's the humidity. It turns my hair into cork-screws. They just spiraling wildly off my head."

"Well, go ahead and use the whole bottle of hairspray. Plaster your hair down hard as a board. You know the Fructis stuff isn't cheap."

"Who buys it? You or me?"

"You."

"Well, then."

Sarah lifted the green bottle, working the pump madly, while Priscilla plopped down on the bed, leaned back on her hands, and rolled her eyes.

"Go load the corn and lima beans a while. Dat got the spring wagon out. Go. Go on!"

"Your hair isn't the only thing out of control!" Priscilla shot back and started for the stairs.

Laughing, Sarah could hardly see to comb her hair, so she leaned on the dresser, giving in to the mirth, and was shocked to find herself crying and laughing at the same time.

Alright. This was enough of this stuff, as dear Mommy Beiler would say.

She raked her hair back once more, plopped her covering on top, pinned it, and without another look, ran down the stairs, through the empty kitchen, and out to the spring wagon, where Levi and Priscilla sat waiting.

Dat stood at the horse's head. "My, Sarah, we've been waiting." But he was friendly, smiling. If he felt impatient, he'd never show it, his emotions about such minor things always on an even keel.

"It's my curly hair."

Dat laughed and leaned sideways to look through his bifocals at the now severely plastered hair.

"It looks pretty straight to me."

Sarah laughed. "*Ach, shick dich* (Behave yourself)."

It was nice to have that reprieve of normalcy before the mile and a half to Ben Zook's farm, or what was left of it.

They arrived to the stench, the smoke, the milling about of people with stiff, numb movements, eyes full of dread or horror, caring, or disbelief. They arrived to the fire trucks, the engines and hoses, the black water draining away, carrying flakes of ash and the remnants of this proud old German barn that had been destroyed by a flick or two of a lighter.

Fire and water—two life-giving elements that humans needed to survive. But in out-of-control quantities, both devastated unlike anything else. Sarah saw the muddy flood waters churning over Mervin's head. She shivered and heard Dutch's screams as the raging fire overtook him.

And when Matthew Stoltzfus walked over to help Dat with his horse, she heard the distinct cawing of the crows.

Chapter 13

"Morning!"

"Good morning, Matthew. Good to see you. Hey, if you don't mind, I'll get the horse if you help the girls unload. Would you see that Levi has a comfortable chair somewhere? Maybe here by the fence?"

"Morning, Matthew," Levi chortled.

"How's it going, old boy?"

"Good. I'm real good."

"Hey, Priscilla," Matthew said, grinning down at her.

She didn't bother answering, intent on rescuing Mam's cakes from beneath the seat.

"Hello, Sarah."

"Hi, Matthew."

She smiled and looked gratefully into his brown eyes, so glad to see him, her whole world lit by his smile.

"Only Mam would bake a layer cake. Black walnut with caramel icing," Priscilla mumbled.

"Something wrong?" Matthew asked, bending to put his face close to Priscilla's to hear her better.

"Oh, nothing."

Matthew's arm went out, for only a second, a half circle about her waist. Blushing furiously,

Priscilla yanked at the cake, grasped it, and pivoted out of his way.

Matthew laughed and looked down at Sarah. "Boy, your little sister is growing up!"

He whistled, watching her retreating form.

Sarah giggled and thought how kind Matthew was, always thinking of others, and of someone like Priscilla, who had been so saddened by the loss of her horse.

"She'll likely take this barn fire hard."

"Matthew! I want down!" Levi yelled.

"*Ach*, Levi. I forgot you, talking to Sarah."

Oh, what hope! What a true cemented hope sprang in Sarah's heart, hearing those words. He had just admitted that she was a distraction. She mattered so much that he forgot about Levi! Imagine. The morning was now filled with pure, unadulterated sunshine, birdsong, monarch butterflies, grass as green and flowers as pink and blue and purple as Sarah had ever seen.

The scene of devastation at the barn faded into the background. Sarah shucked the corn all by herself in Ben *sei* Fannie's garden. She threw the husks across the fence to the three pigs they were fattening, about the only animals they had left.

As her hands ran swiftly across the ears of corn, removing the silk with a stiff bristled brush, she thought of Matthew. When she carried the first dishpan full of golden ears into the kitchen, her smile was dazzling, her face glowing.

She wasn't even aware of the cluster of women at the kitchen window watching her sister. Priscilla stood, still as stone, gripping the picket fence with white-knuckles. The color drained from her face as she relived the horror of her own personal barn fire, the one that had trapped Dutch in its fiery claws, making him suffer as no horse ever should. Her Dutch. Priscilla smelled the burnt bodies of the cows, the huge draft horses, and she remem-bered.

Levi sat a few feet away, his straw hat pushed back on his head so he wouldn't miss a thing. Men shouted as trucks moved among the gigantic black hoses. Cameras flashed as reporters skulked about, knowing they would soon be asked to respect the Amish men's wishes.

Flames still broke out in the charred wreckage. Blackened stone upon stone—the mortar that had held them together for centuries now crumpled by the intense heat—was all that remained of what the forefathers had built by the sweat of their brows.

"That girl is going to have to go for counseling."

"Not Davey Beiler's girl. He's better than any counselor."

"She looks awful."

"Somebody should go get her."

"You can't help her."

"Oh, my heart goes out to her."

"Where's Malinda?"

"That poor woman has had enough. She doesn't need to be here."

"Priscilla brought two cakes in. She made a black walnut cake."

"*Ach*, that Malinda. She is something else."

"Her caramel icing is a tad too sweet, though." This comment came from the owner of the community's top roadside bakery, Henry *sei* Suvilla, completely uncontested by any other.

Amos *sei* Leah stuck a skinny elbow into Danny *sei* Becca's ample side, causing her to jump with an almost inaudible little squeak. Two eyebrows shot up, and when Suvilla glowered at them, Leah quickly brought a hand to her mouth as she turned away.

Well, no wonder. Suvilla may have quite a business at her roadside stand, but nobody made walnut cakes with caramel icing the way Malinda did. And her being so genuinely humble.

Half these tourists didn't really know what good shoofly pie was. They bought Suvilla's dry old things and thought that's how shoofly tasted.

"Oh, my! No! Here comes a reporter. Straight up to Priscilla!"

"Oh, *siss unfashtendich*! (This is just sense-less!)"

"Somebody go get her."

"Where's Sarah?"

A flurry of searching followed but to no avail. It was too late. The reporter, carrying a whirring black contraption on his shoulder with straps dangling, bore down on the unassuming Priscilla.

She was completely unaware, lost in her own sad world of memories and loathing of anyone evil enough to murder these faultless animals. They had never done anything except serve their masters—giving their creamy milk, pulling the plow or the hay rake or the balers—servants that made a living, a way of life. Wasn't that check in the mailbox because of them? Wasn't the milk possible because of the horses' hard work, their beautiful heads nodding, their harnesses clanking, doing what God designed them to do?

So the fortunate person with the camera captured the innocent young Amish girl and all the horror mirrored in her eyes and sold the picture to the prominent Lancaster newspaper with Priscilla's own words in the story.

"No, I do not forgive him. I hope he spends the rest of his life in jail."

The repercussions were terrible. Amish people all over the United States gasped in disbelief—except for a handful who felt the same, Ben Zook among them. The Beiler family knew nothing of it, unaware that day at the barn raising.

The next day was different. Priscilla stayed home with Levi and Suzie, who had both come down with a stomach virus. Mam said it was the dog days of August, what else could you expect?

She didn't understand the politeness, the cold

distance between her and the good womenfolk until Hannah, bless her heart, drew her aside and whispered, "Did you see the paper?"

"Which one?"

"Here."

Hannah shoved the article under Malinda's face. Sarah leaned over to see, and both of their faces blanched.

"Oh, my goodness," Sarah said, slowly.

Mam lifted tortured eyes to Sarah. "Why? Why was she left alone?"

"I was probably shucking corn."

Malinda compressed her lips and stared out the window as tears sprang to her eyes.

"And David thought to warn them all. The children." She sighed, then squared her shoulders.

"Well, it is what it is now. We can't undo it. We'll just have to take the beating, the humiliation that will follow this article."

"It's because of Dutch," Sarah said wildly.

"We know that. But the world doesn't," Mam replied.

And where was I? Sarah thought miserably. I didn't even see her. I had my head in the clouds the whole blessed day, thinking of Matthew. And what had he done on Sunday? Nothing. Not one solitary thing. He never said hello or smiled or anything. As far as he was concerned, Sarah may as well have fallen off the face of the earth.

She stood in Ben Zook's kitchen, picked up one

chocolate cupcake after another, and spread chocolate icing on each one before placing them in a Tupperware container, seeing nothing.

Her heart ached for her parents. Priscilla had said the wrong thing, sparing no one. Those words were not her upbringing, not the Amish way. No doubt Dat would be accosted, over and over.

The yellow, pine-scented skeleton of the new barn grew beneath the hot, August sun. Once again, men clad in black joined forces with men in jeans and plaid shirts or T-shirts, wearing shirts out of respect, when, anywhere else, they might have gone without.

Hammers pounded, chainsaws whined, men shouted, tape measures snapped shut. Women moved back and forth, keeping the large orange and blue Rubbermaid coolers filled with fresh ice and water, with plenty of paper cups beside them.

It wasn't more than midmorning before David Beiler's neighbor, Sammy Stoltzfus, grabbed Dat's sleeve as he hurried by on his way to get a box of nails. He shoved the distasteful newspaper clipping under Dat's nose.

"Your Priscilla, *gel*?" he asked, in a voice oiled with sarcasm.

Dat stopped, searched his pocket for his handkerchief, and mopped his dripping face before tilting his head to look through his bifocals.

As Sammy peered shrewdly up at David's face, searching eagerly for signs of outrage, another man, Levi Esh, came on to the scene and stopped, curious.

David Beiler's face remained inscrutable. He might as well have been etched in stone, that was how still he stood, reading the article slowly, taking his time.

Before he'd finished, Sammy couldn't take the suspense a second longer and blurted out, "Is that what you teach your children?"

Still Dat stood unmoving, reading. Slowly, he folded the paper and handed it back.

"It's a pretty poor light, for the Amish, don't you think?" Sammy asked intensely.

Dat looked at the ground, moved his foot, then lifted his gaze beyond Sammy. "Yes, it is," he said finally.

"I thought so!"

Sammy fairly bounced in his aggressiveness.

"So. What will give?"

Levi Esh extended a hand to Sammy, and he handed over the evidence.

"I don't know. She's only fourteen."

"Well, somebody should have to confess."

"She's young, Sammy. Her horse burned in our fire. She's having a hard time getting over it."

"So now you stick up for her. That makes you every bit as bad as her. I hope you know this is being talked about all the way out to Wisconsin. My brother's out there. He left a message. Said he hoped I'd *fer-sark* this."

Levi Esh lifted his head, pursed his lips, narrowed his eyes.

Dat took a deep breath. "Sammy, I'm sorry. This is not what we teach our children. But she's hurting. She was very attached to her horse. He was a pet. She'll get over it, but give her time."

"Girls shouldn't be allowed to have horses. They didn't used to, in my day. You need to show better leadership. God didn't spare your Mervin, you know."

Sammy sniffed indignantly and rocked back on his heels, his hands clasped behind his back.

Then Levi spoke. His words were modulated but carried a certain authority. "I think we need to be careful here, Sammy. This newspaper article alone is punishment enough for David. It's unfortunate, yes, but we know why Priscilla said that. She's only fourteen. A child. Her pet was brutally burned. Don't you think your measuring stick should reach a bit farther?"

"What do you mean?"

"Just that. Go home and read it in the Bible."

Sammy knew what Levi's words conveyed, but he had the bit in his mouth and wasn't about to give up.

"Well, I told Ezra I'd take care of this. You know as well as I do it can't be forgiven until someone confesses."

With that, Sammy stalked off, dead bent on doing the right thing no matter what. Levi Esh placed a hand on David's shoulder and wished him well. The days and weeks ahead would be turbulent.

When the nine o'clock coffee break was announced—actually closer to ten o'clock—David was stopped again. This time it was by a well-meaning elderly lay member who was completely disturbed by the photograph and accompanying words.

"The world and her ways are encroaching on the young generation. God help us," she lamented.

Dat agreed and tried to explain, but he was rebuked with a stern warning to heed his role as a leader.

Dat had no more than taken up a cup of coffee and was reaching for a warm cinnamon roll when Henry King unfolded the same article, inquiring about Dat's knowledge of it. Dat nodded again, and again he bowed his head as pious judgmental words pelted him, hurting every bit as much as jagged rocks.

He was not doing his duty as a father—and certainly not as a minister of God—if he didn't have a better hold on his children than that. This came from a man who had three sons who had deserted the Amish way of life and chosen to live their own lifestyles.

Over and over that day, as he pounded nails, the sweat flowing freely in the ninety-degree heat, Dat prayed for the power to forgive those who were well-meaning but unkind in their rebukes. Yes, Priscilla had done wrong. But oh, how his love for his daughter throbbed in his heart!

Priscilla had always been emotionally frail, crying all the way to school that first day. Tears had dripped from her face as she wrangled her way through her first poem at the Christmas program. To be subjected to two great tragedies at the tender age of fourteen was almost more than he could bear on her behalf.

Dat struggled mightily against the urge to lash out in words of self-defense. Pushing back thoughts of Jesus' words to the scribes and Pharisees, he persevered in his work and self-control.

In the house, Mam stirred the corn and lima beans, added a stick of butter, and told Hannah she could take over. Mam wanted to walk home. Hannah told her she couldn't in this ninety-degree heat, and Mam said she'd be better off melting away down the road than staying here fuming. Hannah laughed good-naturedly and let her go.

Mam told Sarah to tell Dat, and then she walked the whole way home. When she arrived, she slammed the *kesslehaus* screen door as hard as she could. Kicking off her shoes, she sat down in the hickory rocker by the stove, lowered her face into her hands, and cried and cried, releasing all the humiliation and the disappointment in human nature.

Priscilla found her mother there, shocked to see her tear-stained, swollen face. They unfolded the newspaper article, pored over the story, cried, laughed, then cried some more.

Levi wanted to see, so they showed it to him, and he shook his head, grimly prophesying a sad future for Priscilla for letting someone take her picture.

"I didn't know, Levi!"

"Yes, you did. You were looking straight at him."

"Not on purpose."

"Yes, you were."

"No."

They let Levi have his say and then started making supper. Mam cut open a succulent watermelon and a warm cantaloupe, while Priscilla apologized, saying she hadn't thought.

"But is that really how you feel?"

"Yes."

"But you know, you must forgive others or our own sins cannot be forgiven."

"I'm being very careful until I decide to forgive."

"Priscilla!"

"No, I mean—how can I say this right? I know I have to forgive the arsonist. I plan on doing that. I actually have started the process. I'm not as mad as I was. But Mam, it's so awfully hard to move on. Especially now, since it happened again.

How many more fires before we all . . ." She stopped. "I may as well admit it. I'm not sure about our belief in being nonresistant. Are we just going to stand by and let that man or men or whoever just go along and burn barns?"

"It's only happened twice. Perhaps it will stop."

"And what if it doesn't?"

"We'll have to wait and see."

Priscilla shook her head.

Five days after the fire, Ben Zook had a new barn. The red barn was trimmed in gray with a gray roof, fancy by Amish standards. It did not complement his white house, but it was another beautiful symbol of fellowship and hard work.

By the last week in August, when the children traipsed eagerly back to school, a new diesel engine purred in the sturdy shanty attached to the back milk house wall. The only thing that kept them from milking was waiting for the new bulk tank. Once that was in place, they could purchase a new herd and get back to business.

With his horses and buggy gone, Ben Zook jogged or ran everywhere, his thick hair becoming steadily woollier as the days went by. His straw hat sailed off his head all the time. His anger had subsided, but he remained huffy, wary of anyone who tried to convince him to forgive and forget.

Sarah offered to help Ben *sei* Anna with her peaches and apples, scootering over the Thursday after school opened. Anna was short and as round as a barrel, with a pretty face—a match for her husband with her unbridled energy.

Her house was fairly new—they'd remodeled—but with nine children under the age of fifteen, there was a lot of wear on the new linoleum, she said.

"I'm not much for mops," she said. "The only way to clean a floor is on my hands and knees."

"Your house is always so clean."

"Puh!" Anna waved her hand, dismissing the praise. "My sisters say I have OCD, but I don't," she said, looking over her shoulder as she washed her hands. "Here, come wash your hands before we start to peel the peaches—Emma! Pick up the Legos. They don't have to be all over the floor."

As they peeled the soft, juicy fruit, Anna talked about the fire, explaining in minute detail the explosion that had woken them, the burst of terror, the feeling of desperation, followed by acceptance after the knowledge of helplessness.

"There is simply no feeling quite like it. To stand by while your whole means of making a living sizzles and flames and roars its way to total destruction. It's just unreal. You know, I told Ben, I was literally heartbroken. I was so upset I threw up that night. But, you know, God giveth us richly all things to enjoy, and I suppose he thought it was time to take some back. I don't know. Why does bad stuff happen? You can't figure it out. Ben got so mad, it wasn't funny. He says this is just going to go on and on, unless someone tries to stop it. He says he's going to sleep in the barn. Huh! That won't last long."

All morning, she talked, her words punctuated by another pretzel or cookie or peach stuck in her mouth. At eleven, she shrieked and said she forgot her brother, Lee, was here for dinner, and she had nothing ready.

"Well, he's not hard to cook for. I'll make chili and cornbread."

Cupboard doors slammed, pots sizzled, the can opener cranked, and plates crashed onto the kitchen table with alarming force.

"Oops! Here they come. And Ben's in a hurry. He hops, like a rabbit, when he's in a hurry. Shoo, I hope he likes chili. He's sorta picky. Come, children. Mary, come. Wash your hands."

Sarah helped little Mary wash her hands, then emerged from the bathroom, wiping her hands on her bib apron. She looked up—straight into the eyes of the person she'd toppled at the volleyball net.

"You're?"

"You?"

They both laughed, she blushed, and he looked tremendously pleased.

"You know each other?" Anna asked, her head swiveling from one to the other.

"I think we met once," Sarah said, smiling at him.

And he thought he had never been so close to ecstatic as when she looked at him and parted her lips in that perfect smile. It was not lost on Anna, who looked from Sarah to Lee and promptly stuffed a slice of cornbread into her mouth to ease the stress.

Chapter 14

Cousin Melvin picked Sarah up early Saturday evening. She wore the customary black. She also wore sneakers, as volleyball became a bit competitive on Saturday night, although she knew she'd play barefoot most of the evening.

In addition to her traditional garb, Sarah wore an air of disquiet. Her eyes seemed haunted from lack of sleep, and a certain unhappiness, a subdued quality, hovered just below the surface.

Melvin greeted her with the usual, "Hey, Cuz!"

"Stop calling me that."

"I wish you weren't my cousin. I'd marry you right off the bat."

"I know you would."

"Seriously, there aren't many girls like you."

"Yeah. Well . . ."

Sarah stopped, turned her head, and blinked back the hated wetness that rose too easily to her eyes.

"Well, what?"

"Nothing."

"What?"

"Nothing, I said. It's nice if you think I'd be okay to marry. Nobody else does, evidently."

"Ah-hah! I knew something was wrong. Your eyes were too flat when you climbed into the buggy."

"Too flat! What does that mean? Duh!"

"You know, Sarah, I'm going to stop right up there at the Tastee Freez, and we're going to eat ice cream and talk. I have a hunch that you and I are in the same boat, paddling like crazy with one oar in opposite directions, and we're so hopeless. Whoa, Buster!"

The light stayed red for too long, so Buster pranced and bucked and tossed his head, rattling his bit. But Melvin said not to worry. It was all harmless, and Buster just did it for fancy.

They pulled up to the hitching rail beneath a spreading crepe myrtle that was blooming profusely and humming with honeybees. Melvin declared it completely unsafe. He made her get back in the buggy and waited through the red light again with Buster acting as crazy as before. Melvin tied him to a tree on the opposite side of the street.

"Give me your hand to cross the street. People will think we're a couple," he said, grinning at her.

Who could be unhappy in Melvin's company?

He ordered a banana split with two spoons,

and they sat outside in the waning summer light. The ice cream melted and dripped while he went back for napkins. He met a friend and talked so long that Sarah had to keep scraping the melting ice cream into her mouth.

When he finally sat down again, Melvin paused for a long moment of indecision about which side would be his, the strawberry or the chocolate, and wondered which one she liked best. He didn't include the vanilla with the chocolate syrup as he hoped he could eat that all by himself. He finally reached the conclusion that she could have the strawberry side; it was girlish.

"You know, like Strawberry Shortcake. That coloring book and doll character. It's for girls, so you have the strawberry."

"You know what? I wouldn't tell just anyone this, but I love strawberry ice cream. Mommy buys it all the time from the Turkey Hill down the street. Their ice cream is the best—better than Schwan's."

Clapping a hand to his forehead, Melvin squinted and rocked from side to side with pain in his eyes. He said he didn't know why, he never got a brain freeze no matter how fast he ate ice cream. And he also just remembered he had forgotten his volleyball.

Sarah watched him and then burst out laughing. She spluttered and pointed her plastic spoon at him and said he could just quit that.

Melvin laughed and laughed and said yes, he had a horrible case of brain freeze. They finished their banana split and ordered French fries, loading them down with ketchup and salt. They ate every last one and even dipped the tips of their fingers into the white cardboard container and licked off the salt.

They talked until the lights blinked and wavered and cast their steady blueish glow into the night. Clouds of insects swarmed around the hypnotic light, smacked madly against the hot bulb, and fizzled to their deaths.

Melvin said she could hide nothing from him —that she never got over Matthew. She said no, she didn't, that she was exactly like one of those insects and Matthew was the pole light.

Melvin snorted and said he wished Matthew was a pole light. He'd smack his bulb out.

"You know, Sarah, I can hardly stand it. Every little thing he does, you take as sincere. He knows it. He just keeps you dangling. You're always thinking that around the next bend, he'll break up with Rose. You know he won't. She is as sweet as she's beautiful. I don't think she has a mean word in her vocabulary. Is that how you say vocabulary?"

Sarah lifted her face to the night sky and laughed a laugh of genuine amusement. Here was a person who was completely straightforward. He was as simple to read as a child's book—

uncomplicated, nothing hidden, content to be who he was, thinking he was quite cool and handsome when he really wasn't. Not much, anyway, and so lovable because of this rare trait.

Too many people, especially youth, were so desperate to be someone they absolutely weren't. In the process, they lost their genuineness, the only thing that actually was real.

Melvin was so real.

"Okay. So now you figured out my life. Let's start on yours."

"Ah, no."

"Come on. Who is it?"

"She's dating."

"She's dating? No wonder you said we're in the same boat."

"Yep. We are."

"Let me guess."

Sarah lifted her face, rubbed her nose, and hummed. She threw a covering string across her shoulder then remembered to tie it before tossing it back.

"Not Lavina?"

Melvin pursed his lips and nodded, his brown eyes liquid with sincerity.

"Yep. Her."

"But . . ."

"I know exactly what you're going to say. Eggs-zackly! She's too cute for me."

Aghast, Sarah stared at her cousin in disbelief.

"Too cute? But . . . Melvin!"

"Don't you think so?"

"Well, yes, of course. If you do. I just can hardly believe you would consider Lavina Esh."

"Not Esh. Not Lavina Esh. She's . . ."

"Well, Melvin, I wondered."

They laughed, the sound of understanding. When he said Lavina Fisher, from below Christiana, Sarah couldn't picture her.

"I don't know her, do I?"

"You do."

The calm night was ripped in two by the wail of a fire siren. Instantly, Melvin's head came up, and he grimaced.

"You know," Sarah said. "It doesn't matter where we are or what we're doing. That sound will never be the same for us. We can no longer think it's someone else. Someone English who we don't know."

"It totally gives me the shivers."

Sarah nodded, then confided in Melvin about the newspaper story of her sister.

"Yeah," Melvin agreed. "It's tough for your dat. That poor man has had more than his share of late. It's hard to understand, a family like yours, and Mervin's death. Why does God allow these things?"

"Melvin, we're not perfect. I can write a whole list of ways we could improve. Other people don't know, can't see, but we have many faults.

A whole bunch, to be exact. I truly think God chastens those He loves, to make us better, more loving, kinder, *mit-leidich* (understanding)."

Melvin nodded soberly. He wiped his mouth very carefully, adjusted his collar, brushed imaginary crumbs from his trousers, and sniffed.

"See, Sarah, I wish you weren't my cousin. You're such a treasure."

Sarah laughed and watched the insects' wild flight around the hypnotic pole light, but she said nothing.

They left the Tastee Freez and arrived late at the volleyball game. Dozens of buggies and a few vehicles were parked in the lower pasture, the horses contentedly chomping hay from a flat wagon. There were three nets set up. Huge battery-operated lights illuminated the night. Color-infused movement pushed back the soft, velvety curtain of darkness.

As always, her face tightened searching for Matthew. She was not content to enjoy her evening until she knew he was there. As always, he was front and center, his height a great asset to his ability. As usual, Rose stood beside him, dressed in the lovely color of the flower for which she was named, her blonde hair sleek and gleaming in the strong light.

Sarah sighed, a tiny sound of resignation, like the flutter of a despondent moth. Why did she stand here with her older cousin Melvin, putting herself through this week after week? The futility of her longing loomed before her, an impenetrable wall without end. She could not climb over it, or dig beneath it, or walk around it to the right or to the left.

He didn't know she had arrived, and if he did, would it make a difference? How did one go about extricating one's self from a spider web so effectively spun? She was as helpless as a dead fly.

Melvin, beside her, glanced at Sarah's face as Matthew successfully spiked the ball. Rose squealed and turned to him for a congratulatory high five. Melvin watched the pain and jealousy move across Sarah's features in a numbing wave. It was a shame.

As usual, the life of the evening was partially extinguished for Sarah. She half-heartedly entered a game on the side that needed players, which was not Matthew's team, of course.

She spoke to her friends, smiled, laughed, greeted others in a daze of sorts, her gaze constantly going to Matthew's game.

"Hey, watch it!"

A girlish yell broke in on her incompetent play, and she whirled to face the admonition.

"Sorry," she murmured miserably as the ball bounced away unheeded.

"You want someone else to play?" the girl asked, not completely without anger.

Sarah turned and sized up her challenger. She was tall, wide in the hips, tanned, freckled, with hair that should have been red but looked like it was toasted. She had a full, generous mouth, a prominent nose, and at the moment, she was not completely thrilled to have Sarah on her team.

"No, I want to play."

"Well, then, keep your mind here, and stop watching the other game."

Sarah was humiliated beyond words. She blinked rapidly to dispel the hot tears of frustration. She glanced again at the tall freckled girl and decided she knew exactly who she was.

That's Lavina. Lavina Fisher. The one Melvin wanted. But she was dating someone else.

Hmm. Sarah's eyes narrowed, watching her. Lavina played aggressively, pounding the volleyball with solid "whumps," moving quickly, shouting her moves to the other players. If she was English, she'd likely go far as a volleyball player, Sarah thought. Whew. Melvin better think about someone else.

After that, she forgot Matthew and played, putting her heart into the game. She kicked off her sneakers. She'd show that big bossy Lavina.

When the evening was over, Sarah had pushed her way into Lavina's good graces. She had whirled and twisted and dove, fists extended, helping their side win two straight sets. When the last game was over, they found themselves seated side by side on the ground, propped up by their hands, legs extended, as they talked about the game.

"You're Lavina Fisher, right?"

"Yes. I am. And I know you—Davey Beiler's Sarah, right?"

Sarah nodded.

"You just lost your little brother. I'm so sorry. It must be very hard. And didn't your barn burn too?"

"Yes."

"It must be tough."

"It is."

"Little brothers are so precious. I have three, and they're the delight of my life. I teach school, so naturally, they're my pupils. And what a challenge, teaching them!"

Sarah laughed.

"You hungry?"

"Not really."

"Oh, come on."

"No, I just had a banana split at the Tastee Freez with Melvin."

"Melvin? What Melvin?"

"My cousin."

"That older guy who lives alone with his widowed mother?"

"Yes. That's him."

"He's your cousin?"

"Yes. My mother's oldest brother Alvin's son."

"I know who he is."

This was spoken in haste, the words hard, pelting. Sarah raised her eyebrows and turned her head to look at Lavina.

"Why does that make you . . . whatever?"

"What?"

"Why did you get mad, thinking of Melvin?"

"I didn't. Well, maybe. I didn't want to let it show. It's just that . . . if you wait for someone for so many years, you finally come to the long overdue, sane conclusion, that he doesn't want you, doesn't even know you exist. And so, you move on. I moved on. I'm dating happily now."

Sarah tried hard to hide the incredulity she felt. Oh, my goodness.

"I'm glad you're happy," she said but only as a soothing message, a sort of space between them until she had time to absorb the power of Lavina's words.

So. Is that how it was with Matthew? Is that why the attraction was so powerful that day? What if Matthew was like Melvin and wanted her, but he was too shy to ask? That was how it was with Melvin. And Lavina had wanted him all that time.

She drew up her knees, smoothed her skirt over them, and shivered with happiness.

So when Matthew dropped down beside her and said, "S'up?" Sarah turned to him with a shining face, her hope renewed, and asked how he was doing. When he said, "Fine and dandy," she fell in love with him all over again. Especially when Rose remained standing beside the table loaded down with homemade pizza, grilled hot dogs, cookies, bars, and whoopie pies and continued talking to Elmer Zook.

Sarah would be patient, bide her time, unlike poor Lavina, who hadn't waited long enough.

Should she speak to Melvin about this?

"You're not even listening to what I'm saying," Matthew said.

"Oh yes, I was. You were saying it's Rose's birthday."

"Mm . . . hum. Now. What would be a good gift? If you were my girlfriend, what would you like?"

Oh, the radiance of the night! The unbelievable thing he had just spoken of! Sarah giggled.

Lavina watched her, shrewdly, her eyes missing nothing.

"Well, I've always wanted one of those oak tea carts. Or a clothes tree. Both of them make nice gifts for someone who has been dating a year or so."

"A clock. I can't wait to give her a clock."

Sarah's radiance was dashed to the ground by a black hand—a hand so large and so capable of ruining all her hopes. She could not answer, could not think of a word to say.

A clock, Matthew. No. A clock was an engagement gift—the Amish version of a diamond ring. The hoped for, long-awaited gift of commitment desired in every young girl's heart. Please don't say that, Matthew. She looked into his face, startled that she hadn't said the words out loud.

"Why? What's wrong with a clock?" Matthew asked.

It took every ounce of willpower to recover, to speak normally.

"Nothing. Of course. Nothing. It's perhaps a bit soon. That's all."

"Yeah."

Lavina jumped to her feet and said, "Come on, Sarah. I'm hungry."

Sarah sat, refusing to go, until Lavina reached down and grabbed her hands and pulled her to her feet.

"I don't want to go alone."

There was nothing to do but leave Matthew, so she did.

They filled their plates, although Sarah thought she might as well have scooped a nice pile of sawdust onto hers, so unappealing was the thought of any food at that moment.

Lavina led her away from the groups of girls, away from the glare of the unforgiving lights.

"Sarah, I know I don't know you very well, but . . . is that Matthew your friend, or . . ."

"Friend," Sarah broke in, hurriedly pulling the curtain of oblivion abruptly between them.

"A bit more?"

"Look, Lavina, you don't even know me. Stop

asking impertinent questions that are none of your business."

With that, she flung the white Styrofoam plate to the grass, sprang up in a quick movement, and walked quickly away, the mind-numbing events of the battered evening spurring her on. When Lavina called after her, she ran.

Sarah ran the whole way through Elam Lapp's lower pasture, stumbling over rocks until she found the field lane that led to the large white barn. Her breath was coming in ragged gasps as she approached it, her heart pumping out her despair.

When she reached the road, the narrow macadam country road to Ronks, she noticed how the enormous white barn stood close to it, only a strip of well-manicured lawn between the road and the building. This was the kind of setting the fire marshals had warned about. In a few short minutes, barns like this could easily be ignited by the occupants of a vehicle stopped along the lonely road on a dark night.

Sarah shivered. And then—because their barn had burned that awful night, and because Mervin had died, that dear, innocent, tow-headed little soul—she began to shake uncontrollably. She sank to the dew-laden grass by the barn, overcome by the power of the tragedies coupled with Matthew's disclosure of his desire to present Rose with a dumb clock.

Suddenly, she hated Matthew with an alarming, powerful sense of revulsion she had never thought possible. He had been her captor far too long, holding her hostage, her whole life held in his hands. His hands—when it should have been God's hands.

Well, let him give Rose a clock. She hoped he'd be happy. Suddenly the knowledge that he would be happy brought a hoarse cry to her throat, and she buried her face in her hands, her body shaking, dry sobs escaping her.

That was where Levi Glick, known as Lee, stumbled across her as he walked home, envisioning Sarah sitting with Matthew again, her eyes vivid, her features animated.

"Oops. Oh."

He jumped back, apologizing and alarmed.

"I'm sorry. I didn't see you. Who . . . ?"

He bent, and she twisted away from his gaze, swiping a forearm viciously across her face, then using the hem of her apron, as she breathed hard, struggling for control. It was too dark to see who sat before him until yellowish headlights on the road suddenly appeared, starkly illuminating Sarah, her face swollen from the effects of her painful realization.

Lee stood, waiting for the car to pass. It was a small white one, traveling only a few miles an hour, and they both thought it would roll to a stop. Seemingly, the driver spied the two figures, accelerated smoothly, and continued on his way, leaving them enveloped in the still, hot August night.

Awkward. That's what this is, Sarah thought, grimly. Lee made the transition smoothly.

"Do you want to go back?" he asked kindly, completely ignoring the fact that she had been distraught, knowing how mortifying this chance encounter must be.

She shook her head but then realized he couldn't see her and whispered, "Not really. Melvin won't know where I am."

"Who's Melvin?"

"My cousin. He brought me."

Lee said nothing, just stood beside her, gazing off into the summer night sky, and waited.

"Will you be okay? I don't want to leave you here by yourself. It is the middle of the night, after all."

"I'll be alright."

Indecisive, he remained. The sense of loss was too great if he left, but to stay might pose a whole set of new problems.

What had caused her to become so upset? What was the puzzling aura about her? This girl fascinated him. All the turbulence in her green-gray eyes was drawing him—but to what?

Resigning himself to what he knew was best, he walked away.

Chapter 15

It was actually Hannah, Matthew's own mother, who was the next to completely wreck Sarah's fresh new resolve. She came breezing in on a tempest, the winds of October bringing gusts of hurricane force. They sent maple leaves skidding wildly across the porch and smacked them up against the wire fence in the pasture, shoving them through the white picket fence in the front yard.

Hannah wore a headscarf over her white covering, smashing it flat against her hair, which wasn't far from its usual appearance as she had no time for a matter as unimportant as a covering. Her heavy sweater was buttoned down the front, and she pulled off a light pair of gloves as she walked into the kitchen.

"Chilly out there."

Mam looked up from her pie dough, or rather, the flour and Crisco she was mixing into pie dough.

"Hannah! What brings you?"

"The wind. It blew me straight up the road. I can't imagine getting ready for a wedding. Just think of all the plywood and plastic being nailed into place. I bet a bunch of men are chasing after their hats," she said, chuckling.

Lifting her glasses, she peered into the bowl containing the pie crumbs.

"Crisco or lard?"

Mam laughed, a good-natured, relaxed chuckle of comfortable friendship, of years of having Hannah living just down the road.

"You know which one."

Hannah laughed with Mam, and Sarah smiled to herself.

"Matthew wants me to try and make those fry pies. Some people call them moon pies. But why go to all that bother if one large pie gives you the same exact taste? He says Rose's mother makes them. She dips them in glaze, like a doughnut. Well, whatever she does, you know, is how it's done."

She rolled her eyes, a gesture of impatience.

"And now . . . *ach*, I don't know why I start. I was always hoping he'd see the light, and . . . well, you know what, it isn't nice, but Rose will not always be easy. He'll have to take care of her, no doubt. He's talking of giving her a clock, and they've only just been dating a year."

Her voice rose on a panicked note, ending in a squeak of desperation. Immediately, Sarah listened closely, now keenly aware of Hannah's wishes.

Mam remained quiet, the sun and clouds changing the light in the kitchen as they played hide and seek with the wind. Mam's covering was large and very white, her face small and serene, the blush in her cheeks a sign of her healthy way of life. Her navy-blue dress was cut well, the neckline demure, the black apron pinned snugly around her waist. Mam's strong arms turned the lump of dough.

Sarah could not picture her mother being like Hannah, their differences so obvious. Yet they remained true friends, the bond of love between them as strong as steel cable. They defended each other fiercely. And yet, where Matthew was concerned, Mam would not speak her mind, and Sarah knew why: she did not approve.

In her wisdom, she kept her peace. She knew every Monday morning Sarah had subjected herself again to a useless struggle, like a trapped sparrow beating her wings against a window, when all she had to do was turn away and escape through the wide-open door.

A small smile played on her lips as she scooped some flour from the container, scattered it on the countertop, pinched off the proper amount of dough, and patted a small addition on top. Taking up her rolling pin, she plied it lightly over the dough in an expert circular motion. Hannah shrewdly observed over her shoulder.

"You know your dough wouldn't crack like that if you used lard?"

"Now, Hannah!"

Hannah poked an elbow in Mam's side and laughed.

"You know, Malinda, Mommy Stoltzfus always said the beginning of the end of all good pies and doughnuts was the exclusion of lard."

"Our generation will live longer, thanks to good, clean arteries."

Hannah sniffed indignantly.

"Who wants to live 'til they're a hundred? Folks caring for you, helping you in and out of a carriage, being a burden to your children. See, that's another thing. I cannot imagine that *piffich* (meticulous) Rose taking care of me when I'm old. Matthew always says he would be the one to care for me, and he would, bless his heart. He's such a sweet boy."

Mam discreetly waved a bright warning flag of caution, but Sarah's eyes turned to pools of yearning, imagining Matthew caring for his aged mother. Mam knew the tightrope that extended between sons and their wives. It was a balancing act to be negotiated with great prudence. And wasn't that Matthew a spoiled one? Ah, but the consuming jealousy one would battle. How well she remembered those days.

Many Amish lived double—one might call it. An addition to the house accommodated the son and heir, who would farm the home place. The new bride he brought home would start out optimistic, so in love, convinced her Daniel or John or Sam would love her unconditionally. But she only became bewildered, then hurt, then angry, when she found her young husband visiting with his mother, when his rightful place was with his wife.

Hadn't Mam and Dat navigated those treacherous waters themselves and counseled many troubled newlyweds since they were called to the ministry?

Oh, Sarah.

Mam rolled her pie dough expertly, her old wooden rolling pin clacking at both ends. She draped the round, flattened orb across the pie plate with the ends hanging unevenly and took up a dinner knife and sliced them off so fast Sarah could hardly see her turning it.

Sarah finished peeling apples, set aside the peelings, and began cutting the apples in small slices, filling the pastry. Mam stirred the pie filling of brown sugar, butter, milk, vanilla, and water as it bubbled to a caramel-like consistency. Then she poured just the right amount over the freshly sliced apples.

"That does look good," Hannah observed. She watched Mam roll out the lid, the pie's top crust, which had small indentations cut into it to allow the steam to escape. She flipped it neatly on top of the filling, and Sarah's fingers worked the dough into an even crimp.

"Boy, Sarah, you sure can *petz* (pinch) pies, for someone as young as you are."

"Thanks," Sarah murmured.

"Did you know my sister Emma needs a worker?"

Sarah's head came up. "Where?"

"Her bakery in New Jersey. That farmer's market there. You should apply. You'd make an excellent worker."

"Oh, Mam! Why can't I? You could manage. Levi is doing really well. Priscilla is home."

Her eyes pleaded with her mother. Hannah looked from Mam to Sarah. Mam pursed her lips.

"Oh, Sarah, I depend on you so much. It's not just the work. It's the companionship, the support. You've always been here."

"Now, Malinda, that's not fair. Maybe it's Priscilla's turn to support her mother. I think Sarah needs to get out and see the world a bit."

"Maybe you're right."

At the supper table, Dat ate two hefty slices of warm apple pie with vanilla ice cream, telling Mam between mouthfuls that it was the best pie she'd ever baked. Mam smiled back, and her cheeks flushed slightly. Levi whooped and hollered and raised his fork and said she shouldn't have sent a pie to Elam's.

"Hannah doesn't need our apple pie. She's big enough!"

Dat pushed back his chair, his eyes twinkling merrily at Levi.

A resounding crack came from the front yard. Suzie dashed to the window and gasped when she saw the heavy limb lying across the driveway.

"It must be terribly windy out there."

Dat's face became sober.

"I certainly hope there is no fire tonight. A barn would be gutted almost immediately, with the power of this wind. It seems that once you've gone through it yourself, you're just never quite the same. I shiver to think of a fire tonight. I have half a notion to sleep in the barn, just to be safe."

"You'll do no such thing!" Mam's voice was terrible, and they all turned to stare at her, shocked.

"Davey, you know what a sound sleeper you are. You'd never wake up. You know better!"

Dat nodded. "Perhaps you're right."

Silence remained after that, its presence calming, comfortable, as each member of the family remembered the night of the fire, the storm, the horror, the grieving, as if it had all happened yesterday. Only a short summer season had passed since then, but they had all learned so much. Like gleaning sheaves of wheat, the knowledge of others' suffering and loss felt ten times keener now.

Dat's hardest trial had been the laymen's bickering, each one convinced his opinion was the one with which Dat should agree. The disturbance over the newspaper story had subsided to wary muttering about Davey Beiler protecting that girl. It was, after all, only a horse.

Sammy Stoltzfus called his brother in Wisconsin and left a message telling him that if Levi Esh dealt with him in this manner one more time, he may as well start looking for a farm out there. After all, the closer the end times came, the worse people would become, and if Davey Beiler knew what was good for him, he'd take that daughter firmly in hand.

After the second barn fire, a decided change had blown in. An unwelcome fog of suspicion shrouded the congregation. Dat desperately tried to turn a blind eye to it, but it was there nonetheless. On one hand, the fires had united them in love and brotherly concern. On the other hand, unsound theories pervaded the community that had formerly been innocent and childlike in its trust.

Mannie Beiler put padlocks on all his barn doors, and Roman Zook bought a Rottweiler, a huge slobbering beast with a massive head and wide paws. It barked and growled and muttered to himself all day. Eli Miller slapped his knee and laughed uproariously, thinking of an arsonist caught by the seat of his pants by that dog.

And David Beiler was saddened by all of it. There was no use being touted and admired by the world if the truth was decaying, a spoiling mold growing unobtrusively within two members of the church and spreading among the others as the weeks went by. Where was true forgiveness?

Each and every time he stood up to minister to his people, David exhorted the truth. "In our hearts we are a peaceful people, so let us be very careful, not boasting of revenge, not assuming something we are not truly sure has occurred."

He also knew human beings were often doing the best of their ability, and he overlooked many things, measuring each person through eyes of love.

The story of John Stoltzfus's Ivan was repeated time after time and never failed to bring a smile to Dat's face. Ivan was only eight years old, but he was determined to protect the family farm and his small flock of sheep. He unfolded his sleeping bag in the haymow, a powerful Makita flashlight beside him, a Thermos bottle of water, and the latest Bobbsey Twins book.

Why his parents allowed the courageous little third-grader to sleep there in the first place was beyond Dat's comprehension, but that was beside the point. The poor little chap had been awakened by the cruel wail of fire sirens. He panicked and ran through the sheep pen in his underwear, terrifying the creatures to the point that one of them got hung up on the barbed wire, and they had to call the veterinarian.

Other stories and questions—and the attitudes behind them—were not so humorous. There were those who believed the Amish way of forgiving did not apply when one's livelihood was in danger.

"Yes," David said, "Yes. You're right. But what will you do? Does unforgiveness and threat bring back the barns, cows, and horses? The balers and wagons and bulk tanks?"

Each evening he prayed for wisdom to weave a thread of unity and peace in a world that was slowly unraveling through suspicion and fear.

That evening, Sarah said evenly, "Dat, Hannah's sister, Emma, has a bakery at a farmer's market in New Jersey. She needs help. May I go if they ask me?"

"I guess that would be up to Mam."

Priscilla looked up, her eyes alight. If Sarah was allowed to go, perhaps she would be too eventually.

Mam shook her head ruefully, then admitted to her own selfishness, wanting Sarah with her. "But, of course, she may go. Let's wait and see first if Emma actually needs someone. You know Hannah."

It was said fondly as her friend's fussing and stewing about life was a great source of humor in her life. Dat nodded, understanding softening his eyes.

"Oh!" Priscilla gasped.

"What?"

"I forgot. Ben *sei* Anna left a message last night. She needs you to help with applesauce on Wednesday, which is tomorrow. Sorry, Sarah."

"It's okay. I guess I can go. Right, Mam?"

Mam nodded, already gathering the dirty dishes and drawing the hot water to wash them.

"Wouldn't know why not."

Through all of this, Levi sat somberly, making no effort to include his own opinion, which was highly unusual. He remained hunched over his card table, shuffling his Rook cards, his large head swinging from side to side as he talked to himself. Finally tears began to roll down his cheeks, and he dug in his pocket for a red handkerchief, which he used to blow his nose repeatedly.

At bedtime, as Mam helped him with his pajamas, he told her that she'd likely never have to do it again.

"Levi!" she said, shocked.

"No, you won't. I'll just pass away now. I'll go to heaven to be with Jesus and Mervin."

"Don't talk like that, Levi. We'd miss you too much. We couldn't bear it, after losing Mervin."

"Well, my time's about up—especially if Sarah goes to market. That will be hard for me to bear."

"*Ach*, Levi."

Mam patted his shoulder. She made a big fuss about his ability to dress himself and brush his teeth and said they'd be just fine without Sarah.

The next morning, Sarah scootered the mile and a half to Ben Zook's and was shocked to find ten bushels of Smokehouse apples in the washhouse. Anna had her breakfast dishes already washed, the Victoria strainer attached firmly to the tabletop, and the first apples cut and on the stove.

"Morning, Sarah!"

"Morning!"

"Didn't you get cold, scootering?"

"I dressed warmly."

"Did you have breakfast? I saved some casserole for you. Let's have a cup of coffee before those first kettles are ready to put through the strainer."

"You put your kettles through?"

Anna laughed, her stomach shaking. She moved with surprising speed, her round form fairly bouncing with energy as she poured two mugs of coffee, lifted the creamer bottle, and raised her eyebrows. Sarah nodded.

She set a glass dish between them, steam rising from a deep, delicious looking casserole that was covered in buttered corn-flake crumbs. Taking up a spatula, she cut a huge square, slid it expertly on a small plate, and handed it to Sarah.

"Oh, I had breakfast, but it's been an hour. I can always eat some more."

She laughed, helped herself to a generous serving, and took a hefty bite. She rolled her eyes and said this recipe could not be beat, now could it?

Little Mary climbed on her mother's lap and promptly became the recipient of a nice sized mouthful of breakfast casserole.

"*Gute, gel*?" Anna chortled happily.

The door banged shut, and in walked Anna's brother, Lee, who was taken completely by surprise, his reaction to Sarah's presence a complete giveaway. He was holding his forearm firmly as he nodded in her direction.

"What's wrong with you? You look terrible!"

Anna rose to her feet, dumping Mary unceremoniously onto the floor.

"Cut myself. It's pretty deep."

"Let me see."

As he slowly lifted the clamped hand, blood spurted from a wide cut on the underside of his arm. Immediately, Anna's face blanched. She made small mewling sounds and sagged back into her chair, then slid to the floor below.

"She's fainting!"

Sarah stood, helpless. Lee said she'd be alright, she always did that. He seemed completely at ease with his sister crumpled to the floor.

Sarah looked from him to his sister, then moved quickly to the medicine cabinet in the bathroom. She found all kinds of salves, gauze, and adhesive tape. She grabbed them all and hurried back to the kitchen.

"I think the most important thing would be to get the bleeding stopped. You sure you didn't cut a vein?"

"No. Just wrap it tightly."

"With what?"

"A small towel would work."

Sarah grabbed a towel and pulled it as tight as possible, watching his face for any sign of discomfort.

"Still okay?"

"Yeah."

But he sat down, his face contorting.

"Does it hurt?"

"A little."

Mary began crying, so Sarah scooped her up and sat facing Lee, who lifted the towel and peered underneath.

"Shouldn't you go have that stitched?" Sarah asked.

"I doubt it. We'll stop the bleeding, put butterfly bandages on it. That should fix it right up."

Sarah was relieved when Anna muttered and coughed, and raised herself to a sitting position, still mumbling to herself.

"She's coming around."

"You sure don't worry about it," Sarah said.

"It's normal. I told you."

Fully awake now, Anna said, "Shoot, I passed out. Boy, I hate that. It happens so easy. *Ach*, my. Now I'm sick to my stomach. Shoot."

She lifted herself from the floor and wobbled dizzily to the bathroom. Lee shook his head.

Sarah bent and removed the towel, astounded by the size of the cut.

"You'd better go have that taken care of," she said.

"You think?"

"I do."

"Ah, just stick a few of these on. It'll heal." He grabbed several butterfly bandages.

"It's going to leave a scar."

"That's alright. It's just my arm. No problem."

So as he held the cut together, Sarah concentrated on applying the bandages just right, holding the edges of the cut uniformly. She held her breath and bit her tongue as she did the best she could, then straightened.

She looked at him fully for the first time ever, the blue of his eyes taking her completely off guard. His eyebrows were perfect, like wings. His nose was stubby and wide but somehow also just right.

He looked back and saw clear eyes of green flecked with gold and gray and bits of brown. At the lowering of her eyebrows, her eyes clouded over with a hint of bewilderment. Her breath came in soft puffs as her heart beat a notch faster.

Over and over, she relived that moment and chided herself. What was God trying to show her? That she was simply swayed by close proximity to any available man? Or was it the beginning of the end of her whole world being wrapped up in Matthew Stoltzfus? Would Lee provide the freedom she so desperately needed?

Ten bushels of apples later, she still had no clue.

Chapter 16

The cooling October winds must have been host to a serious virus. Levi came down hard with a temperature of 102 degrees, his large body lying as still as death, his breath coming in great gasps.

The rasping sound from his bed in the enclosed porch aggravated Sarah's nerves as she did the Saturday morning breakfast dishes. Her arms covered in suds, she scrubbed the black cast iron pan that was caked with bits of cornmeal mush and grease.

The wind had died down, but scattered puffs still blew leaves half-heartedly across the driveway. The strong winds left a residue of straw, bits of hay, a Ziploc bag, bits of paper, plastic, and cardboard strewn around the yard. The day would be busy with the weekly cleaning, Mam hanging out two days' laundry, and cleaning up the messy yard.

Already Priscilla was upstairs, wielding the broom and dust mop. By the sounds from above, Sarah hoped she was cleaning underneath the beds. Priscilla was only fourteen years old, so her cleaning was done only well enough to get away with. This usually meant that Sarah had to spray the bathtub again or remove every object on a hastily swiped dresser and dust it again.

Today, with Levi breathing like that, Sarah became impatient. She whirled away from the dishwater, took up her apron, and dried her hands. Going to the stairs, she told Priscilla to clean the bathtub right this time and let the cleaner on the tub walls while she did the rest of the bathroom.

Priscilla mumbled a reply, the banging resumed, and Sarah could picture the few jabs of the dust mop, leaving disorderly trails underneath the beds.

Turning, she approached Levi's bed and bent to crank his head a bit higher to ease his breathing. He started, his swollen brown eyes opened to a slit. He coughed painfully then asked for a drink. Sarah checked the pitcher on his nightstand and found it empty. She took it to the kitchen to refill it, adding mostly ice cubes.

She lifted the blue straw to his mouth, watched as he swallowed a small amount, and then set the tumbler back on the nightstand. She arranged his pillows to keep his head from sliding to the side, put a hand on his feverish head, and asked if he was alright. Wearily, Levi shook his head.

"Do you want Swedish Bitters?" Sarah asked.

Again, he shook his head and fell asleep.

Sarah brought the broom, a bowl of hot vinegar water, the window cloth, and a bucket of sudsy Lysol water to begin cleaning his room. She set the geraniums aside and washed the shelves, windowsills, and windows, rubbing the glass panes until they shone.

She picked off the yellowing leaves from the geraniums, the dead blossoms following them to the floor, then set the plants back. She stepped away to view the result of her work and decided anew that she would never, ever, have one painted coffee can in her house and certainly not one that was covered in floral contact paper.

Mam was frugal. She viewed every empty tin can as a new flower pot. She bought all her Maxwell House coffee in tins, not the new-fangled plastic containers, just so she would have another flower pot to keep her beloved geraniums through the winter.

Mam couldn't imagine paying five dollars for a geranium. Anna Mae and Ruthie were of the younger generation, and they refused to keep a single geranium in any tin can. They kept theirs in the cool part of their basements, in the same pots that had contained them in the summer. They brought the geraniums back up in the spring, clipped them back, and had beautiful new plants.

It had escalated to an all-out geranium competition, albeit an unspoken one. Ruthie had a large new deck built onto her house with pretty pots distributed across it, many of them containing geraniums bursting with healthy pink or red blossoms.

When Mam spied them she said, "My, oh," but

that was all. She didn't question the method of keeping them "over winter" or ask which greenhouse Ruthie had gone to. She just said, "My, oh." Ruthie and Anna Mae laughed heartily about it but never approached Mam or asked her to change her geranium habits.

Sarah now questioned herself. When will I ever have the chance to clean my very own house? I'll be twenty years old next month and don't even have a boyfriend (or a special friend, as her mother would say).

She'd had chances. Boys had asked her on dates, but accepting was unthinkable. Even though it was one sure way of allowing Matthew to fade from her life, she couldn't do it.

She often wondered why he'd asked Rose instead of her. Obviously, if he was attracted to her beauty, that was the whole thing right there. Sarah couldn't even come close to that blonde perfection.

She took all the things off Levi's nightstand and wiped it well with the Lysol water and then replaced the items.

Well, Rose was so good-natured and amiable— as sweet as she was pretty. So Sarah guessed that it all made sense. But she had immediately picked up on the way his mother sniffed and disapproved. If he listened to his mother, he wouldn't date Rose; he would date Sarah.

But what could Hannah really do? She couldn't

go around telling her children who to marry like they did in some cultures.

Sarah swept the dust and dirt and bits of geranium residue out of Levi's room, then dropped to her hands and knees to scrub the floor. Levi's breathing rose and fell above her.

Perhaps Matthew had no idea how she felt. Was that it? Or maybe, and this was very likely the truth, he had never felt the same thing for her—not when they went to school and most certainly not when they had each turned sixteen, joined the group of youth, and began their *rumspringa* (running around) years. She was just Sarah, his buddy. The thing was . . .

Miserably, she sat back thinking of her burnt hand. That incident had only cemented her longing firmly into place. Likely he'd just been nervous, wanting to get out of the kitchen, afraid Rose might find him alone with her.

Viciously, Sarah wrung the soapy water from the cloth and resumed her cleaning. Reasoning, wondering, she remained caught up in the subject that occupied her thoughts most of the time: Matthew Stoltzfus.

But now there was the disturbing intrusion of that Lee. Uh-huh. She had resolved on the weekend of Matthew's first date with Rose that she would never marry until he did. That was the one and only thing she had never told anyone, not even Mam or Priscilla.

So Lee, who she had now decided was most definitely attractive, may as well not even try. Not that he had. He was always at Ben's when she went to help Anna, who was fast becoming a close friend and confidante. They could easily talk a whole day about any subject, bushels of apples and peaches disappearing beneath their conversation.

She didn't know Lee at all, but she smiled to herself remembering how unconcerned he'd been about his sister sliding to the floor in a faint, looking for all the world like a soft teddy bear thrown against a kitchen chair.

Sarah got up and surveyed Levi's room with satisfaction. Turning to get the brush and dustpan, she saw a dust mop come bouncing down the stairs in a shower of loosened dust followed by three knotted Wal-Mart bags filled with a week's worth of trash can waste.

"Priscilla!" Sarah yelled at the top of her lungs, indignation coursing through her veins. She knew better. Nobody threw that mop down the stairs.

In response, Priscilla called, "Bring me a bunch of plastic bags!"

"No!"

"Come on. You old grouch."

"No. I would if you hadn't thrown that dust mop down the stairs."

"You know I didn't clean the stairs yet. Why shouldn't I throw it?"

"The dust flies all over the house, not just the stairs."

"Girls! Come," Mam called. "Do you want a few cookies? I'm so hungry from the washing."

The girls put aside their differences and joined Mam at the kitchen table. She heated the coffee and got out a container of cream-filled molasses whoopie pies and one of chocolate chip cookies.

Sarah unwrapped a whoopie pie, took a large bite, and said nobody had ever come up with a better recipe.

"You're getting fat," Priscilla said dryly.

"What?" Sarah shrieked.

Mam chuckled as she poured the coffee. Then she laughed outright as Sarah made a mad dash for the bathroom scales.

"135!" she wailed a few seconds later.

"I told you!" Priscilla said jubilantly.

"It's that job at Ben Zook's. Anna eats all day long. Mam, you know how much she weighs? 208. She said so herself."

"Well," Mam laughed. "She has always been that way. I remember her as a little girl, her round little body covered with that wide, black apron. She's never been different, but she had no problem catching a good husband."

"That's for sure."

Dat entered the kitchen with Suzie in tow, their faces flushed with cold air and hard work.

"We're hungry!" Suzie said, her voice low.

241

Since Mervin's death, Suzie had seemingly found solace in becoming her father's right-hand person, the way Mervin had been. Whenever she could, she accompanied him from barn to workshop, from cow stable to haymow, handing him tools, always asking questions.

Dat seemed to appreciate this, his former little companion stolen from him by the cruel flood waters. Suzie, in her childish way, remedied that theft the best she knew how.

"I'm going to finish the cow stable, then Suzie and I are going to go to Intercourse to the hardware store. You need anything?"

"Clothespins."

"Alright. After that, I'll bring Suzie home before I go help Ben Zook. He still needs help finishing up doors, and he said his diesel shanty could still use some work."

They sat dunking their cookies in coffee, lost in thought, until Levi's raspy breathing broke through to them. Dat looked up.

"Is that Levi?"

"He's pretty sick this time."

After they finished up their snack, Sarah resumed her cleaning. Priscilla sprawled across the sofa with the daily paper, which was every bit as annoying as Levi's breathing.

Sarah was aggravated. She weighed 135 pounds, couldn't eat whoopie pies, was almost twenty and still single, and had one annoying fourteen-year-old sister and a brother with Down syndrome who was a lot sicker than even Mam knew. Everything irked her this morning. Melvin hadn't called all week, and she was sick and tired of those stupid volleyball games anyway. What was the point of batting that ball back and forth across the net?

"Get off the couch," she growled.

Priscilla obeyed but promptly sat on the recliner, the newspaper held in front of her face.

"Priscilla!"

"What?"

They were interrupted by the sound of hoarse coughing, which turned into a wheezing of mammoth proportions, as Levi struggled for breath.

Mam hurried into his room, Sarah following.

"Levi."

Mam called his name tenderly, as Sarah smoothed the covers over his shoulder.

"He's so hot, Mam."

Mam nodded, held the digital thermometer to his ear, and lifted it, mutely, for Sarah to see: 104.3.

"Time to call someone," Mam said briskly.

Sarah nodded, grabbed a sweater, and went to the phone shanty with the speed she felt was necessary.

It was Saturday, so the health center was closed. She dialed 911 and calmly told the dispatcher the situation. Inside, Mam was trying to relieve Levi, who was now awake, crying in pain, his massive chest rising and falling as he struggled for breath.

Levi's condition was not out of the ordinary for the Beiler family, so their movements were not panicked, just calmly efficient. They sat him up, offering a drink of cold water, their eyes speaking volumes as they knew it was bad this time.

Levi was whisked away to Lancaster General Hospital. Dat was notified and joined Mam there while the girls finished up the cleaning and prepared to work outside.

They'd call around three o'clock.

The autumn sun had warmed the air, and Sarah soon shed her black sweater, raking the front lawn with long even strokes. The wash flapped in the sky high up on the wheel line, a colorful picture of motion, the green, blue, purple, and pink colors waving back and forth, whichever way the wind sent them.

Priscilla used the leaf blower. Suzie ran in circles, flopped into the piles of leaves, and then helped rake them onto the plastic sheet before they dragged them away to be burned.

The crisp air lifted Sarah's spirits, and she reveled in the perfectly raked yard. She leaned on her rake and admired the brilliant red, orange, and yellow of the chrysanthemums planted in a row along the garden's edge, the cover crop already producing a thick, green lushness.

Another season had come and gone, and the shelves were well stocked in the cellar. Applesauce, peaches, pears, five varieties of pickles, tomato soup, spaghetti sauce, and red beets—the variety of colors a sight to behold. Corn, lima beans, peas, green beans, cherries, and raspberries occupied the freezer in labeled boxes, ready to be cooked or made into pie fillings.

It was a wonderful way of life, and the rich gratitude that flowed through Sarah's veins brought a renewed zest for life, for the Amish way. No doubt it didn't make sense to the English world, and it certainly didn't have to. Sarah knew her people were not out to prove anything or live self-righteously. They weren't looking down their noses with the attitude of the scribes and Pharisees in the Bible.

It was an appreciation of heritage, a rich experience of lives lived before theirs—the stories, the respect for birth, life, and death, for marriage and raising children. It was continuing to live upright humble lives and existing in harmony amid a world filling with more and more confusing and unwanted technology.

Here in the heart of Lancaster County, with all its sprawling development and tourism, Sarah could see the physical results of her labor and enjoy the same house, yard, garden, and outbuildings as her mother, grandmother, and great-grandmother before her.

Except for the barn. She turned and eyed the sturdy new building, and a sadness coupled with appreciation enveloped her. The barn was resplendent. A change had come into their lives, and they had to accept it. She could picture the old barn, so timeless, so beautiful, but it was gone now. A new one took its place, and it was okay.

Missing Mervin was not. How he would have run and leaped into piles of leaves, scattering them untidily all over the yard. Sarah would have chased him, caught him, tickled his sides, rolled him into the leaves until they both fell back, breathless, laughing, his eyes alight with the little boy mischief she loved.

But *so iss is na* (so it is now). Mam's words were tapped into her mind like old Morse code.

Geb dich uf (give yourself up). It was a full time job, giving herself up, but anything else surely led to misery and kicking futilely against walls of restraint. She could kick and pummel that wall with a fist and get absolutely nowhere. It only bruised and battered the spirit, the soul.

Little Mervin was not here to spend his days growing up with them. It was so final—and so real.

Sighing, Sarah turned, called to Suzie, and went to the phone shanty, leaving her rake leaning against its front wall. She spoke to Dat, who told her Levi had a serious infection in his lungs,

246

a bad case of pneumonia, and was in the ICU.

Sarah gasped, tears of pity welling in her eyes. Did she want to come stay with Mam, or would she rather do chores? She'd milk, with her sisters' help.

Dat thanked her and said it meant so much. Mam would be glad if he could stay, at least until Levi was stable.

Sarah soon found herself in the cow stable with a navy-blue men's handkerchief tied over her hair, pulled down almost to her eyebrows, and sturdy Tingley work boots on her feet. She wore an old purple dress and no stockings. She lifted her arms as she called to the plodding cows, their heavy udders dripping with milk.

Priscilla wheeled the feed cart along the alley, dumping scoops of nutrient-rich cow feed on the tiles beside her, the eager cows curling their long, rough tongues greedily around it.

Suzie was feeding the chickens, the sheep, and the two pigs Dat had bought from his neighbor, Elam. They would be fattened for next winter, he said. Suzie loved the pigs, and Sarah told her that if she wasn't careful, she wouldn't be able to let Dat butcher them. She said the cute little pigs would turn into big lazy hogs. Then she wouldn't be attached to them.

Sarah tapped the first cow's hip and was rewarded by a polite lifting of one hind foot, then another. The cow moved over to accommodate her, allowing her to dip the udder in the disinfecting solution, then attach the gleaming stainless steel milking machine.

As the diesel purred in the shanty, the sun began its descent toward evening. The cows rattled their locks, a horse whinnied, and another one answered. The steady chugging of the milkers brought contentment to Sarah, and she smiled happily at her sister.

Priscilla smiled back and gave the feed cart a shove, sending it crashing against the chute. She turned, dusting her hands by clapping them against each other.

"Now what?" she asked, grinning cheekily.

"You better watch it. That's a new feed chute, you know. You probably put a good sized dent in it."

In reply, Priscilla spread her arms and twirled, a pirouette executed perfectly, the lime scattered on the aisle assisting her movement. Sarah stood between two cows, an elbow on one's back, watching as Priscilla leaped and twirled again, just for the sheer joy of it.

Well, you were only fourteen once, she thought, smiling to herself. That time when you were still enough of a child to spontaneously whirl around a cow stable, not yet having to worry about the *rumspringa* years.

Sarah was startled to hear a clapping sound. She looked toward the door of the milk house and saw Matthew Stoltzfus watching Priscilla, his dark eyes alight with enjoyment.

"Bravo! Bravo!"

Priscilla came to an immediate halt, her cheeks flaming, her eyes blinking miserably.

"Keep going!" Matthew shouted, boisterous to the point the cows drew back on their locks, causing them to clank loudly.

Priscilla shook her head, her eyes downcast.

"Hey, Priscilla, you need to come to the . . ."

"She's only fourteen!" Sarah spat out forcefully.

"Whoa!"

Startled, Matthew looked at Sarah, whose eyes were flashing with outrage.

"I didn't see you, Sarah. S'up?"

As usual, the anger dissipated, and as usual, the greeting brought the response he knew it would—a smile returned, a gladness in the green eyes.

"Oh, not much. Levi's in the hospital, so we're doing chores this evening."

"Poor old chap. What's wrong with him this time?"

"Pneumonia."

"Yeah, well. One of these days the old boy will kick the bucket. Mongoloids don't often live to be forty, do they?"

Sarah opened her mouth in reply but was stopped short by Priscilla's clipped tones.

"He's not a mongoloid, Matthew. That word is outdated, taboo. He has Down syndrome. We hope he'll live to be a hundred. You have no idea how much our family enjoys him. He's the star of the household. But you wouldn't know, because he doesn't look nice to you."

"Whew! What a speech!" Matthew clapped a hand to his forehead, and then took off after Priscilla in mock pursuit.

She gave him no chance, standing her ground as obstinately as a pillar of iron, her eyes flashing defiantly. He stood grinning, his hands on his hips, but his eyes fell first. He turned away, the grin slipping away, embarrassed but desperately trying to hide it.

He walked the length of the cow stable, then turned back, and said, "I almost forgot what I came for. Can we borrow your croquet game? Sisters and husbands are coming."

"Sure!" Sarah smiled too brightly, stepped out too quickly. "I can show you where it is."

"You're milking, Sarah. I'll go."

With that, Priscilla ushered Matthew out the door, and Sarah felt the life-giving air leave her body in a whoosh of defeat. He left and never looked back, sending her heart plummeting into another week of lost hope and despair.

When Priscilla returned, she was not smiling, just talking fast and hard and with meaning. She told Sarah that Matthew was about the last reason she could think of to act the way she did. What was wrong with her? He was arrogant, a flirt, and not even worth her time. Furthermore, he was dating, and it was about time she got over him. If she kept this up, sure as shooting she'd be an old maid. She was halfway there already.

She finished with a grand, "So go ahead, ruin your life. He knows everything he's doing to you. You're just another one on his string of starstruck young ladies. It's disgusting."

Sarah was speechless as she watched her younger sister stand her ground, amazed at the resolve she was displaying. When had she managed to acquire this attitude?

And then Sarah realized it was a necessary virtue birthed out of her loss. She had weathered a terrifying episode, dealt with waves of grief, been tossed about by winds of change. But she had clung to her little life raft of prayer and newborn faith. She had come through with flying colors. Bravo, Priscilla, Bravo.

Chapter 17

Levi was in the hospital almost a week. Six days, to be exact. He was everyone's friend, a favorite. He spoke in broken English, his droll sense of humor the talk of the third floor, where he had been transported after the infection in his lungs was under control.

He felt so important, being wheeled down the

wide, gleaming corridors of Lancaster General, as he referred to it. His narrow brown eyes beamed brightly as he smiled, turning his head this way and then the other, trying to check out the occupants of each room they passed.

"What is he doing? Why is she here? What's wrong with her?" Over and over he voiced his curiosity, the nurse's aide at his side answering in monosyllables that were just enough to satisfy Levi.

In his room, Sarah adjusted pillows and pulled a warm blanket over him. Exhaustion crept over his pale features.

"Try and get some sleep, Levi." She patted his shoulder, smoothed back the thinning hair, and wished he could have a good, hot shower.

Levi nodded, his eyes already drooping. Turning his large head, he said, "I can sleep having you here with me, Sarah. I know you'll watch out for me."

He sighed, turned his head, and fell asleep almost instantly. Good. Now she'd find something to eat.

She found the elevator and located the hospital cafeteria, where she selected scrambled eggs, bacon and pancakes, orange juice, and coffee with cream. She paid and found a table, collapsing gratefully into an upholstered booth.

She'd done the milking that morning with Priscilla. It was several hours of hard work, and there had been no time for breakfast. The driver had arrived at eight. She was barely out of the shower and dressed in time.

The cafeteria was crowded with people holding trays and jostling their way to and from tables. Red-eyed doctors, nurses in scrubs, anxious visitors—they all sought a moment's rest and some food to sustain them. She looked up when someone stopped at her table.

"Do you mind if I sit here? The tables are all full."

A shy, nervous young girl, probably about the same age as Sarah and dressed as a volunteer, stood hesitantly at her table.

"Of course. Sit down."

"I'm sorry."

"Don't be. There's room."

"My name is Ashley. Ashley Walters."

"Good to meet you. I'm Sarah Beiler."

Ashley smiled, hesitantly, unsure, and sat down.

That was the one nice thing about being Amish in an area that was the hub of, well—being Amish. The English people around them accepted their way of life and their dress without staring or being rude. It was not unusual, then, for an Amish girl to be asked by a local English girl to share a table. The differences between them were accepted, comfortable, a part of life, as were the farms and the horses and buggies traveling briskly along the country roads.

After Ashley sat down, an awkwardness developed at the table. Ashley began eating, buttering her toast after she'd tasted it, and salting her eggs before realizing Sarah might want to pray.

"Oh. Oh. Excuse me. I . . ." Her drawn features looked even more pinched before she hastily laid down her fork.

Sarah shook her head and reached for her napkin.

"Don't worry about it. Go ahead. We don't always say grace in public. My father says it can be done in silence."

Smiling, she took up a slice of limp bacon and consumed it in two bites. "I'm so hungry," she remarked.

Ashley smiled. "Did you have chores to do?"

"I sure did." She explained the milking, the driver arriving at eight, and Levi.

Ashley nodded, sympathy showing in her brown eyes.

"Poor guy. How old is he?"

"He has Down syndrome. He's approaching thirty-two—old for someone with Down syndrome."

"Oh my!"

She asked where they lived, and Sarah told her. The recognition in Ashley's eyes was followed by an inquiry about their barn.

Sarah nodded and said it was April when it burned.

Ashley nodded. Her eyes clouded with sudden emotion, and she crumpled her napkin tightly and threw her silverware on the blue tray, the eggs uneaten. She whispered, "I . . . I have to leave now. Bye."

"Bye," Sarah said, but she knew Ashley hadn't heard as the other girl rapidly wove her way through the crowd, turning sideways to squeeze between tables, apologizing, her tray held high. She disappeared as quickly as she'd arrived.

Shaking her head in bewilderment, Sarah buttered her pancakes liberally and then soaked them well with syrup from a small, glass pitcher. She cut a substantial square and shoved it into her mouth, chewing appreciatively, and followed it with a long swallow of coffee.

Mmm. She was hungry, 135 pounds or not, and she planned on eating this whole stack of pancakes all by herself.

She wondered if the mention of barn fire had anything to do with Ashley's swift retreat. She doubted it. And yet . . . She shrugged her shoulders, cut another buttery, syrupy chunk of pancake, and chewed contentedly.

Back in Levi's room, the nurses were trying to find a new vein on the back of his hand for his IV, so Sarah stepped back out into the corridor, wincing as Levi began to cry pathetically. *Ach my, Levi.*

Two nurses worked—the one as short and round

as Hannah, the other one tall and angular—talking nonstop. "She's drawing into herself, I tell you. She can't get worse. She doesn't talk."

This was followed by a thumbs-down gesture and a vigorous nodding of her companion's head. "I got her to volunteer here just so I can keep her near me when I can. I'm just going crazy. I don't know what to do."

They smiled at Sarah as she entered the room again. The nurses had taped the IV needle to Levi's arm and said he could soon have his breakfast. He dried his eyes clumsily and sniffled. Then he told Sarah that the nurses about killed him with that long needle.

"You'll be okay, honey."

The largest gray-haired nurse adjusted the IV bag and said that if that needle was not in his hand he wouldn't get better. Levi watched her face, his features inscrutable, and then announced loudly that if he didn't get something *chide* (right) away for breakfast, he wasn't going to make it anyhow. They laughed in delight, both nurses chuckling together, and promised him pancakes.

"I want shoofly!" That really got them laughing, and Sarah laughed with them. "I mean it. I'm terrible hungry for shoofly."

When his breakfast finally did arrive, Sarah watched Levi's face as she lifted the heavy lid on the steaming plate—a small mound of lemon-yellow eggs of some questionable origin, a slice of dark wheat toast, a small pot of fruit cocktail, and black coffee. Poor Levi. It was only a fourth of his generous breakfast at home, and he began crying in earnest.

"*Vill net poshing* (Don't want peaches)."

Sarah glanced nervously out the door toward the nurses' station and explained hurriedly that he could have fried mush and shoofly when he got home, but would he please be good and eat this?

"*Vill chilly* (Want jelly)."

Relieved to find a packet of grape jelly, Sarah spread it on the wheat toast, which seemed to placate his despair. Levi ate the toast and all the eggs, but he refused the fruit, saying nobody eats peaches for breakfast. They are only for supper with chocolate cake and cornstarch pudding.

The small amount of food did seem to lift his mood somewhat, and he drank his coffee obediently before drifting off to sleep. Thankfully, he forgot about the promised pancakes.

Sarah settled herself in the enormous plastic-covered chair as best she could and opened an issue of *National Geographic* she'd brought from home. Dat said it was an expensive magazine but well worth it, with knowledgeable articles from around the world. Sarah loved it and read it carefully from cover to cover.

She immersed herself in an article about the Inca culture and then drifted off to sleep before waking with a start and reading on. Machines clicked and beeped, the voices of nurses rose and fell, carts wheeled past, clanking and whirring.

She was startled to see two doctors enter Levi's room wearing ties and expensive, perfectly pressed shirts beneath their open white coats. Sarah stood up, extended a hand, and answered their greeting. Then she listened politely to their diagnosis.

Levi's pneumonia was the result of his weakened immune system, which went with his declining heart condition. People with Down syndrome often have weak hearts. He would be given the best blood pressure medication and another pill to keep his heart rhythm as steady as possible, but exercise and diet would help as well.

Sarah's heart sank, imagining Levi on a restricted diet. Hoo-boy.

She nodded, answered their questions, and thanked them, relieved to see them disappear. Doctors were intimidating. They were smart, wealthy men who were held in high esteem by the Amish, or most of them.

Sarah could never quite grasp the exact meaning of their medical jargon, which made her feel insecure or embarrassed, sometimes both. She was not well-informed about medical terms. She was just an Amish country girl with an overweight brother who had a bad heart, evidently.

Oh dear. Would Dat and Mam be able to pay

all Levi's medical bills as time went on? Well, one thing was sure: in these matters, when medical expenses climbed out of control, the alms of the church were always there with the deacon kindly offering assistance wherever it was needed.

Her people did not believe in insurance, choosing instead to place their trust in God and the support of the church, as in times past. But as medical costs continued to escalate to exorbitant levels, the Amish had developed their own aid plan—Amish Aid. Sarah knew that church members made monthly payments into the plan's fund. When a family faced a medical issue requiring hospitalization or extensive care, Amish Aid stepped in to help with covering the costs. Sarah also knew that the Aid plan was somewhat controversial. While it was a necessity for some families, it was shunned by others.

Dat had been a man of means, but now? The fire damages had exceeded his Amish fire insurance and put Dat into an unexpected financial free fall. And then there had been the funeral expenses.

Well, Sarah would get a job, that's all. She was still waiting to hear from that Emma. Likely Hannah had made it all up. She had said she needed someone to work at her bakery, but where was she now?

Levi whimpered and burrowed into his pillows. Immediately, Sarah leaped to her feet, afraid he'd pull on some needles or tubes. She watched over him carefully.

Sarah looked up with surprise when she saw Ben Zook *sei* Anna come breezing through the door, her brilliant lime green dress certainly doing nothing to hide her size. Her face was alight with interest, her pretty eyes smiling pleasantly, her white teeth gleaming evenly.

"Sarah!"

"Anna! What brings you in here?"

"Oh, that Lee. He . . . I couldn't tell him a thing. Mind you, that arm is so infected, he plum down has blood poisoning. He could have died. He cut himself with the blade he used to . . ."

She stopped and looked at Levi. "Oh my, he looks so sick. Is he any better at all?"

"Yes. Oh yes. He was moved from the ICU."

Anna bustled over and put her arms around Sarah. She gave her a squeeze, patted her back, and said she had to be off as they were taking Lee to his room from the ER.

"He has a temperature of 102 and everything," was her parting line, her bright green dress disappearing with a swish.

Sarah sat back in her chair. She was staying here at the hospital until morning, which now seemed a bit unsettling somehow. Should she go see Lee? Say hello? She supposed she could walk into his room and say, I told you so, but as far as she knew, no one likes to hear that, especially men.

Oh, she'd stay right here. She wouldn't go. It would be too bold of her with him lying in a hospital bed. He'd be ashamed of the fact that he was there, and she had no business visiting him. No, she wouldn't go.

The day slowly wore on, the clock hands moving to the noon hour. Levi awoke grumpy and hungry, asking for shoofly pie or at least a bowl of Corn Flakes.

Sarah told him he had to wait till lunchtime, when they'd bring his dinner. The meal eventually arrived. On his tray they found steamed fish—unsalted, of course—bilious green beans, and macaroni and cheese. He threw a fit of rage, and Sarah had to call the nurses to adjust the IV tube in his hand.

Overwhelmed and tired of the too-bright room, the green paint, the slippery chair, Sarah scolded him with words of serious rebuke, telling Levi if he didn't behave she was going to call a driver and go home. The scolding left him in such a state of repentance that he ate every bite of the healthy food on his dinner tray, drank all the ginger ale, belched loudly, and said he wanted to watch TV.

"No, Levi."

"Why?"

"It costs something, I think."

"You can pay."

"Dat wouldn't approve."

Levi's eyes narrowed, and he told Sarah that Dat wasn't there, that if he walked in, he'd turn it off as fast as he could. Sarah laughed but remained adamant.

The telephone by his bed rang, and Sarah answered. It was Mam, and she wanted to talk to Levi. He grabbed the receiver and proceeded to air all his grievances about the food, and how mean Sarah was, and could she bring shoofly pie in the morning?

Well, he didn't know. Surely, Sarah could ask the doctors, he told Mam.

After Mam promised to bring him food, Levi handed the receiver to Sarah. Then as she turned her back, he pressed the call bell attached to the rail on his bed. Sarah hung up quickly when a nurse appeared inquiring about Levi's needs.

"I want to watch TV."

Patiently, the nurse brought the remote, showed him what buttons to press, and how to change the channels before she left. Sarah decided to keep her peace and see how well Levi would follow instructions.

First, he pulled himself upright as far as possible, then clutched the narrow, black device, and began a laborious process of selecting the button that "made it go," muttering to himself. When nothing happened, he asked for his glasses, perched them on his nose, and bent over the remote once more. After he located the proper button, the TV flashed to life. Another round of muttering, another painstaking attempt at "something else," and then he found a channel about wild animals.

What wonders flashed before his eyes! It was a storybook come to life, the elephants of Tanzania roaming the plains, their leaf-like ears flapping in slow motion.

He chortled and pointed and said, "*Gook mol*! (Look here!)" over and over until he simply wore himself out. He fell asleep with the remote clutched firmly in his hand.

He told the nurse later that afternoon that he had seen elephants. He hadn't known their ears were so busy. She told him he should have ears that big to keep the flies away. Levi considered what that would be like and then told her that if his ears were that big, his wool hat wouldn't fit to go to church.

Oh, the nurses loved him alright, and Levi enjoyed every minute of their teasing, always coming back with sharp answers.

By five o'clock, Sarah was still making up excuses for herself for not going to say hello to Lee. She was not combed. Her hair was a mess. Her covering wasn't neat. What would she say? She didn't know him. He didn't know she was there. Or would Anna have told him? Probably.

She was ravenous, having skipped lunch. Levi would be alright until she returned, so she told him she was going to get a sandwich and that she'd bring it back as soon as possible. He barely heard her, engrossed in another animal show.

Sarah hurried down the hall with her purse slung over her shoulder. She looked neither left nor right on her mission, the cafeteria.

Again she saw Ashley Walters, who was evidently now intent on avoiding Sarah, and ducked into an elevator with an open door. Sarah wondered why Ashley suddenly seemed so afraid. She wasn't at first, when she sat down at Sarah's table at breakfast. Perhaps she had become ill at ease with Sarah being Amish and all.

Still. Sarah pondered Ashley's hasty retreat after she had confirmed that their barn was one of those that burned down last spring. Did Ashley have some connection, some knowledge of the barn fires? Surely not this sweet, hesitant girl.

Levi came home from the hospital with his ego greatly inflated. His knowledge of wild animals had grown to the point that he took it upon himself to educate every member of the family about lions, giraffes, and just about every other creature that roamed the African grasslands. Suzie was intrigued at first, and Priscilla pretended to be bored, but she actually listened in her own sly way.

So life resumed its normalcy again. Mam finished the housecleaning, and Sarah sewed new dresses for the upcoming wedding season.

When Sunday arrived, Dat's face became

drawn, worry clouding his keen eyes. He sat reading his German Bible, his mouth moving as he memorized and prepared for the sermon he would be expected to preach.

The truth was that his ministry had never weighed heavier on his shoulders. It seemed to drain his life's blood. He was tired from the lack of support from the members of his congregation.

Davey Beiler's *ihr* (own) Priscilla had done wrong, and it was not easily forgotten. Now their Levi had been in the hospital again, Mervin was dead, and the barn had been burned at the hand of an arsonist. It seemed God was concerned about the family. Well, no wonder. Look at his sons, the way they carried on with that roofing and siding business, showing no interest in taking over the family farm.

Although that was the thinking of only a handful of people, to David Beiler it was a handful too many. The intricate pattern of love and fellowship was unraveling, destroying the age-old heritage of one for all and all for one, a beautiful design only God could have woven.

David felt the loose threads when he stood up to preach, and his throat constricted with fear, with failure looming on the horizon like a midsummer hailstorm. The black cloud to the west was predictable, but the strength and fury of the storm was not.

So he wavered, the crumbling of his spiritual

post a genuine threat. His knees shook, his hands clenched and unclenched, and he stood wordless.

Mam, seated in front of him on a folding chair, bowed her head even farther, her lips moving in prayer. Nervous members of the congregation shuffled their feet as the ticking of the plastic clock on the shop wall became deafening.

Someone cleared his throat, which seemed to jolt David back to life. He began speaking, choked, and stopped.

Anna Mae, sitting in the women's row, watched her father's face, and quick tears of sympathy formed. Her Dat had had too much. Sarah was horrified. Please, please. She silently begged for help without forming the actual words of a prayer. Priscilla sat like stone, her face blanched of color.

Then it seemed as if God supplied his needs, and he spoke, softly, lovingly but with power. He left nothing back. He told them of the heaviness of his heart, the silent, cunning way the devil was weaving a pattern of his own, destroying the perfect will of God. There was evil among them, but that evil could not enter into the fold unless they allowed it.

Two barns had burned by the hands of someone who meant harm. A young child had died. Let it not once be named among them to berate, to gossip. Instead, they needed to hold themselves accountable, one to the other.

Small human minds cannot think as God does.

Where there is suspicion, hate, backbiting, and bickering—the devil's own handiwork—the church community needed to replace it with love and forbearance, brother to brother, supporting, upholding, forgiving. God is not mocked.

The conviction that fell was terrible, weighing down guilty members as David Beiler bared his soul. They had never heard anything like it. Old Sylvia Riehl said it was time the poor man spoke from the heart, as she cut a piece of snitz pie at the table later in the day.

For now, God had triumphed.

Chapter 18

Mam stood at her ironing board as the late November sun slanted through the kitchen window. Her right arm moved rhythmically, pressing the new black cape and apron she'd finished that afternoon.

The maple leaves were gone, and the trees looked unclothed, exposed to the chilly winds that warned of snow but were unable to produce it. The brown, dried-up remnants of leaves that clung bravely to the cold branches of the oak trees rustled in the steady breeze, as if their perseverance allowed the Beiler family a tenacious hold on autumn. It was wedding season.

Mam suppressed a sigh of weariness. Every

Tuesday and every Thursday, starting the last week in October, after communion services were over, the weddings moved along in full swing. Fifteen of them this year. That meant invitations to fifteen weddings for David Beiler, who was invited along with Malinda for any number of reasons—as a minister, an uncle, a friend.

Monday mornings for Mam meant laundry. During wedding season that task included cleaning the black *mutza* (suit or coat) and woolen hats, ironing extra coverings and white shirts, polishing black Sunday shoes, and making sure there were plenty of snowy white handkerchiefs pressed and in the top bureau drawer for her husband. Priscilla's job was to wash and polish the buggy.

Sarah had been called to go with Hannah's sister, Emma, and her husband, Amos, to work at their large, bustling bakery at the farmer's market in New Jersey, about a hundred miles away. Every Friday and Saturday morning, the market van picked up Sarah at three thirty and returned her at eight o'clock in the evening. She seemed to float on pure adrenaline now, dashing down the stairs, banging the front door so the picture on the wall rattled, eager to be a part of the new world she had discovered.

Secretly, Sarah felt pretty in her white bib apron. When she learned to ring up orders on the electric cash register, she felt very worldly indeed. A real career girl. She loved the atmosphere of the huge farmer's market. There was a constant rush to mix, bake, wrap, and display the pies and cakes, the bread and cookies, the cupcakes and cinnamon rolls—the list was endless. Sarah rose eagerly to the challenge.

She was a farm girl, her arms rounded, strong, and muscular. So the fifty-pound bags of flour and sugar were no problem, the endless rolling of pie crusts no big deal. She smiled easily and was always friendly and helpful to the other workers. Emma watched and noticed. She wondered why she hadn't asked Sarah to be a bakery girl before.

The only downside was the lack of sleep, which often caused her to doze off during the three-hour church service on Sundays. She also had trouble staying awake late on Saturday nights with her girlfriends.

But she had money in her wallet now and a savings account at the Susquehanna Bank without her parents' names on it. If she wanted to purchase a framed piece of art from the craft shop, she could. Or if she wanted to surprise Levi with a new trinket or game, she could do that too. It was absolutely liberating, this new job.

Now the weddings had arrived, and Sarah found she could exist on very little sleep, returning home late every Thursday evening for just a bit of sleep before the alarm rang in the middle of the night—or so it seemed at three o'clock.

The family was wearing black at every wedding this year, since they were still in mourning for Mervin. Sarah had sewn not one, but two new dresses, capes, and aprons, so she still felt as if she was dressed in wedding finery despite their somber color.

She went to Mam at her ironing board to ask if the coverings were ready for tomorrow's wedding. Mam shook her head.

"That's next."

"What should I do?"

"Well, you can make Levi's bed. Just use the clean blue sheets in the bathroom closet. I doubt if the wash is dry yet."

"I'd rather put on the fresh ones, from off the line."

"Alright with me."

Sarah sat on Dat's chair, leaned back, and watched Mam lift and inspect the new apron. She nodded with satisfaction, folded it in half, then again, and hung it carefully on a plastic hanger.

Sarah opened her mouth then closed it as she gazed through the kitchen window at the brown oak leaves. Finally she said, "Mam."

Absentmindedly, Mam said "Hmm?" as she resumed her ironing.

"Rose and Matthew broke up."

"Did they?"

Mam had not really heard Sarah, her own thoughts preoccupying her. Suddenly she stopped the rhythmic movement of the sadiron and asked, "What did you say?"

"Rose and Matthew broke up."

"Oh, my goodness! Who did it?"

"Rose."

Mam's face went pale, her thoughts whirling, stirred to hurricane force by the ensuing tragedy that was sure to follow. She was scared of the torrential rain, the spiritual and emotional blast that could sweep away her daughter in its terrifying grip. Her lips pale, compressed, she asked flatly, "Why?"

"We talked almost all night, Rose and I. Mam, I feel so sorry for her. She has no real reason. He's everything she always imagined her boyfriend to be. Yet she feels empty and drained, she said. She wants to stay away from him at least a month to see if her feelings change."

Mam pursed her lips, folded the black cape, and hung it neatly on the same hanger. "Oh, they all say that."

Sarah was astounded and looked sharply at her mother's pale face, the too-bright eyes. There was a sharp edge in her soft voice. "She wants someone else. You know that," Mam added.

The words were flung at Sarah with a strange intensity before Mam turned, walked swiftly into her bedroom, and closed the door with a firm "thwack" behind her.

"*Die Mam iss base!* (Mam is angry!)" Levi

shouted gleefully from the sofa, where he lay with a stack of catalogs, looking for horses.

Sarah felt a warm flush rise on her face. She knew. She knew with a sickening certainty what had upset her mother. It was the idea of Matthew being free. Free to ask her. Free to be hers!

Unable to stay seated, Sarah jumped up, ran up the stairs, and flung herself on her bed, her chin in her cupped hands, her feet in the air, the old house slippers dangling as she dreamed.

God had answered her prayers! He had put her through the fire, brought her patience, and now he was delivering her into a brand new day, one of hope, one rosy with the glow of a new future. Her whole room was infused with the light of her love for Matthew, a golden yellow halo that transformed the very color of the walls. Her world had come crashing about her, righted itself, and turned to its original color.

Then the dark form of her mother appeared in the doorway. "Sarah, I'm asking you to listen to me, this one time. I know it may not make a difference to you, but I don't feel right saying nothing at all."

Sarah rolled over, sat up, and pushed her feet into her slippers. The sun disappeared behind a gray November cloud, bringing a sense of unrest and dread into Sarah's bedroom. She looked at the ratty old slippers and wondered why she'd kept them so long. Dropping to the recliner in the corner, Mam squared her shoulders, folded her hands, and began to speak.

"I know how it is for you. You fancy yourself in love with Matthew. You always have. My soft mother's heart wants to tell you that you can have him. God has answered your prayers, and this may be so. I hope it is. But you must face reality. It was Rose that broke up, not Matthew, which means nine chances out of ten, he's heartbroken, and he wants her back."

"You don't know!" Sarah's voice was raw with fierce denial.

Mam remained silent, holding Sarah's intense gaze with the kindness in her own. Sudden confusion caused Sarah to lower her eyes.

"No, I don't," Mam said softly.

The wisdom Mam had gleaned through her years of experience helped her accept the truth: Sarah had built an impenetrable wall of fantasy around herself. She stood up, brushed imaginary dust from her apron, and said, "I wish you God's blessing, my daughter." She walked softly to Sarah's bed and held Sarah in her arms. The moment was warm with love put firmly in place, because it never failed.

Patting the shapely shoulders, Mam stepped back and quipped, "So, if the waters get rough, I guess I'll sit beside you in your little rowboat and row for dear life!"

Sarah smiled hesitantly at her mother, and they

laughed together softly. Why, then, did she flop back on her bed and stare at the ceiling? She didn't know she was crying until something tickled her ears, and she recognized the wetness sliding down each side of her face. Immediately, she sat up, grabbed a Kleenex, and went to the window, gazing out through the gray branches of the maple trees, seeing nothing.

She had never dressed with more care or anticipation. She combed and patted, moussed and sprayed her hair, until finally she achieved the perfect sleekness she sought.

Black it would have to be, but a new black, the fabric full-bodied with a bit of a ripple, not too fancy, not too plain. She successfully pinned the cape after three or four tries, satisfied that each pleat was just the right length down her back. Then she pinned the apron snugly about her waist.

She had just pinned and tied her new white covering on her head when she heard the obnoxious air horn on Melvin's buggy. He had attached it to the twelve-volt battery beneath the floor of the buggy in its own box, riding low above the road.

Dabbing a small amount of her favorite fragrance on her wrists, she grabbed a few Kleenexes and ran downstairs, where Levi sat with his coffee and shoofly pie, yelling lustily that Melvin was there.

"Bye, Levi. You be good for Priscilla!" She

grabbed his arm, kissed his forehead, and left him swabbing the spot with his red handkerchief and a smile on his face.

Priscilla didn't respond. The longing in her eyes was too intense. Weddings were off-limits for fourteen-year-olds, except for cousins or close friends, so her lot was to stay home with Levi, get Suzie off to school, and sometimes babysit her nieces and nephews. That was fun for a while until the day wore on, and they became tired and cranky, and Levi teased them without mercy.

When Priscilla complained to Mam, Mam said Ruthie and Elmer were extremely sociable, staying at weddings until the last song was sung, and yes, Ruthie could be more considerate of Priscilla's long day with the children.

Levi shook his head after the *kesslehaus* door closed behind Sarah. "Boy, the flies shouldn't bother her today," he mused before cutting off a large chunk of shoofly pie with the edge of his fork.

Melvin was in a sour mood, scolding her for being late and saying, "Watch out for the heater, there."

Sarah pressed her knees together and clasped her hands in a grip that gave away her eagerness. Melvin watched from the corner of his eye. Buster trotted briskly, his ears forward in a perfect circular shape, his tail lifted, his steps high.

Sarah smiled to herself. No use wasting it on

vinegar-infused Melvin. Sour old bachelor. It wasn't her fault he hated weddings.

Silence pervaded every inch of the buggy. Not a good, comfortable silence, but one ripe with unspoken thoughts. Well, she'd wait. Melvin could never stay quiet very long, and she knew the subject that he'd tackle the minute he put his prickly pride behind him.

The air was damp, the skies overcast, but there was a telltale line of blue to the west, emerging as the thick gray blanket of morning clouds moved on.

Sarah was glad to see the pretty blue sky approaching. Susan and Marvin deserved a beautiful wedding day. They were both only twenty years old, so young, but they had been dating for more than two years, almost three. The parents had given their consent, saying it was better to marry young than to be dating too long.

They would occupy the small Cape Cod on the Miller farm, paying minimal rent, a favor Dan Miller presented to young couples to give them *an guta schtart* (a good start).

Susan would be so happy, decorating and painting her cute little house and cooking supper for her beloved Marvin with the brand new stainless steel cookware her mother had purchased from the traveling *Kessle Mann* (cookware salesman).

Sarah inhaled happily, then exhaled quietly,

warily watching Melvin from the side. Yes, her chance of marriage fluttered a victory flag on the horizon. Soon. Oh, just soon.

Melvin's voice broke into the silence. "I guess you feel like the cat that got all the cream."

"Why?"

"You know why."

"Why?"

"You know."

Sarah laughed, elation rounding out the happy giggle that rolled from an overflowing heart.

"Well, I can't help it they broke up."

"It was her, Tub said."

"Yeah."

"So, that could mean he's still in love with her. Likely he's heartbroken, his pride shattered. He probably won't be at the wedding, if I know Matthew right."

There it was again. This dark prediction, a pressing insecurity flung about her shoulders by someone she loved.

Instantly, a quick retort rose to push back the cloak of doubt. "You don't know, Melvin. He may not be heartbroken at all. Perhaps he's . . . well, sort of glad it's over. Maybe he was bored with Rose. Her . . . her . . . perfection, or whatever."

Melvin snorted so vehemently he had to lean over so he could extricate his white handkerchief.

"He never once got bored with her!" he burst out.

"You don't know," Sarah countered forcefully.

Then, neither one having the wisdom born of experience, their youth rolling the losing dice, their barbed conversation turned into an argument, albeit a polite one, as cousins tend to do. Buster trotted up to the Reuben Stoltzfus farm pulling a gray and black buggy with an invisible cloud of dissension hanging above it.

Yes, Matthew was there. Sarah watched the long row of boys file in, her fevered gaze latching onto the sight of him with much the same intensity that a drowning man grasps a life preserver. See, Melvin.

Her lips curling with her own sense of victory, she lowered her eyes, afraid to look up, afraid not to. When she dared, she peered between heads and shoulders until she found him, gazing at the floor. Oh well, she had a whole wedding service ahead of her to try to gauge his mood. Hadn't she become quite adept at it over the years?

There was, however, one thing that troubled her. Rose. She'd been so wan and pale, her face aged with the trial she'd gone through, her beautiful eyes clouded with indecision, or fear, or . . . what? Sarah didn't know. What if she wanted him back now that he was no longer hers?

The opening song was announced, and great waves of the ageless plainsong rolled evenly across the clean, painted woodworking shop as the approximately four hundred invited guests joined their voices in the wedding hymn.

Chills chased themselves up Sarah's spine. She joined in, reveling in the opportunity to be one with the group of singers. She loved to sing in church, and weddings were even better. So many voices blended in song were *himmlisch* (heavenly), and she could easily imagine a host of angels singing as they did.

Then she looked up, straight into Matthew's eyes, which confused her so much, she stopped singing. Goodness. What in the world? What was wrong with him? Surely it couldn't be that bad. His eyes were dark pools of misery, so bad, in fact, that she hardly recognized him.

Well, she'd remedy that, as soon as she was able.

After dinner, the single girls stood outside against the shop wall, waiting for the single young men to choose them to accompany them to the long tables to sing wedding songs and have cold punch and pizza or soft pretzels or some other special treat. Sarah was afraid, truly terrified, her breath coming in gasps, quick and hard. She could feel the warmth and color leave her face. She became quite dizzy, her head spinning, but sheer willpower righted it and kept her feet solidly on the ground.

Then they came, led by a young married brother of the bride, who was teasing and laughing to put the nervous young men at ease.

From beneath lowered lashes, she saw a few boys each pick a girl. They walked away together to spend the afternoon seated next to each other at the long wedding table. She watched Lee approaching, surprised to feel a rush of companionship. Merely friendship though.

Through a blur, her heart hammering in her chest, she saw Lee approach Rose, his eyes questioning her. With a small smile, she moved away with him. My, what a couple they'd make! A ripple of teasing and good-natured calls of praise rose from the crowd, and Lee ducked his head, smiling.

Matthew! Swaggering just a bit, desperately trying to conceal his self-consciousness, he strode up to Sarah and extended a hand. She grasped it with fierce possessiveness.

No words formed thoughts, no thoughts could describe her feelings as she followed Matthew to the table and sat on the long bench beside him.

He looked at Sarah, said, "S'up?"

She giggled, shamelessly, gladly, unreservedly.

Oh, just look away, Mam. Just look away right now, with all the senseless fear and doubt in your troubled eyes. Nothing, not Mam, not Melvin, not the tides of time would remove Matthew from within her grasp. Not now. Please. Not now.

They sang together, they talked, they shared a butterscotch sundae, they ate soft pretzels dipped in melted cheese. And all the years of yearning, the prayers, the patience had finally come to fruition for Sarah.

Somewhere, in some distant corner of her mind, a persistent little voice kept interfering, an unwanted dose of reality that she couldn't completely ignore. This thing of going to the "afternoon table" was not very promising, after all. Often young men would choose a friend, someone who was easy to spend time with, an acquaintance. So, for that reason alone, Sarah could not become overconfident. Still, he had chosen her. That knowledge alone overrode the reality, which she put aside easily.

"So," Matthew was asking. "What do you think of me and Rose breaking up?"

Surprised, Sarah looked at him, but his eyes gave nothing away.

"I . . . I don't know."

"Yeah, me either."

The words were dull, flat, weighted down with bitterness.

"She says a month. I told her if she broke up with me I was going to go English. I mean it. If I can't have Rose, I'm not going to stay Amish. There's no point in it."

Babbling incoherently now, Sarah tried to make him see that he couldn't leave his family. He'd break his mother's heart. And mine, Matthew, and mine. It's pulverized already. How could I bear it?

Her thoughts wove themselves painfully into her mind, her mouth speaking the accepted words, her mind thinking the unaccepted ones.

The pain of his words was too great to bear. He was still in love with Rose. Her mind refused to comprehend it. But maybe he only thought he was still in love. Sarah could change him. She could win.

Lifting her shield, adjusting her armor, she prepared herself for the battle of her life, knowing she must be brave and courageous. She resolved to pray without ceasing, and God would bless her. Wouldn't He?

She lifted miserable pools of stormy seawater green eyes and found the blue of Lee Glick's upon her, his blond hair shining like the sun about him. In that blue, there was rest and comfort. She wanted to stay there in that calm. It was mesmerizing, a cascade of pure, clear, no, blue water. She had to tear her eyes away.

And Lee did not know it was possible to feel what he felt for Sarah on that sun-infused November afternoon. It was far more than he imagined love to be. It was a sweet and tender pity, a cradling of her troubled head to his chest, coupled with the wonderful knowledge that God, who was fairly new to him, would do what He would. Lee only had to bow his head and accept it.

Unknowingly, he laid his sacrifice on the altar.

Chapter 19

"Ashley!"

"Sarah!"

Again the two girls met, this time in the middle of the crowded farmer's market. People milled about them, shoving, moving from one stand to another to buy fresh produce or cheese or a pound of freshly butchered grass-fed organic beef or eggs laid by hens who pecked about in pure grasses free of pesticides.

Restaurants at the market catered to every taste—Italian, Chinese, Amish home cooking, American cheeseburgers and fries—a vast melting pot of ethnicity. The flea market stands sold leather goods, jewelry, and antiques. Others sold furniture crafted who knows where but labeled "Amish." The whole market was a wonderful place to walk aimlessly and enjoy the smells, the sights, the people.

Sarah didn't think Ashley would stay to talk, but she lingered long enough to exchange pleasantries. Ashley's father had a flea market stand where she worked. She inquired politely about Levi's well-being but then said she must be on her way.

"We'll likely keep running into each other, won't we?" she asked, backing away, waving.

Sarah gasped as Ashley backed straight into a large column and slid down to the floor, her legs crumpling without resistance. Lowering her head she giggled uncontrollably, her stringy brown hair hanging stiffly on either side.

Sarah hunkered down, pulled her skirt over her knees, and asked if Ashley was alright.

"Oh, yeah, yeah. Jus' fine."

Still laughing, Ashley got to her feet and wandered off with a haphazard wave of her hand. Puzzled, Sarah shrugged her shoulders and went on her way, already five minutes into a half-hour break. She hurried to the Kings' restaurant, where Rose served tables, found an empty spot, and hoped Rose would be the one to wait on her.

Here, in this crowded place with the homey, checkered tablecloths, she could get a twelve-inch hoagie loaded with anything she wanted and a glass of water for five dollars (Pepsi cost two dollars). She rarely spent more than that on her break. She'd eat half of the delicious sandwich, mayonnaise squeezing from the sides of her mouth, pickle juice soaking the crusty home-baked wheat roll, and then take the remaining half in a Styrofoam container to eat later, usually in the van on the way home while she elbowed the other girls away.

Rose came bustling over, clapping a hand to her forehead while sliding into her booth. "I'm beat!"

"Busy?"

"Just run ragged. Where do all the people come from?"

Sarah shook her head.

"You want your usual hoagie?"

"I'm starved. Put plenty of ham on it."

Rose hurried off, her small frame neat and compact, her sky-blue dress and white apron giving her a celestial quality.

When Rose returned with the oversized sandwich and a tall glass of ice water with a thick slice of lemon, Sarah squeezed in the lemon, added a few packets of sugar, and stirred as she half-listened to Rose's encounter with an extremely harried boss.

"So, how are you? For real," Sarah asked.

"I don't know. Okay, I guess. One day I feel sorry for Matthew, the next I miss him. I'm all mixed up."

"Do you want Melvin and me to pick you up Saturday night?"

"No."

"Why not?"

"Oh, I don't know. I'll find someone to take me."

"Whatever."

"Yeah."

With an awkward wave, Rose moved off, her eyebrows lifted a few notches too high in Sarah's opinion. So, she was too good for her and stodgy Melvin. Well, that was fine with her. Melvin acted too bizarre around Rose anyway, trying to impress her with his stretched truths and weird rambling on and on about nothing. But then, most young men did that around Rose. Melvin was only being normal.

After a long Friday at the bakery, the two-hour ride home was a welcome reprieve. The market girls slouched in various positions, pillows stuffed into any available corner, and tried to gain back a bit of sleep. The van moved along with the four lanes of traffic, the lights stretching out from the fast-moving vehicles in an unbroken line, until they reached the darkness of the country.

The back roads of Lancaster County were always tedious, heads sliding, bobbing, as the driver maneuvered the van as efficiently—and as swiftly—as possible.

Half-asleep, Sarah jostled against Rachel Zook, who jabbed her elbow into Sarah's arm.

"Look! What is that?"

"What?"

Sarah blinked, sat up, and peered out the window. She could see nothing out of the ordinary. She kept watching and saw a few lights, some buildings, the night etched in black and gray. Absolutely nothing unusual.

"There it is again!" Rachel hissed.

Sarah pulled back, grimacing. Whew, Rachel must have had Italian food for lunch. A strong garlic odor was escaping from her mouth in great, steaming billows.

"There!"

Rachel pointed, and Sarah turned her head, more to avoid the garlic than to concern herself with the horizon. A grayish, almost white line hovered above the horizon, so nearly the same color as the rest of the night. Suddenly, a reddish glow burst up, like northern lights, and then disappeared.

"I see it!" Sarah whispered.

The van rolled to a stop at an intersection and allowed a car to pass, before continuing on the way home.

"Hey, Ike!" Rachel called, sending the rich odor of garlic wafting across the occupants of the back seat.

"Ew! Rachel, what in the world did you eat for lunch?" Rose grumbled, half-asleep.

Sarah burst out laughing, holding her stomach as tears of mirth squeezed between her eyelids. That was the best thing about market jobs—the companionship in this fifteen-passenger vanload of girls along with a few older people, all contained together in an oblong box of steel and metal hurtling through the night. The close proximity produced a bond of sisterhood.

Only sisters would be so honest as to blurt out about garlic breath, or so Sarah had thought when she first rode to market in that van. She soon learned differently. They fought for doughnuts, scrambled across seats for bits of soft pretzel, pinched, punched, pulled sleeves and coverings and hair, yelled and teased and hooted with joy, then one by one, they all fell asleep. The driver was usually a long-suffering individual who tried to be strict but enjoyed the antics as much as anyone else.

"Hey, Ike!" Rachel screeched again, causing Rose to turn her head and wave a hand furiously in front of her nose. "Look to the left!"

Sarah could see Ike's silhouette leaning forward, alert.

"What is going on?" he said finally.

The van slowed, the driver also craning his neck for a glimpse.

"It almost looks like northern lights," he observed.

"That's close to Bird-In-Hand. Or Monterey. Somewhere along 340."

The van rolled to a stop, heads popped up like corks, eyes blinking, the girls muttering questions. There—another finger of pinkish red, a gray sky stained by a color that was not really supposed to be there.

"Somepin's goin' on!" Ike observed, the driver's jargon rubbing off on him.

They all held their breaths as a sharp whistle stabbed the night somewhere behind them. Quickly, the driver turned the wheel to the right, and they drifted off the shoulder, the van leaning toward a ditch filled with cold, black water. A gleaming red and silver mammoth, flashing the power of its presence, plunged through the night, roaring past them and leaving the van rocking in its wake.

"Has to be a fire!" Ike said decidedly.

The driver pulled back onto the road and asked if they wanted to see what was going on. There were exclamations of agreements and some grumbling went up, but they had little choice— riding in the van being guided by their driver.

Sarah's heart began a frantic hammering as the light steadily grew more orange in color.

"It's another barn, I bet."

"I mean it, seriously."

"If it is, we're moving to New York."

"They can light fires in New York, too."

"You think?"

"Hey, be quiet. This isn't funny."

"Hush."

But only Sarah understood the terror of another barn fire. It was a stake driven through her heart, producing memories of their fateful night. She began to shake uncontrollably as more fire trucks zoomed past, their engines whining and sirens screaming, bringing back memories of the smoke and flames, the charred dirty water after it had soaked the burning timbers and hay and straw. The fire had cruelly licked at the docile cows, annihilated the living, breathing horses, and thrown the gentle, obedient creatures into a living hell of pain and fear.

When they came upon the scene, they stayed back, away from the red-faced, shouting fire-police volunteer who was whipping his green fluorescent flag in frenzied circles. The barn behind him had turned into a massive inferno of pain and torment. The flames whipped away from the barn toward the house, which stood close to the barn, separated only by the driveway and a small block of lawn.

The market workers decided to get out of the van. But Sarah could not move, her eyes pools of horrified memories. A great cry arose from the crowd as the small flames rolled along the asbestos shingles, the house clearly in grave danger.

"Sarah, come. We're walking across the field for a closer look."

"Come on!"

The girls took off across the field as Sarah slowly got up and moved to the van door. Her heart pounding frantically, she gripped the vinyl handle and lowered herself slowly to the ground. Her intentions were to follow the small flock of girls, led by Ike and the driver, but the nausea rose swiftly in her throat and gagged her.

The whole world tilted dangerously to the right, then whirled recklessly around her. She lifted her hands to steady herself, but there was nothing to hold her up. She was being spun into a black vortex, the hot bile rising in her throat. She was as helpless as the brittle, brown leaves whirling through the cold November air. She was aware of making hoarse sounds, then mewling helplessly before she was gratefully erased to oblivion.

She thought she was at home, being sick in her bed, so she leaned over, her hands searching for the small wicker wastebasket with the Wal-Mart bag in it. She retched miserably over and over and tried to lift her head, but the dizziness was too severe.

When the rough stubbles of the alfalfa plants pierced the skin on her cheek, she became half-conscious and confused as someone held her head, stroked her back, and murmured words of comfort.

"It's okay, Sarah. Don't feel bad. It's okay."

A long shudder passed through her, and she turned her head away, ashamed, aware of some person here with her, with these vehicles, these cars, on this dark, windy night. The dancing orange light across someone's head reminded her of why she had become ill and passed out like some eighty-year-old person with a weak heart.

"Oh my. I'm so sorry," she whispered.

Two hands slid beneath her arms, and she was lifted to a sitting position. She struggled to stay upright but kept leaning to the side until two arms held her firmly, a clean men's handkerchief wiped her face as she kept whispering apologies.

It was when he produced a stick of gum and

the sharp smell of the Dentyne was held to her face that consciousness returned fully. Focusing through the haze of her blurred vision, she said, "Melvin!"

"No."

Confused, she gave up, accepted the chewing gum, and sagged weakly against her rescuer.

"It's me. Lee."

She blinked. Who? Lee who? Oh, him. Here she was, held against him by his own strong arms in this cold alfalfa field with the fire blazing uncontrollably beyond them, the now-distant forms of the other market girls silhouetted against the flames.

"I understand why you . . . why you were sick. Please don't feel bad. Your own fire hasn't been so terribly long ago."

In answer, she burrowed her face against his corduroy coat, which smelled of woodchips and steel and shaving cream. She burst into harsh, gulping sobs that tore from her throat, and he held her close and blinked back his own emotion.

"I am so sorry," she said, finally spent of the horror and sadness the night had invoked.

"It's okay."

"Can I get up now?"

"Do you want to?"

"I think I can."

She turned away, and he let his arms fall away obediently. A small cry followed as she teetered crookedly away from him. So he did the most natural thing in the world and reached out with both arms, pulling her against him. He held her there, leaving her with no choice but to apologize.

"The whole world is just spinning so crazily," she gasped.

"Yeah, well, so is mine," Lee answered.

"What? Are you getting sick too?"

She looked up into his face.

Yes, he was, he said, giving a small laugh. "Sarah."

She was startled by the sound of his voice, the deep emotion that rose from his throat.

"I'm sick about that Matthew guy. And you."

Her face was only inches away, her eyes unfathomable, so large and dark and tortured with . . .

With what? Lee's courage failed him, his speech slid away, and silence replaced it. She bent her head. His arms stayed around her. When she lifted her head, she spoke the truth in a soft, quavering voice, the humiliation so heavy, it broke his heart.

"Lee, you have to understand. It's always been Matthew. Through school, through *rumspringa*, and now through Rose. I can't help how I feel about him. I have to wait."

Slowly, she pulled away, out of the unsettling circle of his arms. She turned her head to watch the roaring inferno beside them—the clanking of hoses, the voices of men, the roar of engines—and shivered.

Then she did something so surprising, he carried it in his memory for months. She stepped right back into the circle of his arms, grabbed the lapels of his work coat, and said, "But, Lee."

He had to bend his head to hear her voice. "I won't admit this to myself, hardly. But you . . . you are making this whole Matthew thing easier. Can you understand that?"

As he had never known the depth of his feelings for her, so had he never known the steely resolve, the desperate control he now needed to exercise over his desire to pour out his long-awaited love in a crushing embrace, just once touching his lips to hers, to allow her to feel his love. Just once.

When she stepped back, he gripped his hands behind his back to keep them from reaching for her, the emptiness unbearable now.

"I'll be honest, Sarah, okay? If you say it makes it easier, do you mean I may have a chance someday?"

She was going to say, "Don't wait for me, Lee." She really was. What she said was, "Your eyes are so blue. They remind me of a . . . a . . . This is dumb, Lee." She gave a low laugh. "Your eyes make everything easy. They're calm."

"Thank you, Sarah."

He decided he'd never care much for Ike Stoltzfus from that night on, appearing from nowhere like that, followed by a gaggle of market girls wanting to witness the latest devastation in their community.

The farm was owned by Reuben Kauffman. Everyone called him Reuby. He was a short, rotund fellow with vibrant blue eyes set in a ruddy, glowing face and a benevolence toward his fellow men creating a kind aura about him.

He lost everything. The house was almost completely ruined in addition to the barn.

The vinyl siding had buckled and crumpled as windows shattered into thousands of pieces from the heat of the gigantic tongues of flame. The force of the late autumn gusts that had brought the first serious cold from Canada down to eastern Pennsylvania propelled the fire. They said the plastic pots containing African violets melted down across the shelves straight onto Reuby *sei* Bena's clean, waxed kitchen linoleum. It was an awful mess.

They should have let the house burn to the ground, Mam said. They'd never get the smell of smoke out of the furniture, the rugs, and the clothes.

The following week, Sarah and Priscilla sat on either side of Levi, and Mam sat beside Dat in the spring wagon on the way to the Kauffman farm. The air was calm, harmless, almost an apology in its stillness. As Fred, the family's new driving horse, trotted briskly, the heavy woolen buggy blankets kept them warm against a late frost. They smelled the dry, dusty odor of corn fodder being baled in Jake King's corn field—or what remained of it.

The spring wagon hauled cardboard boxes and bags full of food from Mam's shopping spree. She had been busy visiting her favorite stores, and she beamed with the charity that bubbled from her heart for Reuby *sei* Bena. Poor woman. The poor family, losing everything like that, and they'd never hurt a flea.

Mam bought towels and sheet sets at JC Penney because they ran the best sales. She bought fabric and housewares at Country Housewares and a set of cookware at Nancy's Notions in Intercourse. She wished she'd known the children's sizes, but she bought black coats and bonnets of various sizes at Teddy Leroy's shoe store.

This would all be carried discreetly into the shop, placed quietly with the mound of charitable contributions, and no one would ever know that Davey Beiler *sei* Malinda had spent the more than eight hundred dollars her husband had given her, his heart overflowing with sympathy, driven by the need to help poor Reubys.

Hadn't they been through the same terrifying ordeal? How could they close their hearts or their pocketbooks now, when yet another family suffered an even greater loss? And most unsettling, what new troubles would this barn fire stir up?

David Beiler's heart quaked within him. A twitch began in the corner of his right eye when he drove past the knots of Amish men talking intensely, their beards wagging and hands gesticulating.

A horde of trained personnel came to the family's assistance. State police, some in unmarked police cars, the fire marshal, and the press were all trying yet again to make sense out of an unthinkable deed.

The arsonist, who had now struck three times in less than a year, was determined to create significant damage. He—or they (perhaps it was a group of individuals)—had swept a storm of fear, chaos, and havoc across the Amish community. Anyone starting a fire on a night like that, the wind howling and screaming through the darkness, meant serious harm.

David got down and put the reins through the black ring in the harness. He was not surprised that his hands were shaking. Sarah and Priscilla, surveying the damage, inhaling the smells of leftover smoke and soaked debris, remained seated until Levi said he wanted down off that spring wagon, even if they were going to sit there all day.

Chapter 20

Eager helpers had walled off and insulated a corner of the implement shed. They would eventually install water lines and lay sturdy carpet over the power-washed cement. Reuby and his family would live there until their new home was built.

The women hosed down the furniture and washed it with a solution from the fire company. Then they washed it again with Pine-Sol or Mr. Clean or whatever the ladies of the surrounding area had brought. Then they polished it, but some of it would have to be refinished. They washed all the dishes, but very few of the fabric-covered items, clothes, or curtains could be salvaged.

The men had deliberated, but in the end, Reuby waved an arm and said, "Bring it down!"

It was hard for Bena to give up her home and possessions, Mam said. She'd hoped they could salvage the house and more of the belongings, but Reuby said the dry wall was wet, and the two-by-fours were charred and weakened, even if they were standing. There wasn't a window they could use.

So Bricker's Excavating had gone to work. Bena, short and squat, stood with her children gathered around her like homeless peeps, their faces aged with childish concern. They watched as immense yellow dozers with deafening diesel engines razed their home. Bena lifted her apron and found the white handkerchief she kept tucked away, held it to her nose, blew efficiently, and blinked back the small number of tears she allowed herself. She sniffed then turned, replaced her *schnuppy* (handkerchief), and herded her flock of children toward the implement shed. It was time to get to work.

Sarah, Priscilla, and their sister, Anna Mae, worked with Ben Zook *sei* Anna sorting half-burnt items still dripping from the water of the fire hoses. A large blue barrel marked "trash" stood to their right and cardboard boxes marked "kitchen" or "closet" or "bedroom" to their left.

One of the women filled a wringer washer with steaming hot water and powdered laundry detergent. Another filled the rinse tubs with warm water and Downy. They washed and rewashed the salvaged clothes only to raise them to their noses, sniff, and shake their heads. It was hopeless, so they sent for Reuby *sei* Bena.

"It's just so hard to part with some of these things," she said dully as if she was far away, in a world where she knew nothing of that terrifying night of howling wind that had sent dragons of flames onto her good sturdy house. She had imagined the house would always stand, keeping them safe and protecting them against the elements. She used to think nothing could destroy those four walls and the shingled roof.

Repeatedly, then, the women tossed wet items into the mouth of the blue plastic barrel marked "trash."

Anna looked up from the charred remains of a wooden toy box, the remaining toys lying soaked and blackened, a pile of innocence destroyed.

"Come here."

Sarah went over, looked into the toy box, and shivered. There were the usual plastic rings, trucks, a few Matchbox cars, and a stuffed horse, all shifted to one corner, blackened and gray with soot and soaked with water. A doll stared up at them, one eye opened, another one closed, in an eerie wink, the hair blackened and dirtied by the water, the little Amish dress and black pinafore apron sodden.

Sarah shivered again.

"It plain down gives me the creeps!" Anna said forcefully.

Sarah nodded then gazed out toward the steaming remains of the barn. Small pockets of flames continued to break out, stubbornly refusing to be quenched. In that moment, Sarah realized the Amish community was under siege and needed help from the English world. The danger had been grave before, but now, it was grim. Her beloved Dat could not sort this out alone. A whole band of Amish ministers and laymen could not keep this evil at bay.

Yes, they would pray and place their trust in God, the way they always did, but God was in heaven, and they were down here. And unlike the sparrows, they couldn't just sit on the fence. They needed to use the wisdom that God would provide.

Sarah wondered if this was how people felt in Iraq or Afghanistan or wherever it was that the war was still being fought. It was the falling away of normalcy, the community thrust into uncertainty by the power of barns burning at the hands of an arsonist, a monster without mercy who did not value human life or the lives of faultless animals. Someone who wanted the Amish people to experience horror and fear, ridding them of the only safety they'd ever known: God and each other. For, really, how could God be trusted, if He allowed such tragedies one after another?

"Sarah, come on. Stop standing there like a statue with your eyes bulging out of your head!"

Anna Mae grabbed her arm. Sarah turned and shook free of the whirling mass of fear and doubt.

Ben Zook *sei* Anna straightened her ample body, rubbed her lower back, and asked if there was going to be a coffee break today or what. She was starving. They'd had a fresh cow that wouldn't accept the little bull calf, and she'd had an awful time of it, trying to get the silly thing to drink out of a bottle. Then she had no time for breakfast except a few potato chips while she was packing lunches.

"I'm so hungry I'm going to fall over," she announced, her eyes mirroring her genuine distress.

"*Maid*! (Girls!)"

Anna whirled eagerly to the sound of Hannah Stoltzfus's voice.

"*Kommet, maid*! (Come, girls!)"

Anna dropped everything immediately, slid one arm through Sarah's, and propelled her along. Anna Mae and Priscilla followed, laughing at the round Anna with her arm through Sarah's, tall and thin beside her.

They waited politely as the men served themselves first, grabbing large Styrofoam cups of steaming coffee and a handful of cookies or doughnuts or a granola bar or a chocolate whoopie pie or a slice of coffee cake.

Anna was beside herself with glee. She planned what she would eat long before she could actually help herself to all the baked goodies spread in wonderful array on the plastic table, a dream come true, calories without worry. She'd have a blueberry doughnut first. Dipped in coffee, they were absolutely the best thing ever. But she would have to use a plastic spoon, the way they went to nothing so fast.

Then, after the doughnut, she would have a

chocolate whoopie pie. She knew who made them, and she was talented. Not everyone made good whoopie pies. Nudging Sarah, she asked if she'd ever tasted Elmer Lapp's whoopie pies. The ones they sold at their produce stand? Well, she guessed if those tourists from New York City, the ones in the big buses, if they thought that's what whoopie pies were supposed to taste like, no wonder you couldn't buy them in their big city.

Anna was the first in line, chortling and smiling, stirring creamer into her coffee, when someone approached Sarah from the right, a large being hovering at her elbow.

Turning, she was pleasantly surprised to find Hannah, or Matthew's mother, as she always thought of her.

"Sarah, can I have a word with you?"

"Sure!"

They stepped away, Sarah trying desperately to hide her eagerness, her complete willingness to comply with any of Hannah's wishes.

"Sarah, did you talk to Matthew this weekend?"

"A little. Why do you ask?"

Hannah's eyes were feverish in their intensity.

"How did he seem?"

Sarah could not give her the answer she sought, knowing instinctively what Hannah wanted to hear, so she shrugged, turned her face away.

"Sarah?"

She was alarmed to hear the unprotected panic in Hannah's voice.

"Was he happy? Was he himself? He doesn't seem a bit heartbroken, now, does he? Huh? Does he?"

Without saying a word, Sarah shook her head from side to side, supplying the answer Matthew's mother wanted to hear, which wasn't really lying, just helping to soothe the poor woman's worries. How could she tell her of the devastation in his eyes? How could she stand here and tell his mother of the misery he carried like a shroud, enveloping himself against any overtures even she attempted?

Her face flamed now, thinking of the subtle ways she'd tried and failed. For without a doubt, Matthew was clearly heartbroken, the youthful exuberance gone, replaced with a lethargy, a sick pallor on his normally tanned face. He was hurting far more than Sarah had imagined.

"Well, if he's alright, then, I doubt if he'll ask her again, do you?"

"I don't know."

When Sarah spoke, it felt as if her tongue was covered with a woolen fabric that had thoroughly dried out her throat, and her words croaked, like a frog.

Hannah looked at her sharply.

Sarah cleared her throat.

"You're not telling me the truth," she hissed.

In response, Sarah turned and walked away as fast as she could, her eyes seeing nothing, her face revealing everything. She grabbed a cup of coffee, the array of baked things sickening her now, and rejoined Anna, who was too busy dunking another blueberry doughnut to see the expression on Sarah's face. Looking up, she caught only a glimpse of the fading anger.

"What got into you?" she asked in the forthright manner Sarah had learned to appreciate.

"Oh, Hannah."

"Hannah? Matthew's mam? Oh, I can only guess why, huh?"

Sarah nodded.

"She's probably hurting with poor Matthew. *Ach* my. That's so sad. I hate breakups. Hate them. They're mean and cruel and dumb."

The passion in her voice surprised Sarah. Turning, Anna went back to work, forgetting her heavily creamed coffee with the blueberry doughnut crumbs floating on top. Reuby's daughter, who was only two years old, ambled up to the cement block where Anna had left it, lifted the cup to her mouth, and drank every drop. She took the cup back to her mother and said very clearly, "*Ich vill may coffee* (I want more coffee)."

Anna remained closemouthed, her nostrils distended enough that Sarah knew she was still upset. Why would she be so worked up about Rose and Matthew's break up? What was it to her?

Her mind was taken off the prickly subject by the sight of her father standing with a group of men, his head bent in submission, as he listened to the voices around him. Sarah knew he wouldn't say much. It was her father's way. He'd listen, cultivate what he'd heard, think it through, and talk it over with Mam.

On the way home, the November sun seemed weak and ineffectual as it neared the line of trees to the west. The air was cold, and it would likely be colder tomorrow. She winced as a huge tractor trailer roared past, sending in a draft of frigid air that crept up under the woolen buggy robes, causing Priscilla to shiver.

"Poo!" Levi exclaimed.

"We're almost home," Mam answered calmly.

"They want to hold a meeting," Dat said quite unexpectedly.

"Who does?"

"The men of the surrounding districts."

"What about?"

"The barn fires."

"What are they going to do?" Mam's voice rose an octave, and her bonneted head turned toward Dat, who stared straight ahead, avoiding her intense gaze.

"I don't know. Something, they said. They think we should fight back."

"How?"

Dat shrugged.

"Oh my, Davey. This is very upsetting. How can anyone fight back? There is not much we can do."

"Levi's Abner wants to hire private detectives."

Mam lifted both hands and slapped them down in complete disbelief, sending up a few puffs of dust.

"But even an English detective wouldn't know where to start."

Dat nodded in agreement.

"I'll go to the meeting, likely. I just hope enough of us can come up with a peaceful solution to win over the hotheads."

He pulled on the left rein, an unnecessary maneuver, as Fred leaned toward the driveway without being told. They rode the remainder of the way in silence, then climbed off the spring wagon and walked into the house, each one separated by their own thoughts.

Levi's cough returned after the ride in the cold air, so Mam decided to stay home from the barn raising on Thursday. Emery Fender, the lumber-truck driver, would pick up Dat, so Sarah decided to drive Fred by herself.

Levi was terribly upset about staying home because of his cough. He cried, threatened, and pleaded with Mam, who stood her ground and said there was no way he was allowed to go, and that was that. To ease the pain, she promised him a pumpkin pie if he'd drink his tea with lemon and honey in it.

That evening Matthew walked up to the front door and asked Sarah if she wanted to ride with him the next day. After this unexpected piece of good fortune fell in her lap, she sang, smiled, and whistled her way through the rest of the evening.

Priscilla would go along, but she'd be in the back seat, and that was alright with Sarah. Oh, again, God had smiled down on her and blessed her with Matthew's presence, she thought the next morning as she combed her hair, hovering within inches of the mirror.

Mam asked both girls to mind their business, watch to make sure the men had enough water to drink, and to please stay away from photographers and reporters. She sized up Sarah's hair and covering, her eyes narrowing.

"Sarah, do you have on your good covering?"

Caught, Sarah thought resignedly. "Afraid I do," she trilled, trying to lift her mother to a lighter mood.

"Afraid you'll leave it here," Mam said dryly.

"Please, Mam. My other one fits so stupid. One side leans forward, no matter what I do with it."

"Sarah."

Oh, so she was going to treat her like she was still in first grade, then. Instant rebellion sprang to life, like boiling water poured on coffee granules. "Mam," she said, fast and hard, "You are just mad that I'm going with Matthew. That's the only reason you don't want me to wear my best covering."

Mam opened her mouth, a sharp reprimand on her tongue. But she knew Sarah was right, and she knew she'd been caught red-handed trying to steal the small amount of courage Sarah had outfitted for herself by wearing the Sunday covering.

Wisely, Mam turned away, swallowing the sharp retort. She said no more, allowing Sarah the upper hand. She wisely guarded the open door that led to the complicated world of mother-daughter relationships, viewing the days that stretched both behind her and ahead of her.

How could daughters see right through you like that? How? It was annoying and maddening, all at once. Of course she didn't want Sarah to go with Matthew. She didn't trust him, didn't trust him one bit.

Then, because she was tired from having lain awake until all hours of the morning with her thoughts whirling about her—tormenting her, rendering her unable even to say a decent prayer, the state she was in—she waited till the girls ran out the door. Then she sat down on the old hickory rocker and covered her face with her apron and had a good long cry.

The string of barn fires, the insecurity they had brought, her Davey being so troubled, the loss of Mervin, her worries about Sarah and

Matthew—suddenly and unexpectedly it all took its toll on Mam.

The ride with Matthew was less than comfortable. The buggy had no back seat, the way Matthew had it filled with sports equipment and clothes and all kinds of other stuff. Priscilla had to perch on the door ledge, leaving the cold wind pouring in the open door.

Matthew said if Sarah sat back, Priscilla could fit on the seat between them. But she refused, so she was cold the whole way. Matthew teased Priscilla and spoke only to her, looking at her entirely too much.

Sarah may as well have been a log or a length of stove pipe propped up in the corner, for all the attention he paid her. To make everything much worse, Priscilla continually giggled and smiled but also responded with an intelligence that seemed to intrigue Matthew.

After a few miles of this, he seemed to notice Sarah's lack of input, so he said, "Why so quiet, Sarah?" illuminating her world with the power of his kind, dark eyes.

Oh, Matthew. His eyes made her knees weak with the knowledge of her love. Never would she leave him. Never. She would always be here for him, waiting, hoping, and yes, praying that God would allow her to be his wife someday. His eyes were pools of kindness, of uplifting, of support, a wonderful boost to her faltering hope.

Could she help it, the waves of longing, the repressed love and devotion that held her in its unwavering grip? When she was with him, there was no doubt in her mind: It was always Matthew, and it would always be.

"I wasn't quiet," she said now, breathlessly, in spite of herself.

"Yeah, you were. But that's just you, anyhow. You're not as talkative as your sister. Hey, Pris, when will you be sixteen? When's your birthday?"

"November."

"Really? Wow! You'll be sixteen this month?"

"Fifteen."

"Aw, come on. You mean I have a whole year to wait?"

Priscilla blushed and became flustered. She looked into Sarah's eyes. Finding misery so raw, she did exactly the right thing and asked Matthew what he was thinking. He was way too old for her, seriously. And she no longer giggled.

Cold, disenchanted, her hopes dashed for the thousandth time, Sarah waited until Priscilla stepped down from the buggy before following her.

"Hey, don't I at least deserve a thank you?" he called after them.

"Oh, of course."

Sarah stopped, walked back, and thanked him, looking directly into the deep brown of his eyes, shoring up her resolve for the uncertain days and weeks and months ahead.

As if in another world, she heard the truck engines and the shouting voices, smelled the sharp odor of the new yellow lumber, as the many men dressed in black trousers and coats swarmed around the building site. They had already erected the main beams.

She guessed her love for Matthew was a lot like the barn fires, wasn't it? Dashed hopes destroyed by something so much larger than herself, only to be rebuilt, started anew, and continued on. But there was a growing uneasiness, a cold and dreadful realization, circling, circling, like wary wolves intent on their prey. She was keenly aware of Matthew's disinterest. She just couldn't let that control her hope. She had to keep moving. Fresh courage was her shield, her weapon, against the circling doubt. All was not lost.

The sound of hammers ringing against steel, the high whine of the chainsaws, the voices calling to one another—was it really happening again? The only thing that seemed real to her was the sound of the women, talking and laughing as they bent over the folding table with the dishpans containing potatoes and water, paring knives flashing as they peeled.

A stainless steel bucket piled full of potatoes fed a hundred, wasn't that right? Or was it two? And the same old spirited argument, paring knifes versus those Tupperware peelers. Or were the Pampered Chef ones best?

Aaron Zook *sei* Mary said what did it matter, a peeler is a peeler, and none of them work. A great clamoring of voices ensued, and Sarah smiled. She began cutting peeled potatoes and put her troubled thoughts to rest.

Here she was at home.

Chapter 21

The actual speed with which the barn took shape was unbelievable this time. The women stopped mid-morning to observe. There were more men than usual, they decided.

This third barn fire was attracting a lot of attention. Concerned members of the Old Order from as far away as Ohio and Indiana wanted to help, share their views, extend their charities.

The house was cleared away for the most part, but Reuby and Bena were still planning, knowing that if they rushed through that stage, it would spite them later on, Bena said.

The barn must be rebuilt first; Reuby's livelihood came from milking a herd of cows. By the time dinner was served, the metal sheets were being screwed into place on the lower end of the forebay.

"My oh," Grandmother Miller said from her

vantage point at the stove, waving the great wooden spoon and causing quite a stir among the women and girls.

Someone observed flatly that it was no wonder the new barn was going up so fast, with all the practice they'd had since early spring. It was sobering, all agreed.

Grandmother Miller shook her head, saying, "*Die lenga, die arriga* (The longer it goes, the worse things get)."

They made dire predictions. The end of the world coming any day now, according to the Bible. Mankind was going awry, and evil was prevailing. Mind you, the world is in such a state of sinful activity.

Sarah drew into herself. Yes, there was a certain truth in their words, of course. But what about the overwhelming response among the Plain people when tragedies did occur? Didn't that count for something? But she stayed quiet, being only a young single girl and outnumbered by her older peers.

Amid their prophesying, the women mashed the potatoes, which they kept warm and ready to serve along with gravy, ham, meatloaf, and chicken.

Kentucky Fried Chicken in Lancaster had donated twenty large containers of their chicken, with its distinctive taste—the best, in Dat's opinion. He called it Lucky Fried Chicken because he felt lucky every time someone brought some home or he got to eat at one of the restaurants. Sarah smiled, thinking of Dat.

No doubt, all the Amish would be touched by this generous gesture from the English people. The support from *die ausrie* (the outsiders) was indeed phenomenal, and it humbled the Plain people.

At a time like this, Sarah thought, the line between the English and the Amish was blurry. There really was no line. All over the world, every culture, every religion, understood loss and tragedy, horror and fear. There was always the good in man to combat the evil of men, and so it was this time. After a triple dose of disaster, the good poured in over and over, endlessly. It was truly an indescribable feeling.

Wolf Furniture brought two La-Z-Boy recliners with brown upholstery. Poor Reuby *sei* Bena told the driver he had the wrong place. He showed her the address on the delivery sheet, but she said, no, he had it all wrong, and he may as well take them back; they couldn't afford them.

He said, "Ma'am, I think they're donated."

She burst into tears and wiped her eyes with the corners of her *kopp-duch* (head scarf). Reuby came on the scene and shook the driver's hand so powerfully that the man had to keep taking it off the steering wheel and flexing his fingers the whole way back to Reading.

After dinner, they washed kettles and bowls and cleaned up as best they could. The temporary living quarters in the shed were almost impossible to keep clean, with the mud and the cold and the number of people stomping around.

The girls grabbed their coats and sat on the sunny side of the corncrib to watch the men, refilling the water jugs whenever it was necessary. The frame of the barn was all but completed, rising like a yellow skeleton into the blue November sky.

In the east, a wall of gray was building, rolling across the blue, changing the atmosphere slightly, as if the sun wasn't quite sure of itself. A wedge of geese honked their tardy way across the sky, like schoolchildren who knew they were late but kept hurrying along. Inexplicably, the hammering slowed as the men and boys watched the formation of Canadian geese, then pounding resumed.

Matthew walked by with Amos "Amy" King, one of his friends, and asked Sarah when they'd be ready to go.

"Whenever you are."

"In an hour or so? I have to feed heifers tonight."

"Sounds good."

Matthew smiled at her, then at Priscilla.

"How are you?" Amos asked.

"Good. I'm good."

"This your sister?"

"Yes. Priscilla, this is Amos."

"Hi."

Clearly flustered, Priscilla smiled up at Amos before quickly and shyly averting her eyes, as most fourteen-year-old girls do when introduced to a young man who was old enough to be *rumspringing*.

Sarah was glad to see this shyness in Priscilla. It spoke well for her character, and Sarah hoped she'd keep that sweet trait, even when she was sixteen. Too many pretty girls lost their shyness after receiving too much attention from the young men. And Priscilla was certainly noticeable, with her blonde-streaked, honey-colored hair, blue-green eyes, and round features.

She had a calming quality about her, an aloofness actually, that seemed attractive to some, like Matthew, Sarah admitted in spite of herself.

Watching Amos now, she could see the admiration, the way his eyes lingered on her face. And Sarah was glad—for a short time, anyway, until Matthew stepped over to Priscilla, reached down, and tweaked her ear.

"Yeah, Amy. Sarah's little sister, huh? She's not even fifteen yet. Not quite."

He lowered himself beside her, as close as possible, turning his head to watch her face. Amos smiled and watched Matthew, wondering what Sarah would say.

She said nothing, just stared straight ahead, her

features inscrutable, as the November sun took on a dim quality and the gray bank of clouds moved in from the east.

The men were moving in double quick time now. Some pulled out cell phones and checked the weather. Yes sir, ice coming. Ice and rain and about anything you could expect, they said. Well, they'd have this barn under roof by tonight.

There was quite a buzz about the weather. With renewed effort, friendly banter, bets called on and off, the men quickened the work pace.

Sarah watched and saw Dat, proud of his ability to straddle a beam with the best of them. Then she saw Uncle Elam and Paul Stoltzfus, the roofer, pulling steadily on a sheet of metal.

A gray truck pulled up to the barn, dispatching two young men who hurried to the side of the truck, extracted leather tool belts, buckled them on, and adjusted them, looking steadily up at the barn the whole time. Sarah guessed that men buckled tool belts the same way women put on aprons—easily, without really looking, having done it so many times.

One young man threw his cap into the truck, his blond hair gleaming in the cold sunshine. She wasn't aware she'd drawn a breath sharply. It was Lee.

He had no time to look around, intent on getting up on a beam and helping. Together, the two young men sprinted to the back of the barn, ran up the ladder, and were lost among the dozens, the hundred other men. Sarah sighed.

Matthew was still busy showing off his knowledge of Priscilla to his friend, Amos, with absolutely no help from her. Suddenly, a bolt of anger shot through Sarah, and just as suddenly, she concealed it.

What was Matthew doing, sitting right there like a spoiled school boy, flirting shamelessly with poor Priscilla, who by now looked as if she didn't really know what to do with him? Why didn't he get up on that roof and help? Or why didn't he go over and offer help to the men on the ground? There was so much he could be doing.

But, of course, when he was attentive and charming on the way home, Sarah's heart melted within her all over again. Her love for him was real and steadfast. Priscilla stayed in the background, quiet, watching their faces, wondering if Sarah would ever attain the love of her life. Only time would tell. But with the wisdom of her fourteen years, almost fifteen, Priscilla decided she wouldn't waste a week's worth of Fridays on that loser. He was a charmer, and she'd almost been under his spell that day, but no longer.

How could she help Sarah best? She couldn't believe her ears when she heard Matthew ask Sarah if she wanted to go along to Ervin Lapp's on Saturday evening.

Sarah's face turned from its normal color to a

pasty white before a spot of color reappeared on each cheekbone. She stammered a bit but said, "Why, yes, I'd be glad to go with you," and he said, "Good, good."

When they walked into the warm kitchen, Levi was coughing, and Mam's eyebrows were arched at a 45-degree angle, the tension heavy enough to cut with a knife.

Priscilla was dismayed to hear Sarah tell Mam about going with Matthew on Saturday evening, cringing as Mam gave her a tight smile and said, "Oh, did he?" Mam then turned away and began folding clothes with a vengeance. Sarah ran upstairs as fast as she could and flung herself on her bed and breathed a deep sigh of complete happiness that could only come from a dream fulfilled, at long last.

Yes, it was not a real date. And yes, he was just offering her a ride. But it proved to Sarah that he enjoyed her company, wanted to spend time with her, and would just maybe show Rose, who was bound to be there, that this was what he'd wanted all along.

The heights she rode on wings of joy! Over and over, she thanked God for His deliverance from the river of misery. He set her feet firmly on higher ground, where the view was infused with stardust and the birds sang in harmony with the praise that poured from her soul.

She read her Bible in English, the words of

comfort and praise in the Psalms more meaningful than ever. God was so good, so kind, to help her rise above the doubts that had been her constant companions for far too long.

Her elevated reverie was broken by her mother's voice, calling her rather urgently, saying there was someone on the phone for her.

Instantly, Sarah slammed her Bible onto the nightstand, slid off the bed, and raced downstairs. Shoving her feet into a pair of boots, she grabbed a sweater off the hook, and kicked open the screen door as she pushed her arms into the sleeves before racing across the lawn to the phone shanty.

The black receiver lay on its side beside the telephone, and she picked it up swiftly and breathed, "Hello?"

"Hey, watcha doin'?"

Melvin.

"Oh, not much. I just got home from the barn raising at Reuby's."

"Oh, you were there? How'd that go?"

"Really amazing this time. It's like the women were saying—it's sad to have to admit it, but practice is in good supply. I mean, think about it, Melvin. Three barns since April."

Melvin's voice was serious, intense.

"Well, since no one seems to care about the arsonist, he'll just keep it up, thinking he's doing something right. We need to do something, get organized, get moving."

"How Melvin? Do you have a legitimate plan?"

"Sure. If you have a barn full of expensive milk cows, then sleep out there. Every night. Equip the barn with some first class smoke detectors. Call the police every time anything out of the ordinary happens. Anything at all. Whatever happened to Levi seeing that white car the night your barn burned. Did anyone ever see another one? Did anyone think to ask?"

Sarah sat down on the cracked vinyl seat of the old steel desk chair, tipped it back, and gazed at the ceiling as Melvin rambled on.

She had to admit, he was a mover and a shaker, and he got things done. He was smart and ambitious—too much so, Dat said.

When she could finally get a word in edgewise, she said she'd ask Dat to invite him to the meeting that would be held the following Monday evening. Instantly, Melvin drew back, saying he was the youngest in the bunch, unmarried, and his theory would mean nothing.

But Sarah would hear nothing of his attempt at being modest. He wasn't humble, and she knew it. Any effort of modesty was completely invalid, where Sarah was concerned. She knew Melvin well, and humility was not one of his attributes. He knew he wanted to be at that meeting, and he also knew the thought of speaking out there was extremely challenging.

So she let him talk, adding an mm-hm, okay, or

yes, whenever she felt they were needed. She got down a lined tablet from the shelf, crossed her legs, and wrote "Matthew Ray Stoltzfus" over and over, with hearts and daisies and other doodles portraying her happiness.

Finally Melvin's subject of the barn fires ran dry, and he quickly asked what she was doing Saturday night.

"Matthew is taking me to Ervin's."

The line went silent with his inability to respond appropriately, so Sarah waited, her lips curved prettily with the victory that was so securely in her possession.

Finally, "Matthew?" It was an awkward sound, a squeak, a balloon releasing the air.

"What's wrong with that?"

"Oh, nothing. Nothing."

"Well, then?"

"But, they just broke up."

"It's not a date."

"I know."

Strangely, then, silence returned, the line quietly humming in their ears but sizzling with the unspoken instruments of hurt wedged between them—truth unable to be spoken on Melvin's side, defense rearing its shield on Sarah's.

His voice drained of any bravado, Melvin finally said, "Well."

"What?"

"Well, I guess that makes you happy."

"Yes, it does."

"Good for you."

"You don't mean that."

"But I do, Sarah."

She laughed, a short expulsion of disbelief. "No, you don't."

Melvin hunkered down on the hay bale he was sitting on and decided the fat was in the fire now. If she was going to act like that, then he'd just tell her, swimming along in her total blindness, swept away by that current named Matthew.

"Alright, Sarah. I'm only telling you this because I care about you. I worry about what will happen to you. You're my favorite girl in the whole world. You know that."

He stopped, allowing the dramatic statement to claim her.

She wiped her mouth with a thumb and forefinger and grimaced. Thinking what a complete professional Melvin was, she felt the first twinge of unease.

"Matthew is a nice guy, but he's likely using you to make Rose jealous."

The truth in his words came down on her like a whip, slicing through the innermost region of her conscience, that place that vibrated with tiny blue, pulsing lights, so irrelevant they were once easily covered up by her own beautiful words of love and longing, the yearning piled safely on the entire mass of her own security. Now a hot anger shot through her, alarming in its resonance. She almost hung up on him, but the training in good manners she had received from her parents restrained her.

"I'm sorry you have to feel that way, Melvin."

Melvin shook his head. Her words were as artificial, as slyly sweetened, as deplorable, as any he had ever heard. Enough was enough. Touché, Sarah.

"Well, I'll see you there, okay? I'm looking forward to it. You know the oldies team is going to win, don't you? We're going to whip everyone!"

This was pure Melvin, enthused, back on track in his unbridled zest for life, the competition of the upcoming ping-pong games erasing all the bad feelings between them.

Sarah smiled, then laughed, shoving back the ill will, and they chatted happily about ordinary, mundane things, the darker subjects of Matthew and the barn fires behind them now. As always, friendship prevailed, and theirs was a rare and precious thing, too valuable to shatter with the resounding click of a receiver slammed down in anger.

Sarah shivered, drew the sweater tightly across her chest, and leaned forward to warm herself. She glanced at the lowering sky, the world turning from a white gray to a darker gray as the sun set behind the heavy layer of restrained ice and rain or whatever would be released on the cold, brown earth lying dormant now, awaiting its cold winter cover.

Melvin was still talking, but her mind was on the solidness, the new stronghold of Reuby's barn, just put "under roof" today. How grateful he must be! The ice and snow could assail it now, pound it, and bounce around on it, and the men would have a protected place to complete the job.

She thought of Bena's reaction to the La-Z-Boy recliners and smiled, remembering her short, round form, her purple *kopp-duch* (head scarf), her misshapen everyday sneakers of questionable origin, her sagging black socks, the way she dipped her head in true humility after acknowledging that the recliners really were given to them, delivered by this English man.

"You're not listening," Melvin whined.

"Yes. Yes, I am."

"What was I saying?"

"You were talking about this new schoolteacher at the school across the road from your house."

"But what did I say?"

"That she's from Perry County."

"No, she's not. That's not what I said. See, you weren't listening at all."

"Oh, you said Dauphin."

"Well, yeah."

"Don't act like I'm two years old, Melvin. You know I hate that, when you sound so condescending."

"I didn't know you knew what that word meant."

"Smart, aren't I?"

"Not so much."

Sarah laughed and told Melvin she was freezing. There's nothing colder than sitting in an unheated phone shanty.

"I'm in the barn. I'm not cold."

"Well, lucky you. See you Saturday night, Melvin."

"Bye."

She could hardly open the door fast enough or race back to the house with enough speed, hurling through the kitchen door and moving swiftly to the coal stove in the corner. She shook her hands above it, as chills raced up and down her spine.

Levi observed all this from his chair, where he was patiently waiting on the casserole to come out of the oven.

"You were out there over an hour," he said dryly.

Mercifully, Mam had her back turned, putting carrots in a dishpan to peel and cut. She pinched her lips into a grim line, her eyes dark pools of worry and hard-earned restraint.

"Yeah well, Levi, you know how Melvin talks."

Levi nodded, smiled.

So, it was Melvin. Mam relaxed visibly and turned to ask Sarah to peel the carrots. Sarah moved obediently to the kitchen sink. She told Levi about Melvin wanting to be at the meeting and that he should be questioned more thoroughly about the white car.

Levi lifted his shoulders, shifted in his chair, and cleared his throat with great importance. "I'd be glad to go to the meeting. I can answer questions if they put them to me."

Sarah smiled, noting the *gros-feelich* (proud) cadence of his words.

"I'm sure Dat will want you to go, Levi."

"I think Monday night would suit me alright," he answered, looking across the kitchen at the calendar, his eyes glistening.

Chapter 22

The predictions from the weather forecast proved deplorably accurate. Tiny bits of ice mixed with cold, wet rain drove in from the east, relentlessly battering the new metal siding of Reuby Kauffman's barn. It fell on the half-frozen debris-filled troughs of mud and water blackened by the charred bits of wood, twisted nails, corkscrewed metal, and chunks of blistered tile and drywall and concrete. It swirled and eddied around potholes in the broken macadam and pooled in deep ruts left by the fire trucks and bulldozers, creating a slick, glistening other-worldliness by the time Reuby awoke the following morning.

David Beiler was one of the first people to arrive, his old wool hat bent and dripping, the droplets hovering on its brim as if undecided about whether to freeze or slide off. He threw the leather reins across the horse's back, reached for the *shtrung* (leather straps connecting the harness and buggy), clicked the backhold snap, and looked up to find Reuby striding through the mud.

"Morning, Davey."

"How are you, Reuby?"

"Good. Good."

Dat looked out from beneath his hat brim, his gaze warm with the compassion of a person with *aforeung* (experience). He was shocked to find Reuby's normally vibrant eyes clouded with fatigue, defeat—and what else? Dat shivered, shaken to the core by the gray pallor on Reuby's face.

"Reuby, are you sure you're doing good?"

In answer, Reuby half turned, his mouth working, as he fought to gain control over the debilitating despair that threatened to squeeze the life from his veins. He swallowed, nodded.

Dat came around to Reuby's side and placed his gloved hand on the wet black shoulder, a gesture of pleasant understanding, of deep sincerity, and compassion.

"Reuby, it seems impossible now, but it isn't. You'll receive help. God will provide. He always does."

Deeply moved, Reuby's shoulders began to shake, as the control he held onto so firmly slipped from his grasp. Dat's hand remained on his shoulder, the other held the bridle of his unquestioning Fred, who stood obediently in the cold wet rain until his master would lead him to shelter.

Reuby's head came up then. He shook it back and forth, produced a red, wrinkled handkerchief, and blew lustily. He placed it quickly back in his pocket, as if the disappearance would hide his shame at crying when he was, after all, a man who viewed the whole world through rose-colored glasses of love and charity.

"How can a person go on?" he mumbled brokenly.

"God will see you through."

"But I'm already deeply in debt. So deep, in fact, I don't know if it's wise to rebuild. The Amish fire insurance will never cover it all. I feel perhaps I should just give up, rent a small home, get a day job."

"In the Old Testament, God told the children of Israel to be patient, to stand by, that he would show works of wonder for them. If you rebuild in faith, God will bless you, like Abraham of old. His belief in God was rewarded many times over."

"I'm not Abraham."

There was a tinge of bitterness in Reuby's

words, so Dat told him to come to the meeting on Monday evening. A group of men were assembling to figure out a solution of sorts. They would talk about finances as well. Already, there were trust funds established at two different banks, the generosity of the people reaching unbelievable levels.

Reuby nodded and yawned. He peered at Dat with bleary eyes and said, yes, he'd be there. Then he yawned mightily once more. Dat knew Reuby had barely managed an hour's sleep, the enormity of his situation keeping him awake long hours as the icy rain pelted the shambles of his home and pinged and clattered against the metal roofing of the makeshift quarters in the implement shed.

"The sun will shine again, Reuby. God never makes us suffer more than He gives us the strength to bear."

Reuby nodded and watched dully as more teams appeared. Dat knew he was tired, discouraged, and moving in a fog of disorientation and would be for a while longer.

"Be thankful no lives were lost," he said.

"I know, I know. You lost young Mervin, and nothing can replace that kind of loss."

"Absolutely," Dat said.

Far from the site of the barn raising, Sarah shivered as she sat uncomfortably in the back seat of the van, wedged between Ruthie Zook on her right, and Anna Mary Fisher on her left. Both were sound asleep, their pillows stuffed haphazardly into the corners of the back seat, their mouths hanging open in the most unattractive manner.

The ride to market was risky, unnerving at best, the driver hunched over his steering wheel, staring into the night at the slick and dangerous roads. Massive dump trucks crawled along, their beds lifted as they swirled salt, calcium, and cinders onto the roads for the edgy motorists trailing behind.

If Ike Stoltzfus would close his mouth for one second, Sarah thought. As if the driver knew he had support from the back seat, he turned and told Ike to keep his opinions to himself. He was the driver and he would decide the speed. It was no big deal to be late; the market wouldn't exactly be booming with customers in this weather anyway, so just shut it. Ike slouched back in his seat, crossed his arms, and began to brood, glancing balefully at the streaks of ice and rain in the glare of the headlights.

The van veered crazily as the driver swung the steering wheel to the left, then right, but they stayed on course, the speed significantly reduced yet again.

Ike yelped but remained quiet, his eyes sliding to the tense profile beside him.

Anna Mary's head swung back against Sarah's shoulder. Her eyes fluttered open, and she gasped. Ruthie's head slid forward, she righted it awkwardly, and went right on sleeping.

Sarah sipped her lukewarm coffee from the tall travel cup. Anna Mary leaned over and asked if she could have a swallow of it. Handing it over, Sarah grimaced as she engulfed the lid with her heavy lips, slurped, and handed it back.

End of the coffee for me, she thought.

"You can have it."

"You sure?"

"Yeah."

"Thanks."

The ride was stretching into its fourth hour when they finally rolled up to the vast brick building on Progress Street. The Amish had turned the obscure old train station into a bustling, friendly market full of life, sounds, and smells that enticed consumers to buy something from each stand.

Sturdy posts and a mock shingled roof framed Amos Fisher's produce stand. Piles of fresh tomatoes, green, yellow, and red peppers, towers of cucumbers, zucchini, summer squash, carrots, garden lettuce, and new onions created a feast for the eyes. The bonus attraction for modern shoppers was the organic label boasting that no pesticides or insecticides had been used to grow the vegetables. Customers from the big city paid the price, placing their trust in the bearded fellow and his helpers wearing white bib aprons and coverings on their heads.

Despite the numerous meat counters, some customers only bought from the stand run by a Jewish family. Their meats were kosher, prepared according to the requirements of the Jewish law in the Old Testament. Kosher or not, he had the best salami in the market, and a lively mix of customers, both Jewish and English, Amish and Mennonite, bought from him.

Sarah always viewed the Jewish family with a certain mix of awe and curiosity. What she really wanted was to sit down and compare their beliefs. How different or similar were they? Like the Jews, the Amish derived many of their highly esteemed traditions from the Old Testament. She supposed belief in Jesus separated them, but still. Both groups seemed to have a common love of tradition, and that interested her, although she doubted she'd ever have the nerve—or the time—to start a conversation with them.

The largest stand in the sprawling market was the Stoltzfus bakery, where freshly made pies, bread, rolls, cakes, cookies, and cupcakes rolled off the shelves as fast as Sarah and the fourteen others who worked there could restock the spotless white shelves. They covered cinnamon rolls with Saran Wrap before they were properly cooled. But the goods sold rapidly just the same. Sarah chuckled as an overweight lady happily snatched up the fresh buns and scuttled to a nearby table before peeling off the plastic and tucking into the first heavenly mouthful, rolling her eyes blissfully at her companion.

Sarah mixed huge vats of yeast dough and put large mounds of it into the proofer, a machine that produced just the right amount of warmth and humidity to raise the dough to the required size. Then she turned it on a large, floured surface and began forming the quota of bread, rolls, and sweet rolls. Her arms became rounded and well-muscled from plying, rolling, and turning the dough, sprinkling it with brown sugar and cinnamon and walnuts.

There were five sit-down restaurants and many booths where customers could eat food they bought to take out. Leather supplies, a craft stand, and outdoor furniture—all at reasonable prices—catered to many different preferences.

Sarah truly loved her job now, and her devotion showed in her willingness to take on any task. But she was mostly restricted to the "yeast crew."

Now, because of the inclement weather, they cut down on the amount of dough they would mix for the day. And the workers were allowed a forty-five minute break instead of only thirty. At one o'clock, Sarah still had not taken her break, allowing the other girls their turns, saying she wasn't that hungry.

Then quite suddenly, she felt dizzy, her stomach caving in on itself. A half hour later, Ike told her to go on break, just when she wondered whether to collapse or eat dough. Of course, she did neither.

Hurrying along the aisle, her purse slung over her shoulder, Sarah sat down heavily and waited at her usual booth for her friend, Rose, who was having a slow day and came over almost immediately to sit with Sarah. As always, she was beautiful, her hair gleaming in the electric ceiling lights, her skin flawless, her robin's egg dress reflecting her perfect blue eyes.

"Sarah!" She reached across the table, grasped both of Sarah's hands, and squeezed. "I miss seeing you! I could hardly stand not going to the supper on Sunday evening!"

"Where were you, Rose?" Sarah asked, concerned now.

"Oh, I don't know." Rose removed her hands and looked away and then back. She cupped her delicate chin in one hand and shrugged.

"Sometimes it's hard to go to the supper crowd. I mean, I'm happy. Don't get me wrong, it's just that . . . I don't know."

"Well, you've always been dating," Sarah said too quickly and much too easily.

"I guess. I don't know." She brightened then and leaned forward and said, "You know who is just so attractive? That Lee Glick. See, the reason we never knew of him is that he used to be with the Dominoes, that other youth group, and now he moved down here with his sister, that Anna and Ben. Their barn was the second one that burned. Anyway, I went to the dinner table with him. I was surprised he went in to the afternoon table. He picked me, remember?"

Rose giggled, then looked away. "Oh, what can I get you? It's almost two o'clock. Haven't you eaten anything at all?"

Sarah shook her head. "Bring me a bowl of chili. Fast!"

Rose giggled again and hurried off, waving a hand behind her.

The Dominoes? No, he wasn't.

The Dominoes was the name of an Amish youth group. Because of the many youth in Lancaster County, they were divided into groups with different names, like the Dominoes or the Drifters —any name to mark them as a specific group.

The largest was the Eagles, a parent-supervised group attempting a cleaner, better way of *rumspringa*, without the smoking and drinking of past days. Concerned parents and ministers, alarmed at the moral decline among the youth, were attempting a new *rumspringa*, where the *ordnung* still applied. This caused quite a bit of controversy among Amish wary of anything untraditional. A peaceful truce had been reached, although problems still broke out. But as Dat told Sarah, the problems could be solved when each placed the emphasis on giving in to the other in humility and brotherly love.

Rose didn't know that Anna had told Sarah that Lee had been with the Drifters, the older group, not the Dominoes. Sarah was peeved, intimidated by Rose's knowledge of Lee. What would Rose say if she knew about last week at Reuby Kauffman's?

Her face flamed suddenly. When Rose appeared with a steaming bowl of thick chili, a dollop of sour cream and cheddar cheese on top, she looked anxiously at Sarah and asked if she had a fever. Blinking nervously, Sarah said, no, no, she was fine, and lifted the soup spoon to her mouth.

Rose seemed satisfied with Sarah's reply, then asked if she'd seen Matthew this week. Sarah nodded and told her about the barn raising, offering nothing more.

"Well, how does he seem to you? Is he himself? I mean, you know, getting on with his life?"

Rose was nervously folding and unfolding a napkin, the toe of one foot bobbing furiously, her eyes too intent.

"Well, he teased Priscilla a lot, but—you know—that's how he's always been. He seems happy, yes, at least as far as I can tell."

Rose said nothing, folded the napkin again. "Well, I better go. We didn't finish making some of the soups. In this weather, it'll take a lot, later on in the day. Hey, see you at Ervin's."

Sarah nodded.

"How are you going?"

Sarah cringed inwardly, wishing with all her heart that Rose hadn't asked her that one question. Why did she have to know?

"Matthew."

"Oh."

Rose lifted her chin, scowled, turned on her heel, and hurried off, moving faster than she had all day.

Well. So be it, Rose. You're the one that broke off the friendship.

Before long, the chili was gone, so Sarah paid, wandered two aisles down, bought a chunk of chocolate walnut fudge (she'd save some for Levi, his favorite), and was slowly walking past the leather goods stand when someone called her name.

Surprised, Sarah turned. "Oh, Ashley. Hi."

"What are you doing?"

"Eating fudge."

Ashley giggled, then looked ashamed and ill at ease, fingering a key chain, her eyes averted.

"How are you?" Sarah asked.

"I'm okay."

"Good."

An awkward silence followed, and Sarah wasn't sure if she wanted to keep the conversation going or move off. Ashley's thin, fine hair somehow looked hacked off, and her face was white and riddled with acne. Her eyes clouded with anxiety or shyness, Sarah wasn't sure which. She was painfully thin, her gray sweat-shirt hanging as if on a coat hanger.

Suddenly, she lifted her head, as if in desperation. "Did . . . did you know those people whose house burned, like, last week? Did they . . . are they okay? Like, what happened?"

The words were a torrent, unleashed by the force of her curiosity, raining on Sarah so that she could hardly meet her troubled gaze.

"Reuby . . . Reuben Kauffman's?"

"I dunno. I guess."

"Yes, their barn and house—both were destroyed by fire. They're doing about as well as you'd expect. They're good people and are hurting at the loss, of course, but they'll be okay in time."

"But no one was hurt? Or, like, killed?"

"No, nothing like that."

"Oh." Then, "Are . . . are these people going to try and find out who, like, did it?"

"Oh, I don't know. We're having a meeting soon, at my house—my dad's a minister—to try and figure out a way to keep the barns safe. I don't know how we could actually find the arsonist."

"Yeah. Well, I have to go."

She disappeared behind a wall of elaborately tooled leather belts without giving Sarah a chance to say goodbye. So Sarah shrugged her shoulders and moved on, letting the whole conversation go for now. There was too much to see, too many people to greet and talk to, even if only for a minute.

"Hey, Sarah!"

Ray King waved a hand across his cheese display, a beaming elderly woman at his side, her hair parted like the white wings of a dove, crowned by a large white covering. Ray was a big man, larger than Levi, his round face florid, his beard bristling with good humor. A white butcher's apron stretched loosely across his round stomach.

Sarah smiled and moved over to their stand. She stretched on tiptoes to see what free samples they had today.

"Havarti. Swiss. Aged cheddar," she read aloud.

"What? You can read?" Ray boomed, and his mother gave him a resounding smack on his arm, which was as big as a log.

Sarah laughed, sampled them all, and made a face.

"What? My cheese is no good? Don't let my customers see you pull that face."

"No, it's not your cheese. It's eating anything after that extra sweet chocolate fudge."

Ray laughed and said he hadn't eaten any fudge for a while. He was going to buy some, and he left the stand hurriedly, his large frame rocking from side to side.

His mother shook her head, saying *"Eya braucht's net* (He doesn't need it)."

Sarah moved on. She waved to Rachel Fisher at the fish stand, the rich aroma of frying fish whirling around her. The warm, full-bodied seafood smell made her inhale appreciatively.

"Sarah!"

She stopped and waited as Rachel handed her a small cardboard boat with red crisscrossing on it. It was filled with broiled scallops.

"Taste these. Tell me what you think. Too much lemon? Not enough? It's something new."

Gingerly, with thumb and forefinger, Sarah attempted to lift one of the succulent orbs, which was broiled crisply and coated with a clear sauce. Instantly, she pulled back her hand.

"Ow! They're hot."

"Here. Use a plastic fork."

Sarah jabbed a scallop with the fork and blew on it repeatedly before taking a tentative bite. She chewed, held her head to one side, and rolled her eyes before pronouncing them awful, just awful.

Rachel let out a devastated sigh.

"No!"

Sarah laughed and told her she was joking. They were simply the best thing ever.

"Oh Sarah, thank you so much! You really mean it? We got this great buy on fifty pounds of them, and we have to sell some scallops this week. And just look at the weather out there! It's driving me plum crazy."

Sarah said calmly, "You'll make it." She waved and moved on.

Leon and Rachel Fisher were some of the most successful market people and lived in one of the nicest homes in Leola. She'd heard through the grapevine that they sold thousands of dollars worth of seafood each week, although they always complained of the high cost of their lease, the fish, the help. But it was all done in humility, not flaunting their actual success.

The farmer's market was a great part of Sarah's social life now. She made new friends, comfortably joked with other vendors, and became close friends with her co-workers.

As she returned to her work station, her thoughts went back to the timid Ashley, her fevered questions, and wondered at the mysterious traits she displayed. She was obviously not comfortable with who she was. But who could know what her life was like? What had been in her past to create this sense of imbalance?

Dat often told them not to judge anyone unfairly, before actually knowing what their circumstances were. Be slow to judge, slow to pass opinion of someone, and be patient with each other's shortcomings. Mam lived this advice largely by example. She remained kind in situations others probably could not, her uncomplicated manner a healing balm in more than one prickly situation. So Sarah gave her shy, new friend the benefit of the doubt and felt peaceful, at ease, and only curious to get to know her better.

As she thought of that evening, a new joy rose within her, and she hummed along with the beat of the mixer. Matthew coming to pick her up! Imagine!

She hoped Mam's feathers would remain unruffled, but she'd be glad to escape out the front door. Mothers were unpredictable creatures.

Chapter 23

By early Saturday evening, the ice and rain had moved on. The wind blew strongly, and a weak November sun melted the ice on the south and west sides of buildings, trees, cars, or whatever had been covered by the thin coat of freezing water.

It was the kind of day when it was easier to stay indoors, the wind a bit too belligerent for skirts and dresses, the ground either muddy or covered with thin sheets of cracking ice like broken glass underfoot.

Priscilla, however, chose to ride Dutch, his hooves sinking into the mud and smashing the thin ice that stretched across puddles. It was all the same to him.

When Sarah came home from market, Priscilla came running across the driveway from the barn, her cheeks ruddy with the cold and the wind, her eyes dancing beneath her honey colored hair that had been tossed in windblown tendrils about her face. She was shouting as she ran, oblivious to the curious faces pressed against the tinted glass of the fifteen-passenger van.

"Sarah! He cleared the creek!"

"What?"

The wind whipped her skirt about her, tore the single syllable from her mouth, and whirled it away.

"Dutch! He jumped the creek!"

"Priscilla Beiler! How?"

"Oh well, you know. If you go fast enough, he has to do it."

They bent their heads to the wind and moved rapidly to the front porch, bursting through the door, glad to feel the heat and homey aroma of the kitchen.

Mam looked up from the kitchen sink and said, "Hello, Sarah. Home so soon?"

"Yes, Mam, the market was slow."

"I would imagine people are reluctant to leave their houses in this unpredictable weather."

"He jumped the creek, Mam!"

"Your horse? Priscilla, I seriously fear for your safety."

But Mam's eyes shone, and just the smallest hint of pride asserted itself. It was there in the way a small smile played around her lips and made itself at home, the lifting of her rounded shoulders, and her quick movements as she whirled to the stove.

Was it some remembered time of her own? Did she accomplish a neat, heart-stopping leap on the back of a favorite horse, a pleasure forgotten that was now revived by the antics of her daring young daughter?

"Whoo!" Priscilla fist-pumped the air.

Suzie giggled from her side of the card table, where Levi sat facing her, the game Memory between them. Levi viewed his sister with flat eyes and said she was *gros-feelich* (proud), pressing his lips together in righteous indignation.

Priscilla pulled back on his wide, elastic suspenders and let them snap gently against his back. He swiped at her clumsily, almost upsetting his rolling desk chair.

"*Denk mol* (think once), Levi! Here I come, galloping full tilt, and I don't know if Dutch will do it, so I have to prepare myself to stop. But I can feel it this time. His speed increases, he bunches his muscles, and I can tell he's going to attempt it this time. I can't tell you how thrilling it is."

Levi contemplated his sister's words, before saying calmly, "*Du bisht net chide* (You're crazy)."

Priscilla laughed happily and with abandon. "I knew he could do it!"

"Levi, go!" Suzie commanded.

Levi lowered his great head, swung it to the side, hummed, then reached down with his wide, stubby fingers and picked up two cards, blue ones with orange fish imprinted on the heavy squares and said, "Yep! Got it!"

Suzie growled and eyed his stack of cards that was so tall it leaned crookedly. She counted her own meager five sets. "Levi, you cheat!"

"Hah-ah, I don't. I remember stuff, that's what I do. I remember a lot of things in my life, Suzie."

Filled with the knowledge of his amazing memory, Levi puffed out his chest, snapped his suspenders, and chortled to himself.

Suzie overturned a card with a small pink doll carriage on it then hovered over the cards undecidedly. Finally she swooped down, turned one right side up, squeezed her eyes shut, and howled with disappointment.

"I know exactly where it is!" Levi shouted.

Mam walked over to watch, resting a hand on the back of his chair as he pounced dramatically on the two cards that created a set, fairly yodeling in his excitement. Suzie was a good sport, shaking her head at the end of the game. Levi had twenty-three sets to her nine.

Priscilla ate three chocolate-chip cookies with a tall glass of milk. Sarah handed the chocolate fudge she had bought to Levi, who thanked her rather stiffly, completely bowled over by his good fortune.

Mam seemed to be relaxed and accepting of Sarah leaving with Matthew, so Sarah said that, if it was alright, she'd better start getting ready to go to Ervin's. Mam looked at Sarah, smiled, and said yes, maybe she'd better, and inquired politely what time he was arriving.

Well, you had to hand it to her, Sarah thought as she wound her way up the steps, her hand clinging to the smooth wooden railing.

It was already pitch dark, the bony branches of the maple tree scraping across the porch roof creating unsettling sounds. It was not a good night to be going anywhere. But with Matthew at her side, who would notice the wind or the cold or the leftover spitting rain?

The all-important moment of choosing the perfect dress came first. Slowly, she leafed through the multiple colors of sleeves, hanging side by side in a neat row.

Not red. Sleeves too tight.

Brown. No. Ugly color. Or wait. It was November, brown was a fall color, the color of acorns and dry leaves.

Nah.

Lime green. Sick color, no.

Blue. Too much blue. Always wore blue.

Green. Sage green. The color of her eyes. Hate the fabric. Makes me look fat.

Teal. Oops. Sleeve torn at underarm.

Beige. Too blah.

Navy blue. Too plain.

On and on, then back again, Sarah fingered the empty sleeves hanging before her, dissatisfied with every single one.

She would wear black every Sunday until May, but on Saturday night, she was allowed to wear anything she wanted.

Going to the bedroom door, she called for Priscilla.

"She's outside!" Mam answered.

So much for moral support, Sarah thought. Well, she'd shower, wash her hair, clear her head of indecision, and then perhaps choose randomly, like a game of pin the tail on the donkey. But it was important that she look just right, so that probably wasn't a good idea.

In the end, she put on the brown dress but was absolutely put off by the pallor it cast on her anxious face. Instead she chose the brightest dress she owned, a magnificently colored red.

Her hair refused to cooperate, as usual, and she finally had to let the right side be ruled by its disgusting cowlick. Her apron didn't fit right, and all her shoes looked stupid. Every pair was either too big, with the toes pointed skyward, or too old and worn, too tight or too cold. She should have gone shoe shopping.

So then, because her best sneakers had gray and green stripes in them, she shed the red dress and donned the lime green one. She grabbed her favorite coat and ran down the stairs just as two headlights approached the front yard.

Mam smiled and said, "Bye, Sarah. Be careful."

Priscilla, glued to a chair with a book in front of her face, said nothing, paying Sarah as much attention as she would a fly. If it wasn't Priscilla, it was Mam, or the other way around. She thought they must plan together who would disapprove. It was only a minor annoyance, which completely disappeared when she climbed into Matthew's buggy.

"Hey, Sarah." He smiled at her warmly, his white teeth illuminated by the brilliance of the headlights. Her knees went weak with a happiness beyond anything she had expected.

"Hi, Matthew." What a wonderful way to begin this idyllic evening.

Matthew was talkative, entertaining her with vivid accounts of his job and the dinner he had cooked the evening before. Sarah smoothed back her hair and answered smartly, trying to be witty and worth his company.

She was disappointed when they arrived at Ervin and Katie's house, having to share Matthew with everyone else. She didn't let it show as she jumped gracefully off the buggy, politely helped him unhitch, and handed him the halter and neck rope before walking away.

She stopped, undecided now. Should she wait until he tied the horse? Should they enter as a couple? Did he want the crowd of young people to know he had brought her?

The wind whipped her lime green skirt, pulled at her hair, and tugged her covering away from the pins that were holding it. So she decided to move up to the porch at least, before her hair and covering were a complete wreck.

The door was flung open by a squealing Rose, who was in a high state of excitement from having just beaten that Lee Glick at a game of ping-pong. There was a spot of color on each of her cheeks, her smile was wide, her face already glowing.

Sarah always felt her confidence slip away the minute Rose was within sight. Like a ship tossed by one hard wave, Sarah was knocked off course, but she quickly righted herself. She regained her composure, ready to snap on her confidence and enjoy the evening, remembering that God had made her this way. God had endowed Rose with a more startling beauty, and it was acceptable, Sarah thought, remembering her mother's kind words that to base confidence in beauty was like building a house on quicksand.

Quietly, Sarah entered the basement, led by her hostess, Katie, who followed behind the whirling Rose. She bent to say hello to those who were seated, but she entered the crowded, well-lit room without Matthew.

Lee Glick leaned against the paneled wall, his

hands in his pockets, his dark, forest green shirt turning his complexion to an olive hue. He watched Sarah.

The grace with which she moved! Not very many girls could carry off this unconsciousness of themselves, an innocence born of a good upbringing. She was like a calm pool of water in a hidden corner of a forest—ethereal, transparent, cool, and untouched.

Chapter 24

The basement was well lit, with propane gas lamps at both ends and battery-powered lights illuminating the two ping-pong tables. Groups of young men stood against the paneled walls waiting their turns to play, cheering or egging on the other players.

They wore brightly colored button-down shirts, some with stripes or a soft plaid, an occasional T-shirt showing beneath an open collar. And they wore black broadfall trousers with narrow waists and loose suspenders. If a mother complied with her son's wishes, the waist of his trousers fit snugly to allow the exclusion of suspenders altogether.

There was Melvin, dressed in a shocking color of teal, his face red with exertion, doing his level best to "whip" everyone. His hair was beginning to show that gleam of scalp, a dead giveaway of balding. He was yelling much too loudly, moving with reckless abandon, evidently having a hard time "whipping."

He didn't see her arrive, so she sat down on the arm of a sofa, beside Rose, and watched. After numerous exertions of arms and legs, his face turned an alarming shade of red and he finally managed the game point, raising his paddle high, lifting his face, and yelling a shrill cry of victory before bowing low and then straightening and stomping both feet.

The girls found his display quite hilarious. Rose laughed loudest of all, which pleased Melvin so much that he repeated the whole procedure.

Sarah laughed out loud, helplessly. That Melvin. What an individual!

A girl Sarah had never seen placed a hand sideways across her mouth, giggled, leaned forward, and rolled her eyes at her companion, Arie Beiler, an older girl who had been in Sarah's group of youth as long as she could remember. The new girl seemed to know Arie well, so Sarah wondered if she was the new schoolteacher Melvin had spoken of.

She was dark-haired, and wore glasses with heavy black frames, giving her an edgy, career-girl look. Her mouth was wide with full lips, her dress a charcoal gray, with shoes that were almost sandals but not quite. She was not thin, although she carried the excess poundage well, her hands large and capable, her shoulders wide.

Hmm, Sarah thought. An interesting character, this one.

Later in the evening, she made a point of introducing herself, shyly, but with so much curiosity, she had to carry it out.

"Hi. I'm Sarah Beiler. I should know you, likely, but I have no idea who you are."

"Hi, Sarah. I know who you are. Minister Davey Beiler's daughter, right?"

Sarah nodded, suddenly speechless.

"I'm Edna King from Dauphin County. They had a problem school, near Ronks, so they asked me to teach this year. This is my eleventh term. I do art classes as well—at different schools."

Her eyes were bright with curiosity, her words spoken clearly, no humility in sight, so far as Sarah could tell, but she liked her immediately.

"Yes, I'm Davey's daughter."

No credentials, she thought wryly. No career, no boyfriend, not getting married, just Davey's girl.

"You lost your little brother shortly after the fire, right?"

"Yes."

"Well, that's so awful. It must have been a hard, hard time."

"It was."

"You have my deepest sympathy."

Sarah lowered her eyes, feeling a bit out of her league. This Edna was so well-spoken, so learned, so . . . so English. Sarah felt like some country bumpkin who could hardly speak.

"So, are you healing? Time does help the grieving process."

"Oh, yes. We miss Mervin, especially these winter evenings. But he was so innocent, and he's in a better place now."

"Certainly. Oh, absolutely."

"Winner's pick!"

The call was from Lee Glick, who stood, tall, relaxed, his hair very blond, surveying the crowd, taking his time choosing someone to play. Sarah turned her eyes away, to Matthew, who was slouched on a recliner laughing.

"Sarah?"

It was a question but a calm, assured one, sending a stab through her stomach, creating a tumultuous feeling near her heart, as if her ribs had closed in on its regularity. She looked up and acknowledged the warmth in his eyes, then rose to the challenge, moving fluidly, with unconscious grace. Taking up the red paddle, she smiled at him.

"I never played ping-pong with you. Are you any good?" His question was for her ears alone, and she blushed painfully.

"Of course."

"Alright, then. Here we go."

His serves were atrocious, but Sarah had played enough ping-pong with her older brothers to have acquired the skill of the return. Lee raised his eyebrows, whistled, and realized this was no ordinary girl playing ping-pong.

Lee was an extraordinary player, but so was Sarah. Mid-game, he put both hands on the table, palms down, leaned forward, and asked, "Where did you learn to play?"

"I have four older brothers, remember?"

"I didn't know that."

"They were, shall I say, exacting teachers. Mean, too!"

He laughed, his blue eyes sparkling, and she joined in.

At the end, she won by one point. The score had been tied at twenty, the youth mostly on their feet, cheering. Melvin was completely beside himself, the veins in his neck protruding to the point that Sarah thought he might pop one.

"I should have warned you, Lee. She's a mean one."

Lee laughed and shook his head, breathing hard. Sarah sank onto the sofa, shy now that the game was over, suddenly disliking the attention.

As if Matthew wanted to share the glory, he sat down beside her, his gaze never leaving her face, saying he'd play this next game. And because his eyes were so dark and compelling, and he was Matthew, the love of her entire life, she said of course she'd play. She got back on her feet and picked up the paddle.

As usual, Matthew was no contest. She beat him handily, without too much effort, but she knew Matthew wasn't much interested in sports. He'd rather be cooking or reading, he always said.

She remembered sitting beside him in school, doing anything to gain his attention, even dropping a wad of crumpled paper in the aisle so she could bend over to retrieve it. But his nose was in yet another book, and she may as well not even have been there at all.

In the end, Matthew threw down the paddle, hard, and turned away with no further ado. All the spark left Sarah's eyes, and her smile melted into trembling insecurity before she lowered her head and walked away, misery creeping into her eyes.

Lee had to clench his hands until the muscles rippled beneath his shirt to stop the anger, the overwhelming feeling of helplessness. Sarah, my love.

"Sarah! Pick me!" Edna King raced around the table, and Sarah's face was filled with light again.

Lee's hands unfolded, and he turned away casually, so that no one was aware of the intensity of his emotion.

The evening was ruined for Sarah, however. She had upset Matthew, so the snack that was set up on the side tables may as well have been sawdust and chicken bones as the dryness in her mouth created a sour despair.

Katie had decorated the table with a ping-pong theme using a green tablecloth with a ping-pong net dividing the food from the drinks. She stuck tiny plastic paddles into white icing on top of chocolate cupcakes, and dusted cookies formed in the shape of ping-pong balls with powdered sugar.

Sarah sipped disconsolately on a lemonade, her face a mirror of remorse, until Rose slipped an arm through hers. She leaned close and whispered, "Matthew was a poor sport."

So. She had seen. How well Rose must know Matthew!

"It's okay," she muttered. Rose nodded then giggled when Melvin sat beside her. He leaned across and hissed, "Sarah, introduce me to the schoolteacher."

Sarah examined Melvin's red face and unkempt hair. She wanted to tell him to go outside, stand in the cold wind, cool off, and fix his hair. But what she said was, "Now?"

"Course."

Ach, Melvin. She cringed but stood and moved to touch Edna's elbow.

"Edna, I want you to meet my cousin, Melvin. I think he lives just across the road from your school."

Edna turned, her face alight with interest.

Showing her good manners, she allowed herself to be led to the sofa, where Melvin reclined with Rose, in all his red-faced glory.

Thankfully, he stood and shook her hand, very politely. He didn't hold Edna's hand too long or too hard, and this is what he said: "I've been wanting to meet you for a long time. I often watch you play baseball with the children."

Much to Sarah's complete surprise, Edna seemed to lose all her composure. Her face changed color, and her well-modulated voice slid away into a stammering squeak.

"I . . . Yes. How are you?"

She blinked, adjusted her glasses, sniffed, and then, much to Sarah's chagrin, lifted her apron, found a Kleenex, and blew her nose. Oh my goodness, Sarah thought.

Melvin must have found that whole display of discomfiture a pure delight. His eyes took on that light of familiarity, that cunning beam that was a prelude to a full show of every one of his charms. In his own eyes, Melvin would be the benevolent knight in shining armor, ready to rescue his damsel in distress, that lucky girl who would now be subject to his personality.

"I'm well, thank you! Your name, though?"

Edna may as well have been in the presence of a king, the way she became tongue tied, clearing her throat, stammering, and finally saying, "Edna. Edna King."

"Edna? Oh, I love that name. It's so different. Not many Ednas around. Too many Sarahs and Rebeccas and Suzies. Sorry, Sarah."

Sarah punched his arm. Edna smiled and picked at her dress front, her nervousness only producing more confidence in Melvin, who went way over-board in his introductions. He told Edna his great-great-grandfather was a blacksmith from Switzerland, and Sarah figured it was another one of his stretched truths, feeding off his heightened emotions, laid out for the sole purpose of impressing the worldly Edna King.

She was led away by Matthew, then, who said he was ready to leave, as it was getting late, and they had church tomorrow.

Without a moment's hesitation, Sarah said goodbye to Melvin and told Edna it was a pleasure to meet her. She hurried up the stairs for her coat and purse, thinking she had to dig up enough nerve to help Melvin with his shirts.

Who in the world made those shirts? He'd look so much better in store-bought ones. He always picked a fabric and color that would be truly lovely stitched into a dress for a girl. And with that Edna! Now she had good taste. Understated, but classy. Not out of the *ordnung*, she dressed respectfully, but . . . well, differently.

Why were her thoughts carefully assessing Melvin now? She wondered at this, as she located her purse and shrugged into her coat.

Matthew was hitching his horse to the carriage to take her home, an unbelievable occurrence, a dream come true, and here she was, thinking about Melvin's shirts. What an old maid!

She was stopped at the door by Rose, who was breathing hard.

"Is . . . is Matthew taking you home?"

"Yes. He brought me."

"Oh. Yes, well. That's . . . well. Okay. Have a good night."

"Night, Rose."

Matthew's horse was prancing, so Sarah lost no time running out to the buggy, swiftly getting in, and firmly closing the door. When he released the reins, they were off with a hard jerk, the gravel pinging against the buggy as the horse's speed increased.

Matthew was busy controlling the eager horse, so he said nothing, and Sarah watched his profile, the perfect downward slope of his nose.

She'd go shopping with Melvin. She'd ask him to go along to Rockvale Square to visit a few men's shops. Oh, he'd protest. There would be nothing harder for Melvin to swallow than being told he needed help with his clothes. In his own eyes, he was quite dapper, but if that Edna turned out to be interested, he'd better get a few shirts. Maybe gray, or almost black. A pinstripe wouldn't hurt.

Perhaps that was the reason Edna was in her

eleventh year of teaching. She was almost thirty years old. And she became as flustered as someone Priscilla's age meeting Melvin in his brilliant teal-colored shirt.

"What did Rose have to say tonight?"

Matthew's voice split apart the reverie, and she had to shake off the image of Edna before replying.

"Oh, not much. She seemed thrilled to play ping-pong with Lee Glick."

Intended barbs like that fired much too quickly. They were completely untypical of Sarah, and she knew it. Where they borne of desperation?

Matthew's voice was low and harsh. "Yeah, well. It might be a good idea to eliminate the girls playing against the guys, and you know it."

There was no answer to this, so she remained quiet, afraid she might upset him again.

The night was moving around them, the horse's mane and tail blowing, the weeds shivering beside the road, bushes shaking thin branches at the wind's command. Distant pole lights seemed to blink as branches raked across their beams, and the buggy swayed just a bit as they rounded a curve.

An oncoming buggy dimmed its headlights, and Matthew clicked the dimmer switch on the floor with his foot.

"Old Dutchies are out late tonight," he muttered.

Sarah laughed, hoping to elevate his mood. He

smiled in return, which encouraged Sarah to bring the evening to a better note with happy chatter of her week at the market, launching into a vivid account of her new acquaintance, Ashley.

"I didn't think you were the type to make friends with English girls. Especially not someone like her."

"Oh, but she's so nice. She seems genuinely interested in the barn fires that have been going on all year. She's so caring. I think it really bothers her that we're all going through this together."

Matthew nodded. "You better be careful, Sarah. She might know more than you think. Don't trust anyone, as long as these fires are being lit."

"Alright. I'll be careful."

They turned into the Beiler lane, and too soon, Matthew tugged on the reins, stopping the horse at the end of the sidewalk.

Just when Sarah could hardly bear to lift her hand to tug on the door handle, Matthew's voice stopped her.

"You don't have to go in right away."

Slowly, slowly, her hand slid down, and her breathing almost stopped. The wind whipped the branches of the maple tree. Somewhere a gate clanked against the chain that restrained it. A heifer bawled from its enclosure, a small plastic bag whirled away, causing Matthew's horse to lift its head suddenly, and he tightened the reins.

Then, "Sarah, do you think Rose is unhappy?"

"No." Too quickly, too decisively, the word was placed between them.

"She doesn't miss me?"

"No."

"How well do you know her?"

"We've been friends forever. I know her very well. She is after Lee Glick now."

After the words were out, she felt as if she was sliding uncontrollably into a world where there was no safety, no restraint. Her heartbeat fluttered and accelerated, until she became lightheaded. Oh, but, please God. I'm so close. Please don't take him away.

She wasn't lying. She just wasn't including all the facts. She took a deep breath, steadied herself, and told Matthew that Rose was doing just fine, was happy now, whereas after the break-up, she hadn't been. Matthew listened quietly and nodded speculatively.

There was a space of silence that prickled uncomfortably with unspoken feelings, words that hung in the balance, deciding Sarah's future. If Matthew did not come to a decision tonight, when? Oh, when would he ever?

A gentle nod of her conscience reminded her of the timeframe, that it was too recent that Rose had ended the relationship. But Sarah was afraid that if Matthew didn't commit now, he might never.

Finally he sighed. "Sarah, you know how it is.

I'm still not really moving on. I miss her terribly. But if I know that it's absolutely hopeless, once I find out for sure, will you be my girl?"

"Oh, yes. Yes, Matthew! Of course I will."

Too quickly, too exuberantly again, and she knew it. But like the wind howling outside the buggy, her caution was caught up and whirled away.

With Matthew, all thoughts of right or wrong were confused, the line blurred into a fuzzy gray that her conscience could never quite completely touch.

Why then, when he pulled her roughly against him, his face lowered as his mouth found hers, did she pull back? Was she afraid, with the thought of Mam's warnings forced between them?

"Matthew."

"What? What's wrong now, Sarah?"

She heard the urgency in his voice and succumbed, allowing herself the privilege of being in his arms, blindly erasing the overwhelming feeling of something being not quite perfect.

How many years had she imagined this? How many months had she wondered how it would feel to be in Matthew's arms?

It was Mam—that was all.

A sob rose in her throat, as unexpected as a beam of light on this stormy night. She stumbled into the house, her covering disheveled, her hair windblown, her heart and mind caught in a sweet but indefinable misery.

As she lay sleepless, the branches creaking outside her window, she choked back the mysterious lump that kept rising in her throat. She was tired, that was all. That, and Mam's dire warnings.

Well, Mam knew a lot, but she didn't know Matthew, so she'd get over it eventually. No matter that she was clearly second best. She would be first in his life.

She flipped on her side and was shocked to find tears sliding across her nose. She swiped viciously at them, a fingernail slicing into the skin below her eye. She winced, squeezed her eyes shut as tightly as possible, and tried to give praises to God for Matthew's love. But she found that not quite possible either, like a harmonica with one stuck key, just one note short of perfect.

So Sarah pushed past the mysterious tears, the image of Mam, the warnings, the stuck note that stubbornly refused its song. She prayed the prayer of too many young girls whose hearts and wills are not in complete sync with the will of a loving heavenly Father.

God, please listen to my prayer and give Matthew the love I feel for him. I want him so much. Not my will, but thine, Lord, You know that. All things are visible to You, including my thoughts. Please, bless me with Matthew.

In time, it would all straighten out, she knew. Even if it wasn't perfect now, God would provide. Placing her trust firmly in His hands, she fell into a troubled sleep. But she woke up crying, thinking Mervin had called her.

All this, however, was tucked into a hidden recess of her mind, and the face she presented to her mother at the breakfast table was one of sweet and unconfused innocence. Except for the lurking shadows Sarah was completely unaware of.

Mam watched her daughter and knew how much wisdom and patience it would take to keep her peace.

Chapter 25

By Monday evening, the wind had died down and the air had turned crisp and cold. Dat spread clean, yellow straw in the horse stable, preparing for the horses that would be tied in the stalls.

As he fluffed up the clean bedding, his lips moved in prayer, putting this meeting of minds into God's hands. He knew well how meetings could turn disastrous, with everyone voicing their own opinions, each one different, and sometimes espousing views that were poorly thought out and coupled with passion and self-will.

But it was good they could come together like this, and he walked through the barn with an optimistic outlook. He was glad old Aaron Glick would be among them, and he was pleased that there remained a measure of respect for the older generation.

Levi was in fine fettle, dressed in a blue shirt, his hair shampooed and combed with slow and deliberate care, his glasses polished, held to the light, and polished again. He knew this was a matter of importance, and he knew the fact that he had seen that white car would finally be noticed.

And the biggest highlight would be his mother's warm cinnamon rolls, frosted with caramel icing. She said he'd be allowed coffee, although it had to be decaffeinated. Decaf. That's what people said when they ordered breakfast at a restaurant.

Levi loved to drink coffee with the men. He didn't particularly enjoy the bitter taste. But if he put lots of creamer into it and had plenty of cinnamon rolls on the side, it made him feel like one of the men, sitting there, grimacing that certain way, to show he could drink it hot, like a man.

So when the men began to stream through the door and take their seats around the kitchen table, Levi sat at the end, reaching up a heavy arm to shake hands enthusiastically, so glad to see Omar's Sam and Abbie's Ben's Amos, Davey Esh, and Sammie's Reuben, for he knew them all. Levi rarely forgot a name or a face, usually connecting the two within seconds.

Dat opened the meeting with a moment of silence, and Levi looked very grave when the men's heads were lifted. He knew who God was, and he knew that it was important to include that invisible chap at times like this.

Dat spoke first, as minister as well as a victim. He spoke of the fact that they had no clues at all about the arsonist, other than his son Levi's description of a white car, and he'd let Levi tell them exactly what had occurred that night.

Levi cleared his throat, looked around the length of the table to make sure he had everyone's attention, and then drew his eyebrows down behind his glasses. He sighed with resignation when Melvin appeared at the kitchen door and said, "Come in, Melvin. You should have come earlier." There was friendly chuckling as Melvin slid unabashed into the remaining chair.

Levi waited, then began, his voice low and strong, his demeanor one of pure enjoyment.

"As you know, the night the barn burned, I was sick with *hals vay* (sore throat). I was up and around."

Dat hid a smile, his son so obviously holding court and his choice of words so clearly premeditated.

"I thought it was so strange that a white car would come in the lane at such a late hour."

Here, Levi's eyes narrowed, and he achieved that perfect cunning look of his, the one he assumed when he played Memory with Suzie.

"I went to the bathroom, and when I came out, the car was going past the house already."

Dat's head lifted, his gaze became intent. "You mean going back out?"

"*Ya. Ya.*"

"You never mentioned that, Levi."

"Well, I'm not done, Davey. Maybe you'd want to stay *sochta* (quiet)."

The men exercised great restraint then, no one wanting to upset Levi, but they found it hilarious that he had called his father by his given name. Oh, he was a character, they said after the meeting.

"The shape of the tail lights was sort of round and down low, so I remembered them. I have a whole pile of football cards, you know, and then I started collecting car cards. Vehicles, you know. *Scheena. Mascheena.*"

He had everyone's attention now, the roomful of faces turned toward him.

"Suzie, I need a glass of water." Suzie, seated in the background, blushed and looked frantic, reluctant to be seen by all the *freme* (strangers). So Melvin got up and poured him a cold drink from the pitcher in the refrigerator and handed it to him.

As wily as a small bird, Levi's eyes twinkled up at Melvin. "Is your name Suzie?"

With that, Levi slapped the tabletop with great hilarity, and no one could keep from laughing as he took his time drinking the water, for all the world an imitation of his father when he preached. He then looked around for a place to set his tumbler even though the tabletop was clearly in front of him.

Dat thanked God silently for the gift of his son with Down syndrome and the way he spread humor and goodwill around the table. Just stay with us, Lord, he begged.

"So," Levi resumed, "as close as I can get to it, I think it was a little Volkswagen. An older model from 1978. Like this one."

Taking his time, he pushed back his chair and turned, his wide back bent at a slight angle. Reaching into a drawer, he produced a card with a vehicle showing the distinguishable features of a 1978 Volkswagen.

"It's a punch bug," he said, grinning widely. "I believe the car the arsonist drove was an old punch bug."

Murmurs broke out, but resonantly above the others, Melvin said, "Boy, that would really narrow it down!"

Heads nodded assent. Without being aware of it, Melvin took the floor, Levi listening with a resigned expression. He wasn't finished yet.

"Well, if it is an old Volkswagen the way Levi says, I bet we could eventually find the driver. That wouldn't be impossible. Hard but not impossible, if we get the cops in on this. And in the meantime, we need to take every precaution to stop this arsonist from becoming bolder yet. He obviously isn't worried about anyone catching him setting fire to a barn, or he wouldn't do it anymore. It's just a matter of time till the next one goes up."

"Ah, come on! He's not going to have the nerve," Abbie's Ben's Amos said confidently.

"That's what you think," Melvin shot back. "What's going to keep him from it? We just sit here like a *glook* (hen) hatching peeps, doing nothing, so what else can we expect?"

There was a ripple of assent, but no one spoke up.

"I suggest, if you live close to the road, your chance is about 75 percent higher of having your barn lit. If you don't, it could be lit anyway. So, if I had a barn, that's where I'd sleep."

Voices of disagreement broke through.

"I ain't sleeping out there."

"No way."

"In winter?"

"Nobody could pay me to sleep out there."

Now Melvin's face turned red, his eyes glistening with the need to express himself.

"Well, be that way, then. If your barn burns, don't come crying to me."

At these hotly spoken words, Dat's warning flag waved silently.

Old Aaron Glick was bent, thin, his hair and

beard a banner of white in his old age. But his eyes were bright with wisdom and experience.

"I think Levi here is on to something. The Bible says a child shall lead them. Well, Levi is a man, of course, but we would do well to heed his words. However, Melvin is right. If you want to join the community effort to stop the fires, either sleep out there or spend hundreds—maybe thousands—of dollars installing some smart smoke detectors."

Merv Zook, who was somewhat ill-tempered too much of the time, cut him off. "By the time a smoke detector went off, the barn would be half burnt to the ground."

"Well, then, sleep out there," said Abbie's Ben's Amos, who was still annoyed that Merv had never fully paid him for the last load of straw, the money from which he wanted to spend on a new patio for his wife. The look Merv gave Amos was sadly lacking in brotherly love, but the meeting righted itself and kept moving forward.

Elam Stoltzfus, soft-spoken, ill at ease in a crowd, and never one to voice his opinion, came up with the most workable solution so far. "Could we install a bell attached to a wire that runs across the driveway?"

But without electricity? How would they work?

Inverters. There was a way.

Someone suggested putting an article in the daily paper, warning the arsonist of these three precautions the Amish people would be taking.

Dat shook his head no. "That would not be our way. We don't want to appear as if we're going to battle. I think each idea that has been offered is a good one. Each man must decide for himself. But I do agree with Melvin. We need to wake up, become more aware. No one knows the horror of a night like that unless you experience it first-hand. Let's do what we can to avoid it. Melvin, you're a young man with time on your hands during winter when roofing's slow. Would you be willing to take the responsibility of talking to the police?"

"I could do that."

Sarah was seated in the living room crocheting a white afghan. She looked up and smiled when Melvin spoke, noting the lack of humility, the joy of his elevated position.

"So," Dat continued, "We have agreed to take Levi's words seriously, right?"

Levi nodded vigorously, and Dat smiled at him.

"The rest of us will decide to cooperate with either a bell or a smoke detector or we will leave our good warm beds to sleep in the barn."

Laughter broke out, but everyone was seemingly in agreement. Then Ez Stoltzfus said that if everyone trusted in the Lord with all their hearts, the way the Bible says, there would be no need for any of those costly solutions. An aura of shame arose, and no one had anything to say.

Finally, when the silence became uncomfortable, Dat spoke again, saying that was true, and if Ez's faith was great, then it would be alright for him to do nothing.

Melvin, however, was visibly sputtering.

They exchanged ideas and solutions for another hour, until Levi said he believed he smelled coffee. He turned his head and wiggled his eyebrows at Mam and Sarah, who hurried to the kitchen to serve the men cups of coffee, fresh cinnamon rolls, stick pretzels, and sliced Longhorn cheese.

Levi was so clearly in his element, and it touched a chord in Sarah's heart to see the kindness of these men around him. They knew he was special and treated him as someone who deserved just that. Special treatment.

Abbie's Ben's Amos's wife, Lomie, had sent a package containing a new Sunday handkerchief, two packages of Juicy Fruit gum, and a pair of brown jersey knit gloves for Levi. He was beside himself, since it wasn't even Christmas yet.

Mam served quietly, nodding her head at comments, smiling in that discreet way of hers, always showing good manners, living her life by example. Dat was confident in his wife's dutiful maneuvers. It was clearly a blessing watching her parents interact with the men of the community, Sarah observed in silence.

What set a minister's wife apart? Nothing, and

yet a great deal depended on her support. She needed to supply quantities of it, always striving to build her husband's confidence and his service by *guta-rote* (sound advice) as the lesser vessel. At the same time she was a powerful ally, and Sarah knew the power of her mother's prayers better than anyone.

All she wanted from life was a marriage like her parents' marriage, and Rose had told her not everyone could say that, after she sighed dramatically and rolled her eyes.

Melvin caught Sarah's eye, beckoned her over, and then rose to go to the *kesslehaus*, where a dim kerosene lamp shone from its black wrought iron holder on the side of the oak cabinet.

"So, how's my Sarah?" he asked, grinning cheekily.

"Your Sarah?"

"Yeah. Hopefully not Matthew's yet."

Sarah sighed and let it go. So now there were three of them. Genuine roadblocks. Mam, Melvin, and Priscilla.

"No, not yet," she said quietly with restraint.

"Tell me about Edna."

"Edna King? Oh, she's great! Melvin, she is!"

They stood in the *kesslehaus*, two cousins who shared a rare and beautiful friendship. Under the cold December moon, in a world that had been fractured by three horrifying barn fires, the assembly of men in the kitchen, each one looking out for the well-being of the others, enjoyed warm cinnamon rolls and coffee as they tried to patch together a workable plan.

For Sarah, her personal world was no different —torn with indecision, doubt, and above all, the yearning to be Matthew's wife. It was all she had ever wanted. Now it seemed so near and yet so completely unsure. Was anything ever certain in life?

Now it seemed every barn roof that gleamed in the moonlight on this night was in danger. The Amish men of the community knew this. They had formed a plan of sorts, but ultimately their faith ruled, and they knew it. So nothing was certain, nothing was worthy of confidence, at a time such as this.

It was faith, as stated in the book of Hebrews, that sustained them all: "Faith is the substance of things hoped for, the evidence of things not seen."

Sarah could only rely on her fledgling faith, as she chose to think of it. Her father's faith was like an eagle, soaring on powerful wings, so many years ahead of her in the wisdom and learning she hoped to achieve someday.

Outside, the moon touched each carriage top with a dull gleam, spidery branches etching a pattern across them. Somewhere in the old apple orchard, an owl called, and another one answered, its hushed cry a warning to all the small creatures of the night, burrowed in their warm hollows and caves in the ground.

The warm yellow light shining from the kitchen was a small beacon of life, love, and caring. But the splendid light of human charity was the new barn, perfect in its entirety, the symmetry a banner of God's gift to man—the serenity to accept the things they could not change, the courage to change the things they could, and the wisdom to know the difference.

And somewhere, a white older model Volkswagen puttered along the rural roads of Lancaster County.

The Glossary

Bupplish—A Pennsylvania Dutch dialect word meaning "childish."

Chappy—A Pennsylvania Dutch dialect word meaning "boyfriend."

Chide—A Pennsylvania Dutch dialect word meaning "right."

Dat—A Pennsylvania Dutch dialect word used to address or refer to one's father.

Die Botschaft—A weekly periodical in which volunteer "scribes" report on the events of their communities. Its name is a Pennsylvania Dutch term meaning "The Message." One way in which Amish communities stay in touch is by reading the same publications. In addition to *Die Botschaft*, many Amish families subscribe to the *Connection*, *Keepers at Home*, and the *Ladies Journal*—all periodicals about Plain life.

Fer-sark—A Pennsylvania Dutch dialect phrase meaning "to take care of."

Fore-gayer—A Pennsylvania Dutch dialect word meaning "managers." At a funeral, they take care of arrangements and hospitality for the family of the deceased.

Gaduld—A Pennsylvania Dutch dialect word meaning "patience."

Geb acht—A Pennsylvania Dutch dialect phrase meaning "be careful."

Gel—A Pennsylvania Dutch dialect word meaning "right."

Gook mol—A Pennsylvania Dutch dialect phrase meaning "look here."

Gros-feelich—A Pennsylvania Dutch dialect word meaning "proud."

Himmlisch—A Pennsylvania Dutch dialect word meaning "heavenly."

Ich bin aw base—A Pennsylvania Dutch dialect phrase meaning "I am mad."

Ich gleich dich—A Pennsylvania Dutch dialect phrase meaning "I love you."

Kesslehaus—A Pennsylvania Dutch dialect word meaning "wash house."

Kopp-duch—A Pennsylvania Dutch dialect word meaning "head scarf."

Mam—A Pennsylvania Dutch dialect word used to address or refer to one's mother.

Mit-leidich—A Pennsylvania Dutch dialect word meaning "understanding."

Ordnung—The Amish community's agreed-upon rules for living based on their understanding of the Bible, particularly the New Testament. The *ordnung* varies from community to community, often reflecting leaders' preferences, local customs, and traditional practices.

Phone shanty—Most Old Order Amish do not have telephone landlines in their homes so that incoming calls do not overtake their lives and so that they are not physically connected to the larger world. Many Amish build a small, fully enclosed structure where a phone is installed and where they can make calls and retrieve messages.

Rumspringa—A Pennsylvania Dutch dialect word meaning "running around." It refers to the time in a person's life between age sixteen and marriage. It involves structured social activities in groups, as well as dating, and usually takes place on the weekends.

Sei—A Pennsylvania Dutch dialect word meaning "his." In communities where many people have the same first and last names, it is customary for the husband's name to be added to that of his wife so it is clear who is being referred to.

The Author

Linda Byler was raised in an Amish family and is an active member of the Amish church today. Growing up, Linda loved to read and write. In fact, she still does. She is the author of the *Sadie's Montana* series which includes these three novels: *Wild Horses*, *Keeping Secrets*, and *The Disappearances*. She has also written the *Lizzie Searches for Love* series, which includes these three novels: *Running Around (and Such)*, *When Strawberries Bloom*, and *Big Decisions*. She is also the author of *Lizzie's Amish Cookbook: Favorite recipes from three generations of Amish cooks!*

Additionally, Linda is well-known within the Amish community as a columnist for a weekly Amish newspaper.

Center Point Large Print
600 Brooks Road / PO Box 1
Thorndike, ME 04986-0001 USA

(207) 568-3717

US & Canada:
1 800 929-9108
www.centerpointlargeprint.com